"[*The First Principle*]  what I believe in, no

—*Avi, 15*

"*The First Principle* is fantastic. . . . Keeps you wanting more. . . . A great read."

—*Joanna, 16*

"Loved reading it and hope there will be a sequel."

—*Leah, 17*

"Amazing! . . . I love how Vivica is well known and has to make decisions that may affect more than just her own life."

—*Lexi, 18*

"It was hard to put down. . . . The future that Marissa Shrock writes about could very well happen."

—*Monica, 14*

"Raises good questions about government control and personal freedom. . . . I would recommend this book to my older friends."

—*Rebekah, 13*

"I absolutely loved *The First Principle*, a dystopian story with a Christian twist. . . . Tear-jerking, heart-racing, and beautifully written."

—*Tessa, 16*

# The First Principle

*A NOVEL*

## MARISSA SHROCK

Kregel
Publications

*The First Principle: A Novel*
© 2015 by Marissa Shrock

Published by Kregel Publications, a division of Kregel, Inc.,
2450 Oak Industrial Dr. NE, Grand Rapids, MI 49505.

Published in association with the literary agency of Credo
Communications, LLC, Grand Rapids, Michigan, www
.Credocommunications.net.

The persons and events portrayed in this work are the creations
of the author, and any resemblance to persons living or dead is
purely coincidental.

ISBN 978-0-8254-4357-2

Printed in the United States of America
15 16 17 18 19 / 5 4 3 2 1

*To Mom and Dad*
*Thank you for always believing in me*

# CHAPTER 1

The biggest rebellions begin with the smallest steps, and I took my first small step one December morning during study hall. The quiet drumming of fingers on desktops filled the room as my classmates used keyboards projected from their government-issued multiphone devices to work. I tried to concentrate on writing an essay for my literature class, but the blinding glare reflecting from the sun on the snow outside made it difficult for me to see my screen. I didn't mind. The glare gave me the perfect excuse to let my thoughts wander to Ben Lagarde. Three weeks ago he'd broken up with me, and while I'm not the type to fall in love, I really cared for Ben until he ended our relationship.

In the seat in front of me, Meredith Alderton sat with her chin in her hand, curly brown hair shrouding her shoulders. She was the girl Ben had been hanging around lately. The fact that I'd even noticed meant I needed to find another guy and move on.

A message bubble appeared on my screen.

Viv? U ok? Not much typing up there.

It was from my best friend, Tindra St. John, who sat three seats behind me. She was using the school's rogue messaging system that I'd created during the summer after hacking into my high school's network. The messaging system my friends and I used broke through the school's server blocks and hid inside the network. It allowed us to communicate with each other using our multiphone devices, also known as MDs or docs. The message system was only a fraction of the enhancements I'd made. The one that provided the most possibilities was my access to the grade books. Already a straight-A student, I didn't need my grades altered. However, Tindra did, and we'd made a deal. I changed her algebra grade from a D to a B−, and she quietly promoted my new job to the other kids. I made some extra cash, and my mother had no idea I was breaking the law.

Yeah. I'm fine. Just thinking about Ben.

Tindra's response made me smile.

Don't waste your time. You're too good for him.

The classroom door opened, and twenty-five heads turned. One of the school's government-appointed security guards, Officer Jim, held the door open for a woman wearing a military uniform. Her black hair was cropped close, and her pretty features were marred by the hard expression that settled in her eyes and around her mouth.

Mr. Wilson stood and removed his reading glasses. "May I help you?"

"I'm Officer Martina Ward from Population Management." Her raspy voice was deep. "I'm looking for Meredith Alderton."

Everyone turned to look at Meredith who shrank in her seat. Mr. Wilson pointed to her.

"Stand up," Officer Ward said, and Meredith obeyed. "Come with me."

Meredith gripped the back of her chair. "Why?"

Officer Ward raised her eyebrows. "We'll discuss that later. Come with me."

"No!" Meredith sat down at her desk so hard it banged into mine.

I turned to glance at Tindra whose brown eyes were wide.

Officer Ward crossed the room in three strides, grabbed Meredith's arm, and yanked her out of the seat. "I'm a government employee. You're required to speak with me."

Meredith jerked her arm away. "I'm not going anywhere with you until you tell me why."

Officer Jim stepped in and put a grandfatherly arm around Meredith's shoulder. "Now, Meredith, it's okay. We need you to step out in the hall and speak with Officer Ward." His tone was friendly but firm.

"Then just tell her what she wants to know," I said to Officer Ward. Everyone turned to face me. Meredith shot me a grateful look.

Officer Ward glared at me. "Mind your own business."

I stood. "No. I won't." I caught Tindra's eye. She made a slight hand motion signaling me to sit. "She has the right to know what's going on."

Officer Ward moved closer. "What's your name?"

"Vivica Wilkins."

"The daughter of our governor. I thought you looked familiar." Officer Ward turned to Mr. Wilson. "Is she always this mouthy?" She didn't wait for an answer. "We'll let them have their way. Miss Alderton, it has come to my attention that you are pregnant. As I'm sure you're aware, the Posterity Protection and Self-Determination Act requires that you report to a Population Management Clinic for a termination since you're underage."

"I know what the law says." Meredith raised her chin. "But I'm not pregnant. Don't you have my vaccine record and my test results from last month?"

"Funny you should bring that up"—Officer Ward tilted her head—"since someone tampered with your results."

"I don't know anything about that." Meredith stared the woman down, but her voice trembled.

"I think you do. We recently obtained security camera footage from Officer Jim and discovered you sneaking into the school office after hours." Officer Ward paused and surveyed all of us with a sneer. "Can you believe she was idiotic enough to believe we wouldn't notice?"

Officer Ward's mockery turned my stomach.

"Miss Alderton, you will come with me and comply with the law."

Meredith flinched as if the officer's words caused her physical pain. "You're not going to kill my baby!" She bolted for the open door and darted into the hall. Before either Mr. Wilson or Officer Jim could take off after her, Officer Ward seized her gun from its holster and fired. Meredith's hand flew to her arm, and she moved a few steps before she seemed to hit an invisible wall and collapsed next to the lockers.

A few students screamed and chairs scraped against tile while I ran to the door with several classmates.

"Sit down!" Officer Ward yelled. "It was a tranquilizer gun." We shrank against the wall. Officer Ward looked at Mr. Wilson. "Keep them in here." She pointed at Officer Jim. "Lock down the school. Now."

I couldn't take my eyes off the crumpled heap in the hallway. She was more than a little nutso if she thought she could break the law and get away with it. It's not like you could hide a pregnancy. Why hadn't I ignored the impulse to stand up for her? Why had Ben befriended her? And then the obvious occurred to me—he was probably the cause of her situation.

>X<

I pushed steamed broccoli and carrots around my lunch tray. I'd only managed to swallow one bite of over-baked chicken before my stomach rebelled. I took a sip of vitamin-infused almond milk and wished I could have a brownie, but government regulations rationed sugar and fat for everyone and banned school cafeterias from providing any good stuff.

"You have to eat," Tindra said. "You'll feel better." She'd polished off her entire meal, and her eyes flicked toward my tray. Food always made Tindra feel better, and she was lucky it didn't show on her petite figure. Even though I was tall and slender, I couldn't get away with her eating habits.

"Help yourself." I pushed my tray toward Tindra and moved hers closer to me. The last thing I needed was the cafeteria monitor reporting my lack of consumption. "I can't get Meredith out of my mind." That was half true. I couldn't get Ben *with* Meredith out of my mind. Had he been seeing her while he was with me?

"I can't believe you stood up for her like that." She attacked the broccoli.

"That woman from Pop Management was a bully. But what was up with Meredith sneaking into the office? How dumb was that?"

"I know."

"I can't believe her vaccine didn't work." Every year the government gave each underage girl a vaccine to prevent pregnancy and STDs. We learned in health class that the shots were healthier and more effective than the hormone-based pills women had used years ago, when pregnancy control was optional.

"So what if it didn't?" Tindra asked. "Why didn't she go terminate? Doesn't she want to have a life? A kid would totally ruin everything."

I plucked a strawberry from my original tray and nibbled it. "I don't know." Maybe she just wanted to defy the government. Underground rebel activity had been a problem in our country for years. It was the reason the government monitored everyone and everything. I'd heard of pregnant girls going into hiding with rebel help, but I'd never known one personally. I'd more or less figured that part was urban legend.

"You think she's a rebel?"

"Duh. Why else would she skip termination?"

"Then why wasn't she in hiding?"

"Do I look like a rebel expert? Maybe she was afraid to run away and leave her family." Tindra shrugged and flipped her shiny black hair over her shoulder. "All I know is that if I ever get pregnant, I'm terminating. No worries here."

"Yeah, I hear you."

⋊⋉

When I arrived at my URNA history class, everyone was unusually silent. I took a seat in the third row and propped my doc on the table. The bell dinged four times, and Mrs. O'Keefe rose from her chair, although the screen above her desk that normally held our notes remained blank.

Mrs. O'Keefe tucked a red curl behind her ear and cleared her throat. "I know you've all heard what happened today during fourth hour." She paused and looked at us. I nodded and noticed several other heads bobbing. "I need to read the following message from the principal before we begin." She tapped her doc. "Today during fourth hour, a young lady was placed into a juvenile detention center for attempting to change the results of a government-issued pregnancy test in an attempt to avoid the required termination. Though pregnancy is rare due to the success rate of our vaccination program, we would like to remind you that the Posterity Protection and Self-Determination Act was implemented for the common good of our country. We hope that such an incident will not be repeated, as it reflects badly on our school and community." Mrs. O'Keefe looked up, her expression grim. "Now, moving on—"

"That's bull." Darius Delano crossed his arms. D² was a new student this year, and he always had an opinion.

Mrs. O'Keefe held up her hand. "I know some of you found this incident disturbing, but I've been told that we are not to discuss this issue any further."

"What gives the government the right to tell her she can't have a baby?" D² asked.

"We simply can't discuss this."

D² scowled, and I think he swore under his breath, but I wasn't sure. Mrs. O'Keefe must not have been sure either because she hesitated before she focused her attention on opening the class notes.

"Why can't we?" This time I knew the voice without looking. It was Ben, his tone gentle and disarming.

"Principal Daniels asked that we not." Mrs. O'Keefe's tone was firm, but her thin hands fluttered around her doc. "Besides, it's clear that the student's actions were illegal."

"Can we at least discuss the law and if we even need it anymore? We don't have to talk about Meredith," D² said.

Several people agreed.

"Fine. Darius, since you feel so strongly about the matter, go ahead."

D² sauntered to the front of the class, and Mrs. O'Keefe moved to the side and supported herself with one hand gripping the edge of her desk.

"So, the best teacher ever"—he grinned at Mrs. O'Keefe—"taught us the Posterity Protection and Self-Determination Act, a.k.a. *term law*—'cause of the part that says underage girls and people with too many kids have gotta terminate pregnancies—was put into place back in the day. Our government was trying to get the country rolling after the Great Collapse and the Second Civil War. Too many people were poor and starving, so they had to control population growth." D² shifted back and forth. "The economy is better now. We have food. Why should the government care if some teenage girl has a kid? Or if adults want a big family?"

Claire, who sat in the front row, waved her hand. "You're kidding, right? Do you know how many people *still* live in poverty?

Pop Management regulations ensure we have enough resources to go around. And what about the environmental impact of overpopulation? Besides, you aren't being honest. Adults can have more than two kids if they pay."

$D^2$ crossed his arms again. "It shouldn't be the government's job to provide for everyone, and no woman should have to pay a huge fine or terminate."

"If she can't afford the fine, then she can't support another child," Claire said.

"People like Meredith fight the law because they think the required termination part is wrong," Ben said. "It's not about resources. Or the economy. They don't want to slaughter kids."

I spun and shot Ben a look. *Slaughter?* What was he thinking? Using words like that could cause the government to investigate you for hate speech or anti-government activity.

$D^2$ pointed to Ben. "That's right."

"So, Darius, are you announcing that you're a rebel?" Claire asked.

He scowled. "I'm expressing my opinion. That doesn't mean I'm a rebel."

"Right." Claire rolled her eyes.

Mrs. O'Keefe stood. "Darius, do you have anything else to add?"

"No." He stomped back to his seat.

"Anyone else?"

The room stilled. Even if someone had a thought, Claire's accusation against $D^2$ was enough to silence the entire class.

# CHAPTER 2

"Vivica!" I whirled at the sound of Ben's voice. "Hey, wait up."

The last bell had rung, and students pushed out the front doors, buzzing about their weekend plans. I stopped. My bodyguard waited outside the door in the snow, and if Ben had something to say, I didn't want Bobby to overhear.

"I need to talk to you." Ben sounded sincere.

"I don't feel like listening." I adjusted my bag on my shoulder, and Ben reached over and slid it off. I jerked it back. "What are you doing?"

He held on to my bag. "I'm going to carry this for you."

"No, you're not." I snatched the bag.

"What if I said I'm sorry?"

I smirked in spite of myself. "For . . . ?" A couple of girls from my pre-calc class walked by and gave us a curious look. Rumors would be in full force by tonight. I took a step back. "You need to be specific."

Color rose in Ben's cheeks. "I will. At your house." His chocolate eyes pleaded, but they reflected enough pride that it didn't seem like begging. Why did he have to look so cute?

"Will you leave me alone if I agree?"

"Yes."

I rolled my eyes. "Fine, then let's get this over with." I pushed through the door, and the frigid air numbed my lungs and made my eyes water. The sun reflecting off the snow tickled my nose and caused a sneeze. I nodded toward Bobby. "Ben's coming home with me."

Bobby looked Ben up and down and then led us to the executive car next to the curb. "Got to take a detour. Bad accident." He opened the door, and I slid into the back seat. Ben left space between us, which felt weird because when we had been dating, he would've snuggled next to me. His brown hair fell in soft waves across his forehead. I longed to reach up and brush it aside like I used to.

I stared out the window at the drab scenery that announced the poor section of town. No wonder Bobby usually programmed the car to avoid this route. Graffiti full of anti-government sentiments splayed over crumbling brick walls. Beggars huddled against buildings with boarded windows.

Many people had been destitute since the Great Collapse years ago. After the economy failed, elected officials in the U.S. government spent so much time fighting with each other that they couldn't resolve issues. Riots broke out among starving people. Militias organized and attempted to break away from the government, which led to the Second Civil War.

When Mexico saw the confusion, its military attacked parts of Texas and New Mexico, claiming the land was historically Mexico's. Then Canada was drawn in when millions of United States citizens sought asylum to the north. To bring peace to North America, the Council of World Peacekeepers stepped in and used a nation consolidation model that it had implemented throughout the world. And the United Regions of North America was born.

The Council of World Peacekeepers divided the three former countries into seven geographic regions: the Atlantic Region, the Great Lakes Region, the Coastal Plain Region, the Great Plains Region, the Desert and Pacific Region, the Rocky Mountain Region, and the Caribbean Region. Each region had its own governor. The Nationalist Party dominated, and at the president's recommendation, the Council of Representatives appointed my mother governor of the Great Lakes Region eight years ago.

I thought of the debate today in URNA history. Claire was right. There was still too much poverty. But what did Ben think about the neediness that surrounded us? Did he care or was he comfortable with our affluence? There was a lot I didn't know about him.

The car stopped at a red light where a group of mothers and children waited on the sidewalk. In front stood a little girl whose large, gray eyes looked too sad to belong to someone so young. She held the hand of a woman who had the same eyes, only they contained weariness mixed with the sadness. The girl's face was slender, and her shabby clothes, which were tidy, looked too thin for such a cold day. I grabbed my bag from the seat. "Reprogram the car, Bobby. I want to stop here."

He turned and frowned. "Not in this neighborhood."

"Yes." I rummaged until I found my wallet and withdrew an empty cash card. I removed my doc from my pocket. Bobby entered the commands into the car's computer, and as soon as the light changed, the vehicle maneuvered through traffic and parked along the street.

Ben leaned over. "What are you doing?"

I pushed a few buttons on my doc and activated my bank account, and the allowance that I used for shopping transferred to the card when I scanned it. "I'm helping that child."

Ben glanced out the back window. "What child?"

I jumped out and sprinted down the street waving. "Wait, please!" The group stopped, and I charged forward and bent in front of the little girl. I held out the card. "I want you to have this."

The girl looked puzzled, but she accepted the card. "Thank you," she whispered.

Her mother snatched the card and inspected it before holding it out to me. "We can't take this."

I stood. "I really want you to have it."

The young mother studied the sidewalk. "I know you do. And I appreciate your kindness. But there's no place we can use that card without being suspected of stealing it. The numbers on the card show it belongs to someone in the upper class." She pointed at the card's serial number. "I can't go to jail and neither can my husband." She waved the card, urging me to take it.

I reached out my gloved hand and took it back, trying to ignore the lump that welled in my throat. I was upset by my inability to help, but I was equally embarrassed to be so out of touch. How could I not have known about the numbers?

The woman smiled. "If you donate it to a government-sponsored charity, it can help people like my family."

"Okay, I'll do that."

"God bless you, Miss Vivica." The woman took her daughter's hand and continued down the street. That she recognized me only added to my embarrassment. For the first time since stepping out of the car, I felt the cold and shivered. Ben put his hand on my shoulder.

"Can you believe that?" I asked.

"Yes."

"Did you know they wouldn't be able to take the card?"

"Yes. It's been on the news. People have been falsely accused of stealing after someone tried to help them."

"Then why didn't you stop me? I feel so stupid." Maybe I needed to stop worrying so much about the latest celebrity gossip and pay attention to the news alerts that appeared on my doc every day. "It's been such an awful day. I wanted to do something nice." We walked back to the car.

"I know." Ben opened the door. "I didn't have time to stop you. And you heard the woman. Donate the money to charity."

"I wanted to help *that* little girl." Tears formed, which upset me even more because I didn't usually cry so easily. Plus, I didn't want to break down in front of Ben. I turned away, and we rode in silence.

The slums gave way to our affluent neighborhood, and we passed through an iron gate in a massive stone wall that surrounded our elite community.

Ben lived a few streets over, but he usually took the school's transportation home. My mother considered the shared transportation too much of a safety risk for me, so Bobby escorted me everywhere.

The car passed through another gate and turned onto the winding drive that led to the governor's mansion. It looked more like a fortress than a home, glaring at anyone who dared to travel up the lane. The car parked, and Bobby got out and opened the door.

"Are you getting out?" Ben grinned, his eyes twinkling.

"Yeah." I scrambled out, stuffed the cash card into my pocket, and hurried into the house, letting Ben find his own way.

I grabbed two apples and water bottles from the kitchen, and we headed to my side of the house. Settling on the couches in the sitting area off of my bedroom, I tossed Ben an apple. "So talk." I bit into my apple, the crunch magnified in the silence. I hoped whatever he had to say would help get my mind off everything that had happened.

Ben sighed. "I'm sorry for taking advantage of you."

"What do you mean?"

He twisted the cap off his water bottle. "I shouldn't have had sex with you."

I fought the urge to laugh. Where was this coming from? "In case you forgot, I was a willing participant." I took another bite.

"I know. But it was wrong. I didn't show you the respect you deserve." His eyes searched mine. "I know better than to have sex with someone I'm not married to."

I swallowed before I choked. Some radical religious groups believed sex was only for a man and a woman who were married, but they usually stayed quiet to avoid accusations of hate speech. Now Ben agreed with them? Weird. It was kind of sweet that he felt bad since it had happened only once. After that he'd broken up with me.

"So, you feel guilty now?"

"Yes. What we did was a sin," Ben said.

"Where were these convictions when we were dating?" I sounded harsher than I felt, but Ben confused me.

He blushed. "I was ignoring them."

"And hiding them."

"Yes. But God has forgiven me. And now I'm asking you to." Guilt dimmed the kindness that normally shone in his eyes.

I shrugged. "You're forgiven. No big deal. I get it. You have to hide what you believe or someone will accuse you of hate speech."

Relief flooded his expression before his eyes clouded, and he looked down. "True Christians shouldn't hide their beliefs."

"The smart ones do. Look, I don't really care. I'm so over it."

"Viv, you can stop acting tough. I know I hurt you when I broke up with you. It probably felt like it came out of nowhere."

"Okay, fine. You hurt me. At least I know now it wasn't me. Are you happy?" I drew my knees to my chest.

"No, I'm not happy. I want to be the friend I should have been before I got carried away."

Though his apology was more than I had ever received from most guys, I wasn't sure about us being friends. "Why bother if there's nothing in it for you?"

Ben's shoulders slumped. "Because I care about you. You're exciting. Sophisticated. Smart. Beautiful." He sighed. "And we had fun together before I ruined everything."

We did have fun. From the day he'd worked up enough nerve to talk to me after smiling awkwardly at me for a week in URNA history, we'd been inseparable. He listened to me. I didn't have to put on a facade. I could just be Vivica—not the governor's daughter.

"If I'm so wonderful and you care so much, then why break up with me?"

"Because I don't want . . . never mind. Can you just believe me?"

I tossed the apple core toward the automatic trash disposer in the corner. It hit the metal with a dull thud. The feeling that there was more to his agenda than a simple apology bugged me.

"I forgive you, okay? We can be friendly. But I have homework I need to do."

"I understand." Ben stood and cleared his throat. "One more thing. You're not pregnant, are you?" His cheeks turned pink.

I laughed at the look on his face. "No. You can relax."

"You're sure? Because the vaccines don't always work as well as the gov—"

"I'm sure. The school nurse even gave me my mandatory test a few days after we . . ."

He looked away and shoved his hands in his pockets.

"Besides, if I were pregnant, it would be an easy problem to fix."

Ben nodded slowly, his face a mix of relief and disapproval.

"You obviously have an opinion."

He hesitated. "I don't agree with the term law."

"I'm not surprised based on your word choice in class today." I frowned. "You'd better watch what you say, or you'll be investigated and end up in prison."

"Says the girl who sassed the woman from Pop Management."

I raised my eyebrows.

"Yeah, I heard." His gaze was intense.

"No one's going to think I'm anti-government."

"Not all of us have a mom who's the governor. But we should have the right to say what we believe."

Should we? The laws are meant to protect us from domestic terrorism.

"Whatever." My thoughts turned to Meredith, and I held up a hand. "Wait a second. Why were you hanging around with Meredith?"

"We weren't dating." He rubbed the back of his neck. "She needed a friend. That's all."

"Because she was trying to hide her pregnancy."

"She didn't hide it very well, now did she?" His eyes flicked toward the door.

He knew something he wasn't telling me, but I'd already stirred up enough trouble for the day. "Well, you should be careful what you say. People might get the wrong idea."

"Viv, do you really agree with the term law?"

I looked away. Why couldn't he let this go? "The law is the law. We have to follow it."

"Is that what you really believe or just what you say because of your mom?"

I bristled. "I believe it. Weren't you paying attention when we went through that neighborhood today? Didn't you see how many people need help?"

"The term law has been in place for years. Is it helping?"

I opened my mouth to retort but stopped.

"I saw how it made you feel when you couldn't help that woman and her daughter. And what about Meredith? How'd that make you feel? Don't you want freedom to make your own choices instead of being told what you can and can't do? What you can and can't say?"

There it was—the rest of his agenda. What was with him? It was like there was a totally different person standing in front of me. *This* guy had not been my boyfriend.

"I'll get over what happened today. My mom and I don't always agree, but she's a great governor." I crossed my arms. "If you're trying to convert me to ease your conscience, forget it. That's not me. I know how the government feels about exclusivist Christian whackos. You're crazy to talk about this."

"You gonna report me?"

"No." I couldn't believe he thought I'd do that.

Ben rested his hands on my shoulders. "I'm sorry I was selfish and took advantage of you. I've been a poor excuse for a Christian." He dropped his hands and picked up his backpack. "I'll leave you alone now." He opened it, pulled out a wadded gym uniform, and uncovered a book.

"Where did you get that?" Books made of paper were rare because of environmental regulations restricting paper usage.

"It's an original Bible. Not the government's edited version. Take it."

"No way." I stepped back. "That thing is full of hate speech."

"Viv, there's nothing hateful about it. Why don't you read it yourself instead of believing everything you've been told? It's helped me a lot."

"Fine." I took the book so he'd leave. I could always get rid of it later.

><

"Good morning! Vivica, sweetie, where are you?"

I stifled a groan as I applied mascara. It was too early to deal with Melvin Powers who'd been my mother's faithful assistant since she'd launched her political career as a representative twelve years ago. He'd lasted because he thrived on taking orders. Gaining a bit of influence through my mom probably helped too. He rapped on my bathroom door.

I laid the mascara tube on the counter. "What is it, Melvin?"

"Your mother wants to see you in her office. Pronto."

"Why?" I raked my fingers through my hair and adjusted the pins.

I could hear Melvin's sigh through the door. "Just do me a personal favor and get over there."

"Fine." I owed him for all the times he ran interference for me with my mother. I finished my makeup and tried to guess what she wanted.

I crossed the catwalk that bridged the chasm of living space that separated my rooms from my mother's quarters and ambled down the staircase to her office. Out of habit, I avoided the creaks in the hallway. I stopped at the door, watching her work at her steel and glass desk in

front of a wall of computer screens. Melvin, seated on the couch, jab-
bered on a call with someone important. My mother's black Labrador
retriever, Commander, rose to greet me, and I patted his head while his
tail beat against my legs.

My mother glanced up and waved. "Come in, Vivica." She tapped a
few computer screens, and a map and images from a newscast appeared.
"Let me finish." My mother pursed her lips and studied the screen.

The cameraman focused on huddled masses of humanity that
swarmed in front of a courthouse. I didn't recognize the location, but
from their screams it was obvious something terrible had occurred.

"Melvin!"

He excused himself from his call, hopped to his feet, and wrinkled
his nose as he brushed dog hair from his designer suit. "What do you
need?"

"The media are reporting a rebel uprising in the Coastal Plain Region.
Contact the head of the Department of Security and get a report on the
amount of rebel activity in our region."

Avoiding Commander, Melvin scurried out.

I glanced at the screens. "If you're busy, we can talk later."

"No, I may not have time later." She motioned to the couch.

I sat as Commander collapsed at my feet with a sigh. My mother
relaxed in her chair. *Regal* was what the media called her. It was true.
Her golden hair was arranged in an elegant French twist, and her air-
brushed makeup made her skin appear youthful and flawless. I tried
to recall the last time I saw my mother without makeup and realized I
had no memory of that. There were many who said I looked like her,
and while I shared her golden hair, aquamarine eyes, and height, I had
a long way to go before I could match her flawless elegance.

"What's going on with the rebels?"

Mom's eyes fastened on me. "The Nationalist Party intends to nom-
inate me for president."

I studied the screen above my mother's head. The camera zoomed in
on a crowd of people who pushed and shoved against the government
officials trying to prevent the mob from storming the courthouse. A
rhythmic chant throbbed in the air, but the audio was too low for me

to understand the words. One man held our nation's flag out for the camera while the woman next to him glared into the camera lens and set the flag on fire.

"Vivica. Did you hear me?"

"Yeah. The presidential nomination." I pointed at the screen. "What's going on? Why is there an uprising?"

My mother whirled in her desk chair and brushed her fingers over the screens. The images faded to ebony. "I need you to focus."

"Please tell me what's going on first." I wasn't trying to be difficult, but it was hard to concentrate after the images I'd seen.

"According to my sources, there are food distribution issues in the Coastal Plain Region. The lower class is staging protests, and the rebels are encouraging them. The security in that region is pitiful because their governor is worthless. Now . . . about my presidential nomination."

"What about President Hernandez? I thought the party liked him."

My mother raised her chin as if I'd offended her, which I hadn't meant to do. I was just curious. "They do. But they think after twelve years of Hernandez it's time for someone new. They like what I've done as governor. Besides, Felipe is ready to retire."

In our country the powerful party leaders chose the presidential nominee, and the representatives appointed by the governors of each region confirmed the nomination. "Well, they should like what you've done with security." Our region was one of the most secure in the nation with very little rebel activity due to my mother's policies. She'd be a great president, and I could get used to being the president's daughter. I grinned. "So, the nomination is pretty much a done deal?"

My mother returned the smile. "Yes. Unless something unforeseen happens to prevent it."

⟩⟨

There was always a long line at the school's retinal scanner. I didn't see any of my friends, so I pulled my doc out of my bag and accessed my bank account. My mother had deposited my weekly allowance. Maybe I could take a shopping trip after school. Or I could give the money to a government charity like the little girl's mom suggested . . . I decided on the charity and transferred the money.

When the machine finished scanning my eye, the door opened. I waved to Bobby, who nodded. As bad as it was having him escort me, I was thankful he didn't follow me around the school. Unlike my string of previous bodyguards, Bobby understood a sixteen-year-old girl needed space and instinctively knew what information should be reported to my mother and what information should be ignored. For that reason, Bobby and I got along, but out of habit I operated under the assumption that anything he witnessed might be relayed to my mother.

I entered the lobby where Tindra appeared and grabbed my elbow.

"Good morning." I checked out her cream-colored, lace T-shirt that complemented her olive skin. "I love that top."

"You are totally not gonna believe what I heard."

She pulled me away from the crowd, and we huddled near a screen that exhibited three-dimensional images of trophies as pictures of the school's championship teams scrolled by.

She looked around and then leaned close. "Mrs. O'Keefe got fired for allowing the discussion in class yesterday."

I gasped. "Did Claire tell? I mean she was arguing with D² and made it clear she agreed with the term law."

"I wouldn't put it past her. She's tight with the principal's daughter."

"What about D²?"

Tindra shrugged. "Don't know."

I clutched my purse handle. "Do you think Ben will get in trouble?"

"Why are you worried about him?"

I stared at the trophy case. "He apologized yesterday. He doesn't want to get back together or anything, but an apology is more than I've gotten from some guys."

She shook her head. "Whatever. If it makes you feel any better, I heard Claire has a crush on him, so maybe she'll keep him out of it."

I hoped Tindra was right.

⋊⋉

That evening at dinner I forced myself to take a bite of cod. It wasn't the food. It was my appetite.

"It's my understanding that some interesting events have taken place at your school during the last couple of days," my mother said.

I rested the fork on my plate. "The girl they arrested was in my study hall. I saw her get shot."

"It was only a tranquilizer gun."

"It was still disturbing."

"Perhaps the young lady should have thought of the consequences before she broke the law." My mother dabbed her lips with her napkin and surveyed me. "Is there anything else you want to tell me about that day?"

I took a drink of water and then shook my head. "Can't think of anything." Had someone reported my outburst in study hall?

"I see."

"Wait." I glanced away and pushed asparagus pieces around my plate. "There was a discussion about whether or not we still need the term law in URNA history. I didn't realize people were actually against it."

My mother grimaced. "Only the rebels. The sane people in this country support the law."

"We still need it even though the economy is better?"

"Absolutely. The law was put into place to help reduce the number of people needing government support. Young, single mothers have always been a drain on government resources, and after the Great Collapse, we had to take stopgap measures to bring it under control so everyone could have their fair share. It made such an economic difference, the law became permanent. With young women free of the burden of children, they can further their education or work and contribute to society. Besides, teenage girls have no business rearing children. They should be free to live and enjoy their lives. Imagine being burdened with a child, at your age."

"Couldn't they just have the babies and give them up for adoption?"

"It's too much for the health care system to handle. And there's no guarantee that the children will be adoptable. The rebels have been managing to hide a few lawbreakers"—she smiled—"but they won't for much longer."

"What do you mean?" As long as I asked questions, she'd keep talking.

"With the help of the Global Health Organization, the United Regions of North America is preparing an initiative that will vastly improve health care. Citizens will have biochips implanted in their arms to monitor their health data. Other countries are using biochips already, and citizens are able to have advance warning of, and thus prevent, at least fifty percent of heart attacks and strokes. Diabetics will have immediate access to their glucose levels, making it easier to determine their insulin needs. Another benefit is that if a woman becomes pregnant, we'll know even before she does. And those are just the most immediate and obvious benefits. The entire nation will have an increased quality of life."

Not having to take a pregnancy test every four months would be nice. "How soon?"

"The plan is to begin shortly after I take office. It will be one of the hallmarks of my presidency." Her eyes gleamed as she studied me.

Uh-oh. "Sounds like a great plan. How will—"

"If I ever hear of you showing disrespect to a government official again, I will cut off your allowance for six months."

Busted. "Who told you?"

"It doesn't matter. Do you understand?"

"Yes, ma'am."

My mother and I ate in silence until Melvin appeared in the doorway.

"Excuse me, Governor. I'm so sorry to interrupt your dinner." He held my mother's enhanced multiphone device in his hand. "The security director needs to speak with you. It's urgent."

My mother shoved her plate aside and took the MD3 from Melvin and projected the screen onto the wall next to the table. When I started to stand, my mother shook her head. "Finish your dinner. Go ahead, Director Spiegel."

"Governor, I looked into the rebel activity in our region per your request." He smoothed his comb-over.

"And?"

"It's not surprising that the rebel movement has spread from the Coastal Plain Region to the others, including our region."

My mother swore. "I always knew no good would come of their poor security. If they'd controlled their population better they wouldn't be in this mess now. How bad is it?"

"I have my agents on it, but from what we can tell there are at least five rebel cells in the Great Lakes Region with the biggest one in your hometown. Membership appears to span social classes. Many, but not all, are exclusivist Christians. As we expected based on reports from other regions, they're spreading anti-government sentiments based on old U.S. constitutional principles. The exclusivists are circulating unauthorized print versions of the Bible and claiming our government's Revised Freedom Version is inaccurate."

Ben had to be involved. Where else would he have gotten an unauthorized Bible? Plus, his family had moved into our region two years ago. I forced myself to take a bite and pretended not to listen.

"We're investigating anyone who has moved into your region during the past several years from the CP. However, I'd be careful about trusting anyone, no matter how long you've known them."

"How could this have happened in my own region? How long will it take to find these people? How soon can we have them in custody?" My mother sounded panicky.

"Governor, it could be awhile. But don't worry. The problem has spread all over the country. I don't think it will hurt your nomination chances."

My mother bristled. "Never mind the nomination. How I handle security in my region does matter. Do you need more manpower? More funding? Whatever you need, you have to let me know."

"I think we have enough, but I'll let you know. I'm also sending you a detailed report of our findings."

"Thank you, Director. I'll expect a daily report on your progress."

"Yes, ma'am."

She disconnected. "That idiot is not going to handle this properly!"

Melvin sighed. "I was afraid you'd think that."

"Why wouldn't I? 'It could be awhile'? He ought to know I don't want to hear that. I want people in custody *tonight*, not a week or a month from now."

Melvin rested his hands on the back of a chair. "You may not have people in custody tonight, but you need to do something to discourage the growth of the rebel cells."

She bit her lip. "Schedule a press conference for tomorrow. I have an idea."

Melvin hurried away, and I started to follow.

"Wait." She leaned forward. "Earlier when you were talking about the debate, you implied students were espousing rebel principles. Who were the students?"

My mind churned. D² wasn't a rebel. He just had too many opinions for his own good. I forced myself to meet my mother's eyes. "It was just one new kid. I . . . think his name is Jarvis." I bit a hangnail. "I don't know his last name."

"That doesn't matter. His first name will be enough."

# CHAPTER 3

"I pledge my allegiance to the United Regions of North America and to the Great Lakes Region. I pledge to follow all laws and to give my devotion and loyalty to the leaders appointed to shepherd our great nation. I pledge to stand in unity and maintain peace so justice and liberty may abound for all."

We saluted the flag with red and white vertical stripes and three stars of yellow, blue, and green. Then quiet murmurs filled the classroom as we took our seats.

"Attention students." The announcement blared through the sound system, and the screen at the front of the room displayed the governor's seal. "Governor Wilkins is delivering a special address to the region. Please give her your full attention."

Miss Martinson stepped aside as my mother's image replaced the seal. She stood on our back porch behind a podium framed by massive columns.

Chatter increased and several classmates threw glances my way. I shrugged, even though I knew what this was about. It was easier to pretend I didn't.

Any time my mother addressed the region, class was interrupted, so she didn't choose this time of day often. The only time she interrupted school was when the announcement mattered to everyone, and she wanted to be sure kids heard the message.

"Good morning." My mother smiled and paused. "As you may be aware thanks to the wonderful coverage that our United Broadcast Company provides, there are certain regions in our country that are experiencing uprisings due to increased rebel activity." My mother's gaze grew more intense as the camera zoomed in. "This will not be tolerated in the Great Lakes Region."

Ian, the guy who sat next to me, grinned. "Rebels better watch out."

I smiled. "That's right." I turned my attention back to the speech, forced a smile, and wondered how this news would affect Ben and his family.

"The security of our region is a responsibility I take very seriously. We must provide a safe environment in which our children can grow, learn, and become productive citizens. Rebel beliefs and activities undermine the very freedoms we hold dear."

A whispered conversation took place in the back of the room. Were they agreeing or disagreeing? Or not paying attention at all?

"The United States of America was founded upon Judeo-Christian values that were bigoted and restrictive. Years ago, the Peace and Unity Act liberated us from this narrow-mindedness, protecting our great country from hate speech that spreads intolerance and divisiveness. However, the rebels' negative message resurrects that Judeo-Christian hatred, spreading anti-government sentiment. Most recently, we've seen a proliferation of printed copies of unauthorized Bibles."

I'd always believed the unauthorized Bibles were dangerous, but what exactly made them a threat? No one had ever said.

"We must be a region united against such bigotry. We must be a people willing to do what it takes to defeat those who would destroy our country. Therefore, it is my duty as governor to exercise my best judgment to provide security and order in our region. First, I encourage you to report to your local authorities the names of anyone who expresses anti-government views. This will allow us to investigate and imprison offenders, which will lead to the elimination of rebel cells."

No matter what I'd told my mother, D² was probably in trouble. Ben could be in danger too.

"Second, we must make a concerted effort to locate and destroy all unauthorized print versions of the Bible and supplemental materials that contradict the Revised Freedom Version. Citizens will have three months to voluntarily surrender unauthorized Bibles or related print materials at local community centers. After that period, anyone choosing to retain, obtain, or smuggle unauthorized Bibles will be arrested and subsequently fined or imprisoned. Citizens may continue to find comfort in the Revised Freedom Version on their government-issued multiphone devices. Carefully edited by religious scholars from the United Evangelical Pluralist Association, under provisions set forth in the Peace and Unity Act, the Revised Freedom Version is the only authorized version and contains no restrictive, dangerous, or offensive ideologies. Citizens may continue to use religious books that do not promote intolerance and violence."

It seemed like a fair deal. Why would anyone *want* to keep a version of a book that was restrictive and offensive?

She wasn't finished. "I ask everyone to take a stand for peace and unity. I understand that some of your unauthorized Bibles may have sentimental value. Soon, I will report to my local community center where I will surrender my dear grandmother's Bible, a family keepsake that has been packed away in my attic for years. I cannot in clear conscience risk this book falling into the hands of our enemies. Therefore, I will do my civic duty, and I encourage you to do the same for the common good of our region." She looked into the camera. "Together, we can avoid the frightening prospect of rebels spreading lies and tearing our neighborhoods and homes apart. Thank you for your cooperation."

My mother began to take questions from the press, but since the important part was finished, the screen faded to black. The room was silent. Then someone started applauding and everyone joined in. Did they all really agree or were some of them rebels who were pretending?

>)<

A week later, Melvin greeted me at the front door when I arrived home.

"What's going on?" Before he could answer, my mother's high heels clicked against the tile floor. She appeared at the end of the hallway and held a large book in her hand. "How was school?"

"Fine. What's going on?"

"I'm going to the community center to turn in my grandmother's Bible. The news crew will be there."

Melvin held up a Bible. "I found one for you." It looked like it had never been opened.

"I'd like you to be a part of this," my mother said. "You can set the example for the younger citizens who look up to you."

I thought of the Bible hidden upstairs in my nightstand drawer. Though I'd not even looked at it since Ben gave it to me, the fuss made me curious. I took the book from Melvin. "Thanks."

⋊⋉

Our executive car stopped next to the curb in front of the community center. People of all ages lined the block, even though it was a cold day. A few women and children stood in clusters. The film crew from the local TV station waited near the door.

Surrounded by her security team, my mother led the way to the front door. Some people in the crowd cheered, but I guessed that most were too cold to care.

A short man with a nametag that read *Alan*, motioned us forward and scanned our docs. With fanfare, he opened the door of a narrow, stainless steel chamber. The inside was lined with bricks, and the heat blasted my face. I pulled back and then inched closer to peek inside. It was full of ash. My mother tossed the Bible in, and I did the same. A cloud of soot rose before Alan shut the door and pushed buttons on a panel next to the door. "Governor, these automatic incinerators are awesome."

My mother beamed, and the camera crew recorded everything. "Thank you. However, I cannot take full credit. The Council of World Peacekeepers made these incinerators available to President Hernandez, who in turn made them available to the governors. I only recently thought of using them to solve our problem." Melvin, who stood off to the side with a reporter, motioned for me to join them.

Melvin put his arm around me. "Vivica, Miss Jackson would like to ask you a few questions. Do you mind?"

"No. That's fine."

The reporter was young, and her clothes were stylish and her appearance perfect. I hadn't seen her before. She waved her cameraman over. "I'm Jacinda Jackson." She eyed my outfit in a way that made me feel like I'd put it together wrong, but I raised my chin and stared her down. How dare she question my fashion choices when girls all over the region emulated me?

"I'm here with Vivica Wilkins at the local community center where she and her mother have set a fine example for all Great Lakes Region residents by incinerating copies of unauthorized Bibles. Vivica, how do you feel?"

The right words floated by in my mind, but when I tried to speak, a current of doubt pulled them away.

I'd been interviewed before and had never been speechless. How did I feel? I knew what I was supposed to say, but was that what I really thought? Then there was my own hypocrisy, burning one Bible publicly while another was hidden at home in my nightstand.

Jacinda flashed an encouraging smile. "Perhaps I should rephrase that question. What do you hope to accomplish by being here today?"

I was grateful for the rescue. "I hope to set a good example for the younger generation. It is important to follow the laws established in our country because our safety and security are so important." I took a deep breath. Now that Jacinda had her sound bite for the evening news, my mother would be happy.

"Thank you, Vivica. You're an inspiration." Obviously, Jacinda didn't want to risk me fumbling another question.

I forced a smile. "Thank you. I'm so glad."

The cameraman stopped filming, and he and Jacinda moved on. How much longer would this take?

I found the restroom, shut myself in a stall, and leaned against the metal partition. Maybe I could hide until it was time to go. Two toilets flushed.

I peered through the crack in the door at two middle-aged women who had exited the stalls on either side of me and stood in front of the row of sinks. I studied their reflections in the mirror. One was pudgy and the other had puffy lips from too many injections.

"How do you feel about all of this?" Puffy asked.

"I prayed about it and decided I need to obey the law of the land." Pudgy held her hands under the faucet and scrubbed. "I don't read the old exclusivist Bible anyway. It was my grandpa's. I was brought up as a United Evangelical Pluralist and we always loved and included everybody, so I like the Revised Freedom Version better."

Puffy stuck her hands under the dryer and spoke over the hum. "I'm glad to know I'm not alone. I came to the same conclusion myself." She shook her head. "I don't understand the rebels stirring up trouble."

"Same here. Jesus wasn't a rebel. He promoted peace and unity."

They left the restroom, and I stood thinking about their comments. The exclusivists really were whacko. These ladies were right. Obeying the law was important, so I should've brought Ben's Bible with me. But I had time to get rid of it. I quickly washed my hands and exited the restroom.

Milling through the crowd, I searched for my mother and Melvin.

"Hey! I need a policeman." The man's voice was angry. I scanned the room until I found who'd spoken. The man's nose and ears were red from the long wait in the cold.

For the first time I noticed the police. A few officers rushed from their posts at the door to his side, and the man pointed to an older gentleman who supported himself with a cane and held a Bible under his arm. "Lock this old geezer up. He's standing here spreading hate speech."

The officers exchanged glances. "Sir, is this true?" one of the men asked.

Though the old man had a cane, he stood straight. "Jesus said, 'I am the way and the truth and the life. No one comes to the Father except through me.' You folks can ban the real Bible, but you'll never change the truth."

"You're under arrest for using language that promotes exclusivity and domestic terrorism." Each policeman grabbed an arm and dragged the old man with more force than necessary through the door. The man cried out as his arm twisted at an ugly angle.

I stepped forward. "Go easy on him. He's not resisting."

"Mind your own business." The officer glared, but his expression changed when he realized the protest came from the governor's daughter. He loosened his grip, and I followed them outside to make sure they were careful. As they lowered the man into the car, I looked at his face and saw the saddest pair of eyes I'd ever seen.

>X<

My mother turned off the TV in her office and sat back in her desk chair. "Vivica, I don't know what to say to you right now. I'm horribly disappointed. Why did you interrupt my officers?"

I swallowed, trying to disregard the lump in my throat. At least she was speaking to me again. Until the evening news report from the community center had aired, she'd ignored me. "They were being rough. And the man was really old."

"The man was clearly breaking the law. There were eyewitnesses. You knew that cameras were there. Melvin had to bribe the reporter into not airing your outburst." She motioned toward the TV. "We're lucky she accepted it."

My mother thought my protest reflected badly on her and might hinder her nomination because our region had one news station, and the government-owned national news network managed it. She was making a big deal out of something that people would forget in a few days, but I'd never tell her that.

"I'm sorry," I whispered, and tears welled in my eyes. "I know being president is your dream. I don't want to do anything to keep you from it."

"Fine. You've always been too soft-hearted." My mother cleared her throat. "But I already told you I'd cut off your allowance if you ever showed disrespect to a government official again."

"I wasn't being disrespectful."

"You were interfering. You'll do without an allowance for three months, which will reimburse me for what I had to pay the reporter."

"Okay." I turned to leave before she changed her mind and made it longer.

"While I have you here, there's another matter I'd like to discuss."

I refused to blink because I didn't want the tears spilling over. "Okay." What had I done now? I held my breath.

"Ben Lagarde." My mother said his name as though he were a criminal. "Are you still seeing him?"

"We broke up."

"Did he hurt you?" Her eyes flashed, and I pictured her sending the police after Ben for upsetting me.

"Yes, but he apologized."

"Good. You don't have plans to get back together with him?"

I gazed at the carpet, thankful I could tell her what she wanted to hear. "No, and he doesn't want to either."

"I'm glad to hear that. The Lagarde family may be rebels. I don't need a scandal. It could be an issue that you even dated him." My mother leaned forward. "Did Ben ever do or say anything to indicate that he or his family were rebels?"

I looked into my mother's eyes, knowing it was the only way to convince her. "No."

Her eyes narrowed, and she studied me as if she could determine the veracity of each word that came out of my mouth simply by staring me down. "Fine. You may go."

><

I sat on the edge of my bed, reached into my nightstand drawer, and removed the unauthorized Bible. The old man's eyes haunted me. What was it about the words of this book that made someone risk jail time by speaking them publicly? The old man was crazy, but he was courageous. He was certainly different than the women in the restroom.

Had Ben turned in his Bible? Would he have given me one if the ban had already been in place or would he have just told me to read the Revised Freedom Version? Were the words that scholars removed that important?

I crossed my room and locked my bedroom door. What I was about to do was an investigation to figure out why people would act so stupid for a religion. A comparison of the two versions. That's all.

I removed my doc, opened both versions of the Bible to Genesis, and started reading.

# CHAPTER 4

A few weeks later, as winter surrendered to spring, I continued to read the Bible on the sly, even though I still didn't understand why people risked their lives over it.

The secret Bible reading took second place in my life because it was time for the Governor's Ball. My mother charged Melvin with making the menu, the décor, and the entertainment bigger and better than in the past. She also tasked him with ensuring that I looked like a future president's daughter.

The only detail my mother cared about was the guest list. Politicians from all over the country and people from the upper class in our region would be invited. It wasn't unusual for me to have friends act extra nice in the months before the coveted invitations were mailed. I never let them know it was futile because the guests were my mother's choice.

One afternoon I was working on homework when there was a knock on my sitting room door. Melvin entered.

"Someday you're going to be really embarrassed that you don't wait for me to respond," I said.

He waved a hand. "Oh, it takes a lot to embarrass me, especially from you." He held several dresses covered in clear garment bags. "You need to pick a dress for the ball. Our designer sent over an array."

My mother had a personal designer named Zelda who created her wardrobe, and I had access to her talent as well. I enjoyed shopping, so I only used the designer for special occasions. I took the dresses eagerly. "Am I doing a fashion show?"

"Of course." My mother trusted Melvin to be sure that I was appropriately dressed for every occasion.

I took the gowns. "Has my mother picked her dress yet?"

"No. I tried to get her to do that today and have a little fun, but she was too wrapped up in preparing for her meeting with the rep from the

Council of World Peacekeepers. And we had a report from Director Spiegel."

"Good or bad report?"

"Bad. There's more rebel activity, and she's worried about how that'll appear to the party."

"Is she taking it out on you?"

Melvin didn't answer. He'd never make a disloyal comment about my mother. His thinning gray hair emphasized the lines on his forehead. Why hadn't I noticed he was getting older? I clutched the garment bags.

He perched on my sofa and nodded toward the bathroom. "Let's see one."

My first option was crimson silk charmeuse. I wanted to toss it aside because it reminded me of the color of the walls in my mother's office that I hated. But I liked the body-skimming shape, so I put it on. I could always ask for a different color.

As I pulled the dress up, it was snug, and when I reached around to zip it, I had to hold my breath. That was weird. "Melvin, what size did Zelda send over?"

"Same as always. Four. Are you feeling fat today?" His tone was teasing.

I opened the bathroom door. "No, I *am* fat today."

Melvin started to protest, but his mouth snapped shut when he saw how tight the dress was. "Charmeuse is a difficult fabric to pull off. Try another one."

I sighed and went back into the bathroom. The next two samples were tight and not worth modeling.

I stepped out in a strapless black dress with an empire waist. The beading was pretty, but it wasn't my favorite. Melvin looked relieved. "That fits well. You look beautiful, sweetie."

I looked in the mirror. "I guess this is the one." I could have asked for bigger sample sizes in the other dresses, but the fear of those not fitting either stopped me. "I'm going on a diet immediately."

The Friday before the ball, I was leaving school when Ben waved me over to where he stood by himself watching everyone stream out of the building. I'd avoided him since our last conversation, and he hadn't sought me out. Why was he waiting for me now?

Ben smiled as I approached. "Hey, what's going on?" he said.

My heart jumped, and I hated myself for the reaction.

"You okay?"

I plastered on a smile. "Yes. Sorry."

"I don't want to keep you. I thought I'd let you know my family and I will be at the ball tomorrow night. I hope that doesn't bother you. But you probably already knew."

I was surprised, but I didn't want him to know I hadn't seen the guest list. "It's no problem. I'm sure you'll have a wonderful time."

Ben nodded. "See ya tomorrow."

As he walked away, I mulled over his announcement. Ben's family was part of the upper class, but my mother hadn't invited them to previous balls. I knew she rotated the guest list. But I remembered the conversation my mother and I had about Ben, and I had an uneasy feeling there was more to the invitation. My mother never did anything without a good reason.

The morning of the ball I dragged myself out of bed. I'd been tired lately and slept later than normal, but I still felt sluggish. I hoped I wasn't getting sick. A quick glace in the mirror revealed puffy eyes. Stepping on the scale, I hoped for a good reading and sighed when I saw that I'd gained a pound since last week. I'd been so careful with what I'd eaten.

I rummaged for some eye cream in the cabinet under the sink. I had to look good tonight because the press would be out in full force. The party was expected to announce my mother's nomination next week, so the ball would make the national news.

Where was that eye cream? I pushed a box of tampons aside, and as I did, I caught my breath. Tampons. When was the last time I'd used tampons? I tried to count backward, but my mind was too jumbled to think straight. Signs that had been so easy to overlook now seemed obvious. Weight gain. Tiredness. Crying more easily.

I hadn't had a period since I'd had sex with Ben.

I settled on the bathroom floor. But wait. What about the vaccine? According to the school nurse, the vaccines had a failure rate of less than one percent. Unless the vaccines weren't as effective as the government led us to believe. Is that why we had to take pregnancy tests three times a year?

What else did the government lie about?

I forced myself to think back to November when the school nurse had called my group to the clinic for our mandatory tests. That whole week had been a blur because Ben had broken up with me. The nurse always told us that if we had a brand new pregnancy, the test might not show it.

If I really was pregnant, that had to be the case.

I sucked in a deep breath. This didn't have to be a big deal. It would be embarrassing to tell my mother, but I would as soon as the ball was over. I'd terminate and go on with my life. It would all be taken care of in a few days, and Ben would never have to know.

# CHAPTER 5

I had to tell my mother today because I wanted to get it over with. Even though I was due for a mandatory pregnancy test in a few weeks, I didn't want the school nurse involved in my business.

I padded through the house to her office in hopes of finding her alone. Melvin would know soon enough and I didn't care, but my mother should be the one to tell him. I paused outside of her office when I heard her talking. It was always best to listen first and determine if it was a good time to interrupt.

"Director Spiegel, please tell me you have the teams in place to search tonight during the ball. There will never be a better time to search for evidence of rebel involvement in the upper class, and I want you to be particularly meticulous at the Lagarde home. I've heard rumors."

So that was why my mother had invited Ben's family. How many other people on the guest list were suspected rebels?

"Thank you, Director. I look forward to hearing a report on your findings tomorrow morning."

I fled to my room. Should I warn Ben? I couldn't believe that I was even considering the possibility. If his family was involved in the rebel movement, then they needed to be caught. My country's security was at stake. Even so, did I want to see Ben thrown in prison?

No matter how much I told myself I didn't care about him anymore, I couldn't let him go to jail. The problem was how to warn him. The government monitored everyone's docs, so I couldn't just message him. Sneaking out might make me look suspicious. The best plan would be to take Bobby with me and tell Ben.

I laced my running shoes and went to Bobby's apartment above the garage. I rapped on the door and waited. A few seconds later, the door swung open, and I put on my best smile. "Bobby, I'm dying to go jogging. Is that okay?"

It didn't matter if it was okay. He was hired to be my security guard, and if I wanted to jog, he was expected to jog. I just felt bad about being so demanding.

Bobby smiled, and I was relieved when he didn't seem annoyed. "Sure. Haven't exercised yet today. Gimme a minute."

Soon we moved down the street at a steady pace. The weather had warmed as spring neared and the snow had melted, leaving behind matted tan grass that looked as weary as I felt.

I turned down Ben's street. The houses were stone, and it was as if someone had copied the first home on the block and pasted the same image twenty more times on each side of the street.

I stopped in front of number 220. "Bobby, I need to see if Ben is home. I want to make sure he'll dance with me tonight at the ball." I cringed inwardly because my excuse sounded stupid when I said it aloud.

Bobby shrugged. "Go ahead. I'll be right here." He leaned against a tree and stretched his hamstrings.

I rang the bell. The door opened, and my heart sank when I saw Ben's older sister Faith. A scowl ruined her face, and half of her brown hair hung in ringlets in preparation for tonight's festivities.

I forced a pleasant expression. "I need to talk to Ben for a moment."

"He's not here." Faith started to close the door, but I blocked it with my foot.

"Are you sure?"

"Yeah. I think I'm sure my brother isn't here." She smirked.

I wanted to smack her and pull her perfect curls, but a fight wouldn't help matters. "When will he be home?"

Faith put a hand on her hip. "I have no idea. Probably sometime before the ball since he'll have to change."

"I have to talk to Ben. It's a matter of life and death. Will you tell him I stopped?"

Faith laughed and leaned against the frame. "Seriously? What could you possibly have to tell him that's life or death? Wait!" She held up a hand. "I know. You might die if you don't have a dance partner?"

I raised my chin and refused to let her attitude bother me. "I've never lacked for partners."

Faith's eyes narrowed. "No doubt. If you think you're going to get your claws into Ben again, you're crazy. He knows you're not worth the trouble, so leave him alone." Faith slammed the door.

I whirled and jogged down the sidewalk.

>✗<

I posed with my dress for Tindra. "What do you think?"

She grinned. "Lovely." She unzipped the garment bag that held her own dress. "And mine?"

"Gorgeous."

We'd spent the afternoon at the salon getting our hair, nails, and makeup done, and now we were in my suite until it was time to dress.

"Is Ben going to be there tonight?" Tindra asked.

"Yeah." I hung my dress on the edge of the wardrobe. "But my mother told me to stay away from him."

Tindra laughed. "Like you always do what she says. Where's the rebel who created the messaging system?"

I cringed. "Maybe you should avoid the word *rebel*."

"Oh, right." Tindra giggled and sprawled on the floor to stretch her legs.

I plopped on my couch and pulled a pillow onto my lap. "There's something I want to tell you. But you have to promise not to say anything."

"Oh, this ought to be good." Tindra leaned against the couch. "What is it?"

I picked at the decorative edge of the pillow. "I think I'm pregnant."

"You *think*?"

"Yeah, I'm pretty sure. It's the only thing that makes sense. I mean, when Melvin brought the sample sizes for the dresses, a bunch of them didn't fit. I just thought I needed to run more and eat less. And with everything going on, I hadn't noticed my lack of periods. I've never been that regular anyway."

"The vaccine didn't work for my sister either." Tindra projected the latest celebrity news from her doc onto my wall. "Is it Ben's?"

"Yeah."

"And here I thought you were going to tell me something good." Tindra scrolled through the pictures and stopped when she got to a shirtless picture of Eduardo, her favorite singer. "Do you think there'll be any guys as hot as my Eddie at the ball?"

"Maybe." I rested my hand on my abdomen. "Do terminations hurt?"

She shrugged. "My sister had some cramping, but other than that it was fine and life went on."

"Tindra, your sister got into drugs."

"Yeah, but that didn't have anything to do with it. Why would it?" She examined the flower painted on her big toenail. "Her next boyfriend got her into drugs. Besides, she's clean now." She leapt up and pirouetted across the room. "If I don't get asked to dance, I'll be totally humiliated."

I forced a smile. "You'll be asked. Don't worry."

I should have known my announcement wouldn't shock Tindra. She was right. Like her sister, I'd have the procedure, and my life would go on. But how could I tell her something was bothering me when I didn't even know what it was myself?

# CHAPTER 6

The limousine arrived at the convention center, to a crowd gathered near the entrance where they expected us to exit our vehicle. Bobby adjusted the limo's programmed route, and it detoured to the back of the building where several security guards stood next to a service door. "Right on time," Melvin said. He wore an earpiece, and he paused to listen. "Governor, the event coordinator says as soon as you get inside it'll be time for your introduction. Vivica, follow your mother and then stand next to me." Even though I'd been to many governors' balls, we'd never sneaked in the back, and my mother had never made such a big deal about her entrance. The presidential nomination changed everything.

The guards escorted us down a narrow hall lined with food carts that held plated salads waiting to be served. To our left, the kitchen bustled with activity. My stomach rumbled when I smelled fresh bread and roast beef.

We turned down another hall, arrived backstage, and stepped into the wings. A podium waited in the middle of the ballroom's elevated stage.

The buzz of conversation and clink of glasses quickly stilled as Melvin strode on stage and stood behind the podium. "Good evening, ladies and gentlemen of the Great Lakes Region."

The crowd cheered.

"It's my very great pleasure to welcome you to the twenty-ninth annual governor's ball. May I present everyone's favorite governor and twice-named woman of the year, Governor Genevieve Wilkins."

My mother straightened her shoulders and glided forward. I followed, trying to match her elegance. The crowd stood and applauded, their jewels glittering in the process. Hundreds of linen-clad tables were set with fine china, silver, and crystal. Massive centerpieces of lilies decorated each table, and their saccharine perfume dominated the air. I took my place next to Melvin and waved.

My mother allowed the cheering and applause to continue for a moment before she motioned for everyone to be seated. "Dear friends of the Great Lakes Region, it has been my privilege to serve as your governor for the last eight years."

I scanned the crowd, searching for Ben and his family, but it was hard to distinguish faces, even with my mother's up-do blocking out the light.

"As you know, I am seeking the party's nomination for president. It would be my pleasure to continue to serve you on a national level, and I hope that I will have the opportunity."

Finally, I spotted Ben. He, his sister Faith, and their parents sat at a table in the middle of the room with two couples I didn't recognize. Tindra, her sister, and her parents were seated a few tables away from Ben. Tindra gave a tiny wave. I nodded.

"I hope you have a wonderful evening, and if I don't have a chance to speak with you personally, please let me thank you now for coming out to celebrate our region."

Melvin stepped forward and offered his arm to my mother, who took it. I followed them off the stage to a table near the center of the room by the dance floor. Waiting at the table were five people I didn't recognize. They rose as we approached.

My mother motioned to the first couple who looked close to my mother's age. "I'd like you to meet my daughter, Vivica. Vivica, Governor Jensen and his wife are from the Rocky Mountain Region." I shook their hands and smiled. The governor was balding, and his wife had so much curly hair she never would've missed it if her husband wanted to steal some for his own head. I stifled a giggle at the thought of her curls mounded on top of his wide head.

"And this is Governor and Mrs. Fox from the Caribbean Region." My mother motioned toward two well-tanned people. We shook hands, and I complimented Mrs. Fox on her dress.

"And I'm Drake Freeman." His voice was deep, and his mischievous blue eyes seemed capable of piercing the armor that guarded my secrets.

His blond hair, gelled into spikes, was a suitable crown to his perfect looks, and I guessed he was a couple of years older than me. "I'm from the trouble-making region."

"That seems appropriate." I extended my hand.

Drake laughed and grabbed my hand, drawing it to his lips. I gritted my teeth in an attempt to ignore the shiver that traveled up my arm. "You look beautiful, Miss Wilkins."

"You're not the governor. Why are you here?" I'd met Governor Ellis from the Coastal Plain Region a few years earlier when I was on a trip with my mother.

"I believe the proper response is 'thank you,' but, no, I'm not. I'm the governor's stepson."

Drake pulled out my chair, and I took my seat.

"I'm representing my stepfather tonight at this lovely social occasion because he obviously has more important things to deal with at the moment."

The ball wasn't that big of a deal, but it seemed insulting when Drake said it with a hint of sarcasm. A server placed a salad in front of me, and I was thankful for the distraction.

I tried to think of something to say and blurted the first thing that came to mind. "Are the uprisings in your region under control?"

"That depends on whom you ask." Drake glanced at the governors at our table who were engrossed in conversation. "The governors, including my stepfather, like to think they're in control. Truthfully, they don't have a clue how widespread and well-organized the rebellion is."

"And what makes you an expert?"

"My brother works in intelligence. He can't say anything specific, but he's hinted multiple times that the situation is worse than the governors let on."

Having a brother in intelligence didn't make Drake an expert, and his haughty attitude annoyed me. I paused to drizzle vinaigrette onto my salad. "Things have been better in our region since my mother's improved security measures were implemented."

Drake shook his head. "They only appear to be. I promise you, all that has done is inspire the rebels. I'll be shocked if there isn't a war."

"The URNA army would crush the rebels. There's no way they'd start a war. That's treason."

"Do you study history?"

I studied what was required for school, but I wasn't going to let this guy know that I hated it. "Yes. It's mandatory."

Drake laughed. "I should've asked if you paid attention. Do you remember how the British colonies fought against England to win their independence?"

"That's practically ancient history. But, yes, I've read a little about that. It's not something we've studied in school. The teachers focus on world and URNA history."

"Of course. However, the American Revolution isn't quite ancient history yet. My point, Miss Wilkins, is that the colonists' actions were treasonous. Realistically, they were no match for the British army. But the colonists declared that freedom and independence were worth the risk because they believed in the principles of life, liberty, and the pursuit of happiness."

Drake lowered his voice as he leaned closer. I wanted to back away, but his eyes, which moments before had danced with mischief, were now full of mesmerizing earnestness. "The problem is the governors and other leaders don't recognize that there are people in this country who value those principles as much as the colonists did in the 1700s. And those same people believe they can overthrow the government and create a new one. Or at least reinstate what once existed."

"Overthrow the government? The Peace and Unity Act was put in place to keep us safe. The rebels are promoting hate speech disguised as freedom. Besides, their idea of freedom would saddle people with kids they can't afford. How does that make sense?"

"It's my understanding that the rebel cause isn't just about flouting the Peace and Unity Act. Or the term law. It's about giving the people of this country the chance to experience life, liberty, and the pursuit of happiness without government interference and regulation."

I raised my eyebrows. "Are you sure you aren't one of them? You seem to know a lot."

Drake grinned and leaned back in his chair. "I like the comforts of our orderly society. I happen to believe it's smart to know and understand your enemy. So does my brother." He picked up his salad fork and stabbed a piece of lettuce.

Looking around the room, I wondered how many people shared Drake's opinion. Were there that many rebels among us? People who pretended to be loyal citizens but schemed behind closed doors to overthrow the government?

Men and women dressed in the finest formal wear engaged in friendly banter, adding to the soft roar of voices mingled with the string quartet that played in the background. Yet Drake's ominous prediction cast a pall over the festivities, and the vivid colors in the room dimmed as if I'd donned a pair of sunglasses.

"Drake, I can't believe there are that many people out there who think the government is so bad they want to replace it."

Drake studied me. "Why?"

"Look around. Do these people seem unhappy?"

"Not all of them. But don't you realize that everyone in this room is part of the elite? Everyone who is lower class is stuck because of the educational system."

"That's not true. The placement tests give *all* students the chance to get into college prep schools so they can get good jobs."

"Right. Because there's so much room in the schools by the time the wealthy finish buying spaces for their kids who bomb the placement tests. Middle class parents do the same thing for their kids at the vocational schools." He chuckled. "You're telling me everyone at your school is smart?"

If that were the case, my grade adjustment business wouldn't be thriving. But he didn't need to know that. Or that I'd never given the whole issue any thought.

"Every once in a while a poor kid gets lucky and qualifies for a spot when there's room, but most of the time they can't change their situations with the current system."

I nodded and remembered the little girl I'd tried to help a few weeks earlier. Other than that small incident, I'd never had contact with people from the lower class.

Would the rebels taking over and putting their ideal government in place make things better for everyone? Did the poor know what they were talking about? Or were they just interested in forcibly taking what didn't belong to them so they could wield power?

But if the rebel movement really was about freedom, then that explained why it spanned all social classes and why Ben's family might have joined. I clutched my napkin. What if my mother's team found something in Ben's house?

I pushed my salad away and excused myself. The chaotic gaiety of the party prodded at my nerves, leaving me feeling a wave of nausea akin to seasickness. I rushed into the ladies' room and went to the sink where I wet a towel and dabbed my face.

"Are you okay?" Tindra put her hand on my back.

I startled at her touch. "I'm just a little warm."

Tindra frowned. "Is it . . . ?"

"I don't know. Maybe."

Tindra pulled a tube of lipstick from her purse. "Who's that hot guy sitting at your table?"

I tossed the towel into a basket. "Drake Freeman. And he may be hot, but he's annoying."

"Sounds like my type."

"Whatever. He's from the CP, so good luck with that." I powdered my nose.

"Oh, never mind. There's another guy I have my eye on." Tindra snapped her purse shut. "I'll call you later." She sailed out.

When I exited the ladies' room, I found myself face to face with Ben in the hall. I'd never seen him in a tuxedo, and I liked what I saw.

"I hear you and Faith had an encounter this afternoon."

"That's one way of putting it. Why does your sister hate me?"

Ben looked at the floor. "She blames you for the compromises I made. But I made my own choices. What was so important that you needed to talk to me?"

I looked away. "It's no big deal."

He put his hand on my shoulder. "Yes, it is, if you came over to my house to talk."

I couldn't tell him that at this moment the police were probably searching his house. It was too late. Ben and his whole family would be on their way to jail tonight because I let his sister irritate me.

Ben's eyes were kind. "Whatever it is, you can tell me."

It was a strong impulse, and I tried to ignore it. I'm not sure what possessed me. Maybe it was his eyes. All I ever intended to tell him was that his family was in danger. But before I could think better of it, I leaned forward and whispered, "I'm pregnant."

# CHAPTER 7

Ben's face turned blank for a few seconds, and then his cheeks reddened. He looked over his shoulder. "This isn't something we can discuss right here."

The moment the words left my mouth, I regretted them. "Don't worry. I don't want anything from you. As soon as I can terminate, I will. You don't have to worry. And I'm only 90 percent sure anyway. I still need to take a test and tell my mom."

Ben ushered me into an empty conference room at the end of the hall and slammed the door. His face flushed. "Then you'd better make sure since you had the vaccine. And if you are, you're not going to kill my baby."

*Kill.* Hadn't Meredith used the same word? I narrowed my eyes. "It's my body. I'll do what I want. Besides, you know it's illegal for—"

"I'm so sorry I did this to you, but please don't punish my baby." The muscle in his jaw twitched. "It is mine, isn't it?"

"Yes." I bristled. Why did he have to keep saying *baby*? "You expect me to break the law and go to prison like Meredith? Plus, that woman from Pop Management shot her. Like a wild animal."

Ben closed his eyes. "I know. I wish she'd come to me before she changed her test results."

"Why?"

He looked away.

"Did you get her pregnant too?"

"No." He shook his head. "That's not what I meant."

"Tell me what you mean."

"There are alternatives you've probably never heard about. Meredith came to me about them."

"What alternatives?" Was he talking about the rebels who hid pregnant girls? Surely that didn't really happen. "And why you?"

Ben dropped his hands and walked away from me. He paced for a few seconds before pulling out a chair and straddling it. He rested his head on his hand. "I don't know if I trust you. I mean, the vaccines aren't as reliable as the government wants us to believe, but how do I know you're not trying to trick me?"

"Then there's something else you should know."

Ben raised his head and looked weary. "What?"

I lowered my voice even further. "I didn't come to your house today to tell you I'm pregnant. I came to tell you that my mother invited your family to the ball because your family is suspected of rebel activity. Your house is being searched tonight."

He shrugged. "Let them search."

"Why don't you care?" I was shocked this information didn't yield a bigger reaction.

"Don't you think if we had anything to hide, we'd take precautions?"

"I'm sure you would, but you know the police have been more aggressive lately."

"I know. But it'll be okay." Ben's expression softened, and he stood and pulled me close. "Thanks for watching out for me."

Our lips met, and in spite of all my vows to forget him, I found myself lost in the kiss. I could get used to this again.

When we broke apart, he avoided my gaze.

"What's wrong?"

"I shouldn't have done that. I'm sorry." He buried his head in his hands. "Why do you do this to me?"

"Do what?"

"Put a spell on me. I know that's cheesy, but I don't know how else to explain it. It's like I always make the wrong decision because I want to be with you."

"Why am I so wrong for you?"

"Viv, our belief systems are totally different."

"That didn't bother you before. Be honest. You think I'm not good enough for you."

"That's not it."

Hearing this confession made my heart swell because even though I never wanted to admit it, Ben had captivated me in a way no other guy had before. When he dumped me, I resented him for awakening those feelings.

As long as he was an exclusivist with anti-government views, our belief systems were different. But what if I changed? Would he be willing to try again? I studied my jeweled shoes and wished I could walk away and rejoin the party. Strains of music filled the silence that grew unbearable.

"What were those alternatives you were talking about?" I whispered.

He shook his head. "Not now. We need to get back to the party. They're probably about to serve dinner."

I blocked the door. "Answer my question."

"I'll get back with you as soon as I can." He stared at me, and for a moment I thought he was going to kiss me again. But resolve flickered in his expression, and he straightened his shoulders. "Promise you won't tell your mother yet."

"Promise you'll get back with me."

Ben hesitated. "I've got to get back to my table."

I stepped to the side and let him out. I watched him stride down the hall and wondered if he'd abandon me again.

"That was certainly a fascinating conversation. You're facing quite a mess." Drake Freeman appeared from behind a collapsible wall.

My hand flew to my mouth to stifle a yelp. I shut the door. "How much did you hear?"

Drake laughed. "Enough to know you're pregnant or at least '90 percent sure,' and that your lover all but admitted he's a rebel."

I glared at Drake. "What were you doing in the other room?" My fists clenched. "Who hides in an empty conference room anyway?"

"Perhaps I was having a secret tryst of my own." He leaned against the wall, and the smug expression on his face infuriated me.

"If you were, remind me to warn her to run. Did anyone else hear?"

"No. I was actually planning to make a private call." He held up his doc. "I do have a life back home."

A life with dozens of girls fawning over him, no doubt. "What do you intend to do with this information?"

Drake's eyes twinkled. "I haven't decided yet. Do you want to make me an offer?"

My stomach lurched, and I wondered if the salad was going to make an appearance. "If money would help keep you quiet, I'm sure I could figure something out." It wouldn't be easy with my allowance cut off.

"Relax." Drake chuckled. "That's not my style. I'm just giving you a hard time."

"Why are you laughing at everything I say?" I regretted the words the minute I heard them. I hated this guy and should never have let him see that he was bothering me. He seemed to enjoy toying with me.

"Because you're so amusing. Now, unless you want to be accused of being my lover, I suggest we return to the dinner and act like the acquaintances we are." He opened the door. "After you, my dear."

I narrowed my eyes. "I'm not your *dear*."

Drake shrugged, and we rejoined our table where the main course had been served. My mother looked up from her conversation with Governor Fox. "I was starting to worry about you, Vivica. You were gone for so long."

I opened my mouth to answer, but Drake jumped in. "I found her gabbing with friends, Governor Wilkins. I think she was having so much fun, she lost track of time." He gave my mother a charming smile and patted my knee under the table. I jerked my leg away.

She relaxed and returned the smile. "Thank you for looking out for her, Mr. Freeman."

✖

I endured the main course and dessert while listening to Drake chat with my mother and the other governors. When it was time for the first dance, the three governors led. The men danced with their wives, and my mother chose to dance with Melvin. Some of my friends had often asked me if he and my mother were involved, but I think they thought of each other like brother and sister. Besides, he'd had a few girlfriends through the years, but nothing had ever worked out for the long haul. He probably didn't have time because my mother kept him so busy. Sacrificing love for power seemed to suit him, and sticking by my mother would take him to places he'd never go on his own. He didn't fit the charismatic mold the party preferred.

They swirled around the dance floor, and my foot tapped to the beat of the music. When I turned to say something to Drake, he was gone. Maybe the fear of being my dance partner had driven him away.

When the first dance was finished, the floor opened to everyone. Ben appeared, offered his hand, and led me to the dance floor. He put his arm around my waist, drawing me close.

"What are you doing?" I tried to leave some space between us, but his grip was firm and protective. "Are you crazy?"

"It's common knowledge we're friends."

"I'm not so sure we're friends. You wouldn't promise to help me."

"You want help?" He studied my face with a mixture of kindness and caution in his chocolate eyes. "Why?"

I looked back, unafraid of meeting his gaze. "I'm not sure." The same uncertain feeling I'd experienced when I'd told Tindra about the pregnancy was back.

He twirled me, and we dodged two other couples. "You've got to do better than that."

"It's the best I can give you right now. I need to know more."

The music's tempo increased. "Can you meet me tomorrow night at the cemetery down the street from your house? At midnight?"

Could I? My mind swirled with the music. How would I get there? "I—"

"Excuse me. May I have this dance, Miss Wilkins?" Drake's voice startled me. Ben backed away with a scowl, and Drake took my hand, leading me away from Ben. "Planning another tryst?"

I refused to look at him.

"You know, Miss Wilkins, you and Mr. Lagarde were making your mother quite nervous. If you plan to keep seeing each other, I suggest that you not be so public in your displays of affection."

"My personal life is none of your business."

Drake laughed. "My dear, I don't care about the personal life of a teenager. I'm merely trying to save you from yourself."

At 11:15 I crept through the hallways to the kitchen and listened for any night owls on our household staff who might be lurking. When I heard only the dishwasher humming, I continued.

To a casual observer, it appeared the kitchen had two walk-in pantries on opposite sides of the room. The one to the north was a full pantry that the household staff used. The pantry on the south was lined with shelves, but they were a front for the entrance to the bunker and tunnel. When I opened the pantry door, a floorboard creaked.

I whirled. Commander moved toward me, sniffing. "Go back to bed, buddy," I whispered. He edged closer and licked my hand. "Don't tell, okay?" I slipped through the door and latched it behind me. Commander whined.

I opened the door, rushed to the other pantry, retrieved a box of dog treats, tossed a few to Commander, and raced back before he noticed. I listened for a moment and sighed when claws clicked out of the kitchen.

I depressed a lever on the bottom of the third shelf, and the shelves rotated, revealing steps. I closed the entrance, flicked on a flashlight and batted a cobweb from my face. The bunker had always been creepy, but now its eeriness was magnified by the darkness beyond the beam.

A large room in the middle of the bunker served as living room, dining room, and kitchen. Off each side was a bedroom with an attached bathroom. Straight ahead were the technology and conference rooms. The tunnel entrance was in the conference room.

I pushed on the door and was relieved that it wasn't locked. Before I let the door shut behind me, I tested the lock to make sure I could reopen it. It stuck, and I grabbed a chair from the conference room table and propped the door open.

I needed to hurry if I was going to meet Ben on time. I jogged through the tunnel and twenty minutes later I stood in the chilly night air. I propped open the tunnel door with a rock and wrapped my arms around my waist.

The tunnel exited in the center of a wooded area about a quarter mile from the nearest road. I shivered as the barely budding trees swayed and beckoned in the moonlight. Gritting my teeth and pulling the hood of my sweatshirt over my blond hair, I resumed my jog. Mud squished under my feet, and some of the moisture seeped through my shoes. I came to a clearing where a helicopter could land in an emergency and paused to get my bearings.

I forged ahead and found the road a few minutes later. Staying under the cover of the woods while following the road seemed like the smartest option in case any cars passed.

How would my mother react if I was caught? I cringed. Did I have more in common with the rebels than I realized? The cemetery was ahead through the trees. I paused in the tree line at the edge of the woods. Most of the headstones were old because the majority of people now elected for cremation or, if they had the means to do so, cryopreservation.

A raw wind moaned as a shadow flitted against a monument adorned with a crumbling angel, and I emerged, hoping it was Ben and not a ghost.

"Ben?" I whispered and stopped next to a moss-covered mausoleum.

Behind me, a twig snapped.

"Sorry, my dear. You'll have to deal with me instead."

# CHAPTER 9

"Where's Ben?" Drake had overheard Ben telling me when and where to meet, but I'd never dreamed he'd go this far.

"Ben is currently unavailable."

"What did you do? If you've done something to him . . ." My voice quivered.

"It's interesting how you automatically assume I did something wrong. How do you know I'm not here to help?"

"Why is Ben unavailable?"

Drake leaned against the mausoleum wall. "I can't tell you. You'll have to trust me to help you."

"I don't. This is probably some kind of trap." I turned to leave. Ben would just have to deal with the fact that I intended to obey the law.

"You can relax. I'm an Emancipation Warrior."

"A what?"

"A rebel."

Drake's words caused me to freeze, and it took me a minute to comprehend as I sorted through parts of my conversation with him—his attitude about the rebel cause and a possible war . . . brother in intelligence . . . indifference to the ball . . . contempt for the governors. It all made sense. Except for one thing.

I inched closer to Drake. "What about your stepfather?"

"What about him?"

"Does he know?"

"No."

"Then how are you involved?"

Drake laughed. "So you're saying the child of a governor can't also be a rebel."

My face burned. I was far from being a rebel. "Answer my question."

"My parents are divorced. Let's just say my dad, though he was allowed to have very little influence on my life, had more than my mom and stepdad realized. Being the governor's stepson is the perfect cover. Now can we move on?"

Fair enough. There was something else I wanted to know more about anyway. "Did Ben send you?"

"Ben doesn't give me orders. It's the other way around."

Something from the night of the governor's ball clicked. "At the ball. When you overheard my conversation with Ben, you'd been meeting with him."

"Good observation."

"Is Ben in trouble?"

"That depends on your definition of the word."

"I know for a fact the police didn't find anything when they searched his family's house."

"How do you know?" Drake lifted an eyebrow.

I raised my chin. "I can hack security systems, including the cameras in my mother's office. How do you think I escaped my security detail?" The minute the words tumbled out, I regretted my bragging.

"I'm impressed." Drake's tone held admiration, and I felt more pleased by his approval than I should've. "Now, are you going to let me help you?"

"I'm not sure I trust you. Or that I even want help."

"If it makes you feel better, my organization isn't sure it trusts you."

"Your organization?"

"Yes. The Emancipation Warriors is a unified organization with cells in every region. Our goals are to restore the freedoms that citizens of the United States of America once enjoyed, liberate political prisoners, free children of prisoners from reeducation camps, and win the approaching war."

The whole thing sounded ridiculous. The government imprisoned dissenters to protect our society, but children in reeducation camps? I crossed my arms. "There's no such thing as reeducation camps for children."

"You probably know them as boarding schools. On the surface they seem quite innocuous."

"What about hiding pregnant girls?"

"That's a small part of our operation since the vaccine is fairly effective at stopping pregnancies." He grinned. "But it's not as good as the government wants you to believe, is it?"

I bit back a curse.

"Very few girls want to go into hiding since our society so successfully brainwashes the masses into thinking that child-killing is beneficial to young women and society."

I scowled. How dare he imply that I was brainwashed? Rebels were the ones who were brainwashed. "Termination is not child-killing. It's a safe and effective medical procedure used to improve the quality of a woman's life."

Drake made a poor attempt to stifle a deep laugh. "I'm sorry. For a second you sounded just like your mother."

This time I didn't bother to stop the curse.

"I've been called worse." His eyes gleamed. "Tell me something. What is it that's growing inside you right now?"

"Tissue." I knew what he was getting at, but I refused to go there.

"I think we're done here." He turned to leave, and Ben's face flashed through my mind.

"Wait. Let's say I was stupid enough to want to break the law. What would your organization do for me?"

Drake faced me. "I'm not convinced we can do anything for you. If you run away, you're in for a difficult journey. Young ladies who choose that road have strong convictions about the value of their child's life. They aren't going into hiding to please their boyfriends."

I gritted my teeth. "This isn't just about Ben."

"Really? From what I overheard at the ball you seemed convinced termination is the way to go. That is, until Ben protested and pointed out your differences." He smirked. "What else could it be? Unless this is about flouting your mother's authority."

I stepped closer. "You don't know anything about me, so stop pretending like you do."

"I know plenty about the society that shaped you. And that makes you a danger to my agent-in-training and my organization."

"I would never do anything to hurt Ben."

"Even after he dumped you?"

"He still cares about me as a friend."

"You think by doing this you'll prove you share his beliefs and win him back."

Maybe I did. But was there more to it? Was terminating a pregnancy really killing? If so, did I want to be guilty of taking someone's life? "I haven't decided anything for sure. I'm still looking into my options."

"Then let's go." He motioned for me to follow. "There are some people you need to meet."

"Fine. But I don't trust you."

Drake stopped. His cockiness vanished, and his expression was fierce. "You've made that abundantly clear. I don't trust you either. I'm doing a favor for Ben who has a promising career ahead of him if this little detour with you doesn't mess it up. And I want you to know that I meant what I said earlier when I told you the governors have underestimated the power and organization of the rebel movement. You have the right to change your mind. But if you betray anyone or anything you see tonight, you will pay with your life." Drake's eyes were hard.

"You equate termination with killing, but you're willing to murder me."

"This is a war. If you betray us, you're the enemy. Your child is innocent."

"You have my word. I won't say anything." My voiced trembled, and I was mad at myself for showing Drake that his words affected me, but the threat combined with the chilling breeze made remaining unemotional impossible. "Ben could've come. You didn't let him because you knew he wouldn't be threatening enough." It was the only thing that made sense. The rebels were taking a huge risk, and Drake didn't believe Ben would send a strong enough message.

Drake smirked. "Are you calling your boyfriend a wimp?"

"Don't you dare put words in my mouth. Ben is not my boyfriend anymore. But he's not a wimp because he wouldn't threaten to kill me."

"It just means he has a weakness where you're concerned."

"I know. He told me. But I thought he wanted to help me."

"This may be hard for you to grasp, but Ben wants to do the right thing before God. You're a source of temptation that he's trying to avoid."

"It's not like we were going to do anything." I grew warm.

"It's time to go."

Drake led me to a black sedan parked behind the bushes that lined the road next to the cemetery. He opened the rear passenger side door and motioned for me to get in.

"Lie down on the floor," he said. "I don't need any traffic cams seeing your face."

I obeyed.

Drake got into the front seat and tossed a large strip of cloth at me. "Tie this over your eyes." I complied, and Drake checked to make sure it was secure before he started the car. "If you mess with that, I'm going to drug you."

"I get it. You don't have to be a jerk about it."

We made several loops, and I guessed he was trying to disorient me. About ten minutes later when Drake turned, gravel crunched under the tires.

He stopped the car, and I reached for my blindfold.

"Not yet," Drake said.

"Sorry." But I wasn't. I tried peeking through the blindfold, but a voice inside warned that I might be better off in the long run if I knew as little as possible. Drake led me into a building that smelled as though fresh air had not penetrated its walls for a decade. Moisture lingered in the air and clung to my skin.

A chair scraped across the floor, and Drake helped me sit before he untied the blindfold. The concrete block walls had no windows. I sat behind a table opposite a metal door where Drake stood guard.

"I thought I was going to a meeting with lots of people," I said.

"No. You're meeting privately with some people tonight."

There was a knock on the door, and a woman with a pixie haircut and cat-eye glasses entered. She held a small box and a cup in her hand. Drake exited and closed the door behind him.

The woman placed the cup on the table and opened the box. "I'm here to administer your pregnancy test. We have to be sure you're telling the truth." The woman eyed me, her brow wrinkled. Would she kill me if my test was negative? She held out the cup and pointed to the corner. I took the cup and waited for her to move. She didn't. "Seriously? You're not leaving?" But it was a dumb question because she clearly wasn't going anywhere. Did she really think I was carrying a vial of someone else's urine in my back pocket?

I used the cup to take care of business as quickly as possible, then placed it on the table. The woman stuck the test into the urine. A minute later, the lines in her forehead relaxed. "It's positive." Sadness tinged her smile.

I never thought I'd be relieved to discover I was pregnant.

She left the room and Drake entered. "I see you passed our first test."

"That was so embarrassing."

Drake sighed. "Grow up. If you want our help, then you play by our rules. You aren't just any pregnant teen."

There was another knock, and a slightly older and thinner version of Drake entered.

The man pulled a chair across the room and sat opposite me at the table. "I'm Liam."

"Are you his brother?"

Liam looked at Drake, who shrugged. Liam pursed his lips and threw an annoyed look in Drake's direction. "Yes."

"Drake didn't say anything. It's obvious." I wasn't really sure why I was concerned about protecting Drake.

Liam folded his hands and rested them on the table. "I'm here to tell you about your options. It has come to my attention that you are carrying Ben Lagarde's child and do not want to submit to the mandatory termination. Is that correct?"

"Sort of. Ben doesn't want me to terminate. I'm investigating."

"As a leader in this organization, I'm prepared to offer you asylum, as we do for teenage girls in your situation. However, you know for yourself that you're in a unique position." He leaned back in his chair. "Frankly, it makes me uncomfortable. That's why I'm asking for something in return. We have to know you're on our side."

Liam's expression was intense, but Drake avoided my gaze. "What?"

"How long have you been hacking?"

I knew my bragging to Drake had been a bad idea. "A couple of years. It started as a hobby."

"Mostly black hat, I assume," Liam said.

I crossed my arms. It wasn't like I'd caused destruction, but I had taken advantage of the school's vulnerable system, which was black hat behavior. "Since I helped my friends by altering their grades, they'd probably consider it white hat." I grinned.

Drake chuckled, but Liam's face was stone. "Could you access the cameras in your mother's office from outside of your home?"

I had to think for a moment, but I was fairly certain it could be done. "I'd need to make sure, but yes, I think I can."

"Drake, get a computer," Liam said.

I watched Drake leave. "You want me to do it now?" This situation was getting out of control.

"Why not?"

"What if I can't? Then you won't help me? I mean, if I decide I even want your help."

Liam shook his head. "Then we'll find another way to have you help. But this would be best."

Drake returned with a small touch-screen computer that he placed in front of me. They had top-of-the-line software I'd never worked with before, but I quickly figured it out. My respect for the rebels increased, and the technology reinforced the point Drake had made earlier—the movement was more advanced than I'd realized.

Twenty minutes later I accessed the camera system in the governor's mansion and turned the computer screen so they could see. "Now, what can you offer me in return?"

Liam examined the camera views on the computer and then looked up. "The best option for you would be for my organization to alter your appearance, give you a new identity, and move you to a new location. After the child is born, the organization will place the child with adoptive parents, or you can continue your new identity and bring up the child yourself."

"Won't people get suspicious when a young pregnant woman shows up in town? I mean, even if I'm supposed to be older than sixteen, won't that look obvious?"

Drake grinned. "You're right. That's why your alias will have a husband."

A husband? "This wouldn't be real, right?"

Liam laughed, and I glared at him. Was mocking people for asking questions a family trait? "No," Liam said. "It would be for your protection."

I didn't like the sound of this, but they were right. A husband would sell the act. "So would Ben be my husband?"

"I will." Drake grabbed my hand and looked at me with mock affection.

I jerked my hand away. "No deal. Not if he's involved."

Liam nudged Drake away, and wearing a smirk, he returned to his post at the door, crossed his arms, and leaned against the wall. Had Drake expected me to react this way? A wave of heat flushed through my entire body.

"Ben wouldn't be a good choice," Liam said. His tone was patronizing. "He looks like a seventeen-year-old boy. He's training to be an agent and pilot but doesn't have experience working in the field. Plus, if you agree to work with us, I need a high-level agent supervising you."

"Because you don't trust me."

"Would you trust you?"

Liam's pointed question found its mark. I tried a different approach. "And there's no one besides Drake who could handle this?"

"You are a unique assignment. Drake is the best choice for dealing with your special needs."

I stood so quickly my chair clattered against the concrete floor. "Special needs." I huffed. "I need time to think about this." I pointed at Drake. "I told him earlier that I was exploring my options. I haven't decided anything yet. If I choose this, I'll have to leave behind my whole life forever." I did love my mother, and even though she sometimes made me feel like an accessory for her political life, she loved me. She'd be worried sick if I disappeared. Besides, I had a great life and opportunities for my future. Could I give up everything just to avoid terminating a pregnancy? Was getting rid of tissue really that bad, especially when it would make my life easier and happier? And not just my life, Ben's too, whether he realized it or not.

Liam stood and seemed unaffected by my emotions. "I assume my brother told you the seriousness of betraying anything that you saw or heard here tonight."

I raised my chin with a bravado I didn't feel. "Yes. He did."

"Good." He removed a device from his pocket and placed it on the table. "Here's your courier."

"It's not a doc?"

"Better. More advanced and secure. It'll even throw off your doc's tracker, so the government can't trace you."

I picked it up and examined it. It needed a passcode.

"Drake will give you a passcode. When you make your decision, use the courier to contact him. Good night."

He strode out of the room and slammed the door. I stood immobile. What had I gotten myself into?

# CHAPTER 10

"You're not going to school today." My mother stopped me at the front door. A flush brightened her cheeks, and her eyes glowed.

I let my bag slide from my shoulder to the floor. "Why?"

"I just completed a call with the party chairman, and they're announcing my nomination today." She threw her arms around me.

With a twisting stomach, I thought of my adventure the night before, but forced a smile and returned the embrace. "That's great."

"Go change quickly. Our flight for Union City leaves in thirty minutes." Our nation's capital, and possibly our new home in a few months. Would I be able to run away when my mother was going to be president? I'd miss a lot.

I changed into the light gray suit my mother had hired Zelda to make in anticipation of this day. The skirt was snug across my abdomen, but the jacket covered it.

What would it be like to be the daughter of a president? Would I be able to help people? I thought of the little girl whom I hadn't been able to help directly. What if I could use my influence to help the poor and needy? If I ran away, what good would that do anyone? I slipped on hot pink, patent-leather pumps and shifted the contents of my purse to a matching clutch.

When I went downstairs, Melvin and my mother waited by the door. "Let's roll," Melvin said when he saw me. A grin stretched across his face, and there was an extra spring to his step. All of his dreams were coming true too.

We boarded my mother's private jet, and I was grateful the two-hour flight to Union City would allow me to nap since I hadn't managed to sleep after arriving home a few hours before dawn. Shortly after the plane took off, I nestled into a pillow, careful not to mess up my hair, and closed my eyes.

I awakened and peeked out the window as we landed. Union City was built on the site where Washington, DC, had stood before it was destroyed during riots that followed the Great Collapse. The Council of World Peacekeepers rebuilt the city with a new name to reflect the unification of the countries. Men and women who served on the Council of Representatives lived in Union City and, along with the president, ran the national government.

A bodyguard escorted us off the plane to a waiting motorcade. Bobby held the door open, and we climbed in.

The motorcade moved from the airport to the heart of the capital. Union City's opulence was a testimony to the wealthy who had donated the funds to create a metropolis that would impress the rest of the world, and I never tired of seeing the beautiful landscape. We passed a park surrounded by cherry trees in full blossom, a nod to the trees that once existed in Washington, DC. On the opposite side of the street a shopping complex contained fine clothing and the best the country had to offer in live entertainment. Ahead, the Capitol building towered on the horizon. At night multicolored lights that represented the three united countries illuminated the building that sat next to the Potomac River.

I expected to see more people out and about since it was a warm spring day, but no one shopped and the park was empty. "Why is it so deserted?"

"Security," Melvin said. "Plus, the crowd will be waiting at the Capitol building. President Hernandez announced this morning that he would resign at the end of his term and that the party would recommend his replacement this afternoon."

Though the party backed my mother, the representatives would still have to approve the nomination, but there had never been a case in which the nominee wasn't approved.

The motorcade stopped, and we were in the back of the Capitol building. The security team led us through an entrance and up a broad staircase. When we reached the top of the stairs, a large room with windows on three sides provided a magnificent view of the city. Straight ahead of me were doors that led to a balcony full of empty chairs, and a crowd gathered on the street below where the president would announce the nomination.

The security team member led us to the door and paused. "When I open the door, file onto the balcony and wave at the crowd. President Hernandez, please take your place at the podium."

My mother and Vice President Fortune followed the president and his wife onto the stage. Melvin and I trailed my mother. Bobby and Axel, my mother's primary bodyguard, hovered nearby.

The crowd roared when we waved. President Hernandez allowed the wild adoration to continue for a few moments before he raised and then lowered his arms. A hush began to spread over the crowd, and he waited for silence.

"It has been my privilege for twelve years to serve the people of this great nation. But as I told you earlier today, I am weary. I need time to spend with my family and grandchildren, so I have chosen to retire at the conclusion of my term. On behalf of the party, I am delighted to introduce to you my successor, Governor Genevieve Wilkins." He turned and extended an arm toward my mother who stood. The crowd's cheering resumed, and my mother waved and smiled. When the cheers died away, President Hernandez continued.

"Governor Wilkins has served the people of the Great Lakes Region for eight years. In that time she has developed a security program that is unrivaled by any region. Governor Wilkins has done more to prevent the growth of the rebel movement than any governor I know. As our nation faces uncertainty due to the rebellion of some religious zealots in our midst, this nation needs a strong hand. I am confident Governor Wilkins will provide that hand. Please welcome the governor."

My mother joined President Hernandez, embracing him before taking her place at the podium. "I would like to thank the citizens of this country for their confidence in me."

A distant shout in the crowd caused my mother to pause. A fight had erupted in the area of the shout, and police officers battled to control it. Axel's attention was on the fight, but Bobby stared in the opposite direction, a frown furrowing his brow.

My mother droned on a bit louder to cover the noise of the scuffle. "It is my goal to make the United Regions of North America a better place to live. I give you my word that I will devote my life to—"

Bobby sprang from his corner and tackled my mother.

A dull thump sounded and chaos erupted on the balcony as President Hernandez collapsed. Someone shoved me to the ground where my mother and Bobby rested in a heap beside me.

Blood pooled on the balcony floor.

# CHAPTER 11

I lifted my head, but the bodyguard shoved it down. My whole body chilled when my cheek touched the smooth concrete. The bodyguard crouched over me, the spicy scent of his cologne mingling with the intensity of the moment. The man's arm blocked my view, so I studied his black suit jacket and tried to make sense of the chaotic sounds.

The crowd that had been so enthusiastic had fallen silent. A bird screeched overhead. Were the vultures already circling? Every so often there was a shout from someone in the crowd. Were they searching for the shooter?

Why were we not moving? Shouldn't they try to remove me from danger as quickly as possible?

"Go, go, go!"

A radio screeched. "The governor is secure."

"The vice president is secure."

"Get the First Lady out next."

A chair scraped across the concrete. Feet shuffled. I heard muffled sobs.

"We have a man down."

What was taking so long?

The sound of an approaching helicopter created a horrific duet with the wailing sirens.

The security officer gripped my arm. "Let's go."

I stood and he pulled me along as two more bodyguards surrounded me to trek the five feet to the door leading inside. Bloody footprints blazed the way to safety. We made it through the door, but the bodyguards didn't stop until we were safe in a hall away from the windows. Two of the men immediately returned to the crime scene.

The remaining bodyguard's shirt was splotched with blood. A chill spread over my body, and I started to sway. "Where is everybody?"

He reached out a hand to steady me. "They're coming. Your mother and the president are on their way to the hospital with a security guard who was hit too." His round face was sympathetic. "I don't know any more than that. I'm sorry."

I sagged against the wall and stared at the mesmerizing pattern of the wallpaper, my eyes following black curlicues against an ivory background.

"Vivica." Melvin appeared, surrounded by two bodyguards. He broke away from them and ran to me with open arms.

Encircled in his arms, I sobbed.

✕

Bobby was dead. His quick reaction had saved my mother's life. Axel had been silent since the incident, but grief showed on his face while he stood by the surgery waiting room door. I sat curled up on a couch clutching a pillow and still fighting the pervasive chill that lingered as I replayed the afternoon's events. Though the staff had provided a warm blanket, I shivered, and Melvin, who sat next to me, put his arm around me. A bodyguard told us that when the paramedics loaded my mother into the helicopter she was conscious, but by the time Melvin and I arrived at the hospital, my mother was in surgery. We hadn't heard about President Hernandez.

Melvin's MD3 rang, and he stood and walked past the security guards into the hall. What didn't he want me to hear? When Melvin returned, I pounced.

"Did you find out anything new?"

Melvin's face was gray. "The earliest reports show that the rebels are responsible. That was Director Spiegel. He's doing everything he can. The problem is that there aren't any witnesses to identify the shooter, and there may not have even been a person doing the actual shooting. It could've been a drone."

I scowled. "They aren't sure? I think I have a pretty good idea about how it happened. Somebody started a fight so security would be tied up."

"You're probably right."

"Any word on the president?"

Melvin's Adam's apple bobbed. "He's dead."

I closed my eyes as I thought of his wife and children and grandchildren. It seemed so cruel to murder a president who'd just announced his resignation.

The rebels had to pay.

Melvin ran his fingers through his hair. "I hate to ask, but Director Spiegel recommended that I turn on the TV. There's a lot of unrest right now. You might as well be aware of it."

"Go ahead." There was more Melvin wasn't saying, but that wasn't surprising. The shock had worn off, and my curiosity escalated while I processed the events.

Jacinda Jackson, the reporter who'd interviewed me weeks before at the collection center, was positioned so the camera could show the crowd gathered behind her. The shot was live and the words UNION CITY REGIONAL HEALTH SYSTEM were displayed along the bottom of the screen.

I ran to the window, hoping to catch a glimpse of the crowd, but the only view was the base of a wind turbine. Jacinda exhibited the appropriate concerned reporter expression as she spoke about my mother's condition. Then she gestured to the crowd behind her. "The crowd is full of people wishing Governor Wilkins a speedy recovery." The camera panned the crowd before stopping on a handmade sign that read, "My thoughts are with you, Governor Wilkins."

Seeking the protection of the rebels was out of the question. I didn't want to terminate, but now I had no other choice.

My attention returned to the newscast where Jacinda Jackson stood next to a man holding a sign that read, "Wilkins for President." His face was mottled and angry.

"I'm here with Brylan Fuller," Jacinda said, "who is providing some leadership to this crowd. Brylan, what can you tell me about the overall mood here today?"

Like it wasn't obvious. He looked eager to speak. "Well, those of us who've gathered here tonight are some of Governor Wilkins's biggest supporters. I myself want to see her recover and be our next president.

We're furious about what happened to President Hernandez. Those dirty rebels are going to pay." Brylan turned away from Jacinda to face the camera, and it was obvious he relished this time in front of the media. "Those of you out there listening, we've got a war to fight. I'm sick of these rebels making our lives miserable. I know I'm not alone, so I'm calling on the governors all over our nation to stand and fight."

Jacinda smiled at the camera. "Thank you, Brylan. Now let's head back to the studio."

I looked at Melvin who stared at the news anchor.

"Will this really cause a war?" I asked.

Melvin sat up a little straighter. "Director Spiegel's afraid of that."

"It wouldn't be much of a war. I mean the rebels aren't that organized, and there can't be that many of them." I wanted to see what Melvin would say.

"You're right." Melvin stood and stretched. "But war is war. And we want to avoid it at all costs." Something caught Melvin's attention, and I followed his gaze.

A doctor with his surgical mask pushed down around his neck stood in the doorway. He crossed the room and sat in the chair across from me.

"The surgery went well. I removed the bullet, and there was minimal damage." The doctor looked at me. "Your mother's a lucky woman. She'll make a full recovery but be sore for quite a while." His eyes darted toward the TV before he turned his gaze to Melvin. "Have they found the shooter?"

"Not yet," Melvin said.

The doctor nodded slowly and stood. "I'm sorry to hear that. Someone on staff will let you know when you can see the governor."

⋊⋉

"What is being done to catch the monsters who did this?" my mother asked from her bed as Melvin and I walked through the door of her hospital room. She was propped up even though her face was pallid.

Melvin pulled a chair up to the bed, and I did the same on the opposite side. My mother reached for my hand. "Are you okay? As soon as I woke up, I asked about you, but the nurses made me wait to see you."

"I'm fine. The bodyguards did their jobs." I squeezed her hand. "I'm glad you're okay." I was relieved to see how alert she was.

"Me too," Melvin said. "Are you in pain?"

My mother grimaced. "You never answered my question. What is being done to catch the monsters who did this?" She pointed to her bandaged shoulder.

Melvin sighed. "Not enough. They're still looking. And there's more." Melvin told my mother about Bobby, President Hernandez, the rebels, and the rumors of war.

My mother's eyes filled with tears at the news, and she stared into space for a few minutes. "So Bobby saved my life?"

"We think Bobby saw the shooter right before the shot was fired. He took the first bullet for you," Melvin said.

My mother nodded. "I wish I could thank him. I always felt safe with Bobby looking after Vivica."

As I absorbed the reality of Bobby's death, my chest ached. He'd kept my secrets and even taught me how to fire his government-issued Diablo 87, even though civilians weren't allowed to learn. He'd told me I should have training in case something happened to him and I needed to defend myself. My mother didn't know half of what he'd done to help me. I took a deep breath to steady myself. I couldn't let my grief show, or she'd dig everything out of me.

I handed her a tissue, and she dabbed her eyes. "The president was a good man. So thoughtful." My mother smiled at me. "Do you know the last time we met, he brought a box of dog treats for Commander? He knew how important that dog is to me." Her smile faded and resolve took its place. She held out her hand to Melvin. "Do you have my MD3?"

Melvin handed it over.

"Director Spiegel, Governor Wilkins." She paused, and I could hear the director's expression of surprise. "Thank you. I want constant surveillance on any suspected rebels in our region. If you don't have the manpower, use search drones. I'm doubling your budget. We have to figure out who was behind this treachery." My mother listened for a few seconds. "I don't care. Hire more people. That's why I'm giving you more money." She looked at Melvin and shook her head. "Fine. I'm glad you understand." She tossed the MD3 on her bed. "Sometimes I wonder about that man. He was actually worried about antagonizing the rebels. One minute he wants to execute them and the next he wants to let them walk all over us without a fight."

The MD3 rang. "It's the vice president," she said.

My mother gave the vice president an update on her condition and the security measures she was taking in our region. Then she listened for a while, and when the call ended, she looked worried. She turned on the TV. "Fortune tells me he's ready to take the oath of office so he can finish Felipe's term. He assures me he's going to finish the term and step down, but I don't trust him." She flipped through stations until she found news coverage of the short inauguration ceremony. "He's a snake who'll start angling to keep the job the minute he's sworn in."

"But it's not his decision," I said. "If the party wanted him, then it would've nominated him before."

"Well, there are some who think the nomination should have gone to Fortune." My mother bit her lip. "The party was impressed by my security program. He's done nothing noteworthy the whole time he's been vice president. I hate to think that after all my hard work the nomination would go to that spineless idiot."

"Vivica's right," Melvin said. "If the party wanted Fortune, it would have nominated him. Don't waste energy worrying about it. Focus on getting better."

My mother didn't look convinced. Our platitudes were useless because no matter what we said, the confirmation vote hadn't taken place. We turned our attention to the TV and watched as Cleatus Fortune took the oath of office and became president.

Fortune was small in stature, and when the camera zoomed in on his face, his beady eyes offered a glimpse into a shifty soul. When I saw the smug look on the man's face as he gave his inaugural speech, I agreed with my mother's concern.

# CHAPTER 12

The next day, Melvin escorted me home from Union City so I could return to school. The doctor estimated that my mother would be released in a day or two. Knowing my mother, it would be a day instead of two.

Once I was home, I went upstairs, locked my bedroom door, and groped under the mattress to find the courier Liam had given me. The assassination of President Hernandez and the attempt on my mother's life made my decision easy. There was no way I could accept rebel help. I'd terminate. All the good I could do as the president's daughter made me even more certain. I entered the seven-digit passcode Drake made me memorize before leaving him. When the password was accepted, I dialed the number programmed into the device and waited. After a few rings, Drake answered.

I paced in front of my couch. "Did you hear about the assassination attempt?"

"I know what the news reports are saying, but the rebels had nothing to do with it."

I dropped onto my couch. "Then who did?"

Drake paused and then spoke slowly. "My best guess is that it's someone in your mother's own political party. A person who wanted the nomination to go to someone else. The former vice president? Other governors? Whoever did it knows the rebels are the perfect scapegoat."

In a way Drake's information made sense, and President Fortune's pompous expression from the day before hovered in my mind along with my mother's concerns. "Okay. Let's say you're right. The rebels are a perfect scapegoat. And the press does report what the party tells it to report. But why risk causing a war?"

"Because they think they can eliminate us for good, and a war would give the government a perfect excuse to take us out."

"Sort of a preemptive strike."

"Right."

I chewed my lip. My certainty about telling Drake to take a hike waned.

"So are you going to accept our help or not?"

"I called to tell you no."

"Because you thought we tried to assassinate your mom?"

"Right." I rested my head on my hand. I didn't know what to do now. What if someone else was responsible? Maybe the rebels could help me find out who was at fault. But if I shunned them forever, I might never learn the truth. "I need more time."

"More time won't change the fact that the government will never exonerate us. It probably already knows we had nothing to do with it."

He was right. "At least let me investigate to be sure. We're talking about my entire life. My family and friends."

"And your wealth. And your fame. And your influence."

I swore. "You're not being fair. I've been told my whole life that the rebels are crazy, and now you expect me to blindly trust you."

"I don't have to play fair. I'm trying to help you see reason. Think about it. Would an organization that values life so much that it's willing to go to great lengths to hide you so you can have a baby really kill a president who's resigning? Call me when you've made up your mind." Drake hung up, and I tossed the device across the room. I didn't understand why he couldn't put himself in my position. If I was going to leave everything behind, I had to be sure. Wouldn't he want to do the same thing?

I stared out my window for a few minutes thinking about abandoning my life forever. Drake claimed the Emancipation Warriors could hide me. But with my mother's resources, I wondered how long I could remain concealed before she'd find me and drag me home.

The courier chimed, and my heart hammered as I picked it up off the floor. Ben. I took a deep breath and forced myself to sound calm.

"Are you okay?" The sound of his voice made me smile.

"Yeah, I'm all right."

"I need to see you."

"That's not a good idea."

"Please? It's important. Otherwise I wouldn't ask. I know it's risky, and your mom isn't thrilled about me."

That was an understatement. "What's this about?"

"I'll tell you when we meet. Trust me. It's important."

I sighed. "Okay." I gave Ben directions to the tunnel exit. "And, Ben?"

"Yeah?"

"Make sure you're not being followed."

# CHAPTER 13

Clouds hid the moon and stars. I slumped next to the tunnel exit wondering how much longer I should wait for Ben. Though spring had come during the days, the winter still held the nights hostage and refused to surrender. The brisk air blew through my sweatshirt. A rustle in the distance caught my attention. I sat up and crouched, ready to run. A flashlight glowed through the trees, illuminating Ben's familiar stride. I closed the distance between us.

When he opened his arms, I fell into them. As a sob caught in my throat, he held me while my tears flowed, but after a moment, I stopped. "I'm sorry."

Ben wiped a stray tear from my cheek with his thumb. "You've been through a lot. It's okay."

"Are you sure nobody followed you?"

Ben looked over his shoulder. "Yes. Why?"

I told him about the orders that my mother gave to Director Spiegel, and he frowned but didn't comment. I sat and leaned my head back against a tree. "So why did you need to see me?"

He sat next to me. "I don't want you to terminate."

"Yeah. I know. You've said that before." A wave of anger washed over me. "That is so easy for you. Do you realize you have to sacrifice nothing in all of this? It's all on me. I could do so much good as the president's daughter. I could help needy families."

"Helping needy families will justify killing our baby?"

"Sometimes we have to make difficult choices." As I said the words, a memory, long banished, rose to the surface. Was it the source of my uneasiness that drove me to learn more about the rebels and how they could help me avoid termination? Or did I just want to please Ben?

"Tell me what you're thinking. I want to help." Ben's voice was so gentle and kind that my anger melted.

"It's nothing. It happened a long time ago. But . . ."

"Tell me."

><

When I was eleven and my mother was away at a meeting, I'd wandered to her office, and her oversized desk chair beckoned. I curled up in it, resting my head against the cool leather, breathing deeply and savoring the unique aroma that originated from the combination of my mother's shampoo, lotions, and perfume. I must have bumped the desk because the computer screen blinked to life. It was the one computer in the house that was off limits to me because it contained government secrets. I moved the chair closer. I'd just play games.

Before I could access the games, I needed to enter the password, and it only took me three tries. I reasoned there couldn't be anything that important or my mother would have a better password.

Within ten minutes, I was bored and started looking at old pictures. My favorite was the one of my mother, father, and me on a beach at sunset when I was four years old. The orangey-pink background gave everyone's skin a vibrant glow. It was special because I remembered that moment, and it was the last family picture taken before my father died in a car accident. My parents were relaxed and happy, and I remembered the shells at my feet and the seagulls passing overhead. Like every memory involving my father, it was a shadow. Sometimes the loss seemed worse because I had so few memories to treasure. Why did my mother never talk about my father unless I asked? Had they not been as happy as I wanted to remember? Had her political ambitions taken my father's place? My throat tightened as I pushed the thoughts away.

It had been awhile since I'd seen these photos, and most of them were also stored on a digital photo album I kept on a shelf in my bedroom. There were a few pictures here and there I hadn't seen before. Why hadn't my mother put these on my album?

I scrolled backward and viewed pictures of my birth. There were pictures of me before I was born. The 3-D images were clear, but when I came to one, I hesitated. Like all of the ultrasound images, there was a date in the corner, along with my mother's name. But instead of one fetus, there were three distinct baby shapes, labeled *a*, *b*, and *c*, cuddled together. I clicked the arrow, hoping to see another image, but my fifth grade school picture, taken earlier that year, flashed on the screen instead. I scowled at my dopey expression.

Returning to the image of the three fetuses in the womb, I studied the screen, trying to make sense of what was before me. When I checked the date against my birth date, I realized my mother had been pregnant with triplets. Was I *a*, *b*, or *c*? What had happened to the other two? And why had I never been told?

I should ask my mother, but I wasn't sure if the information was worth the trouble I would be in for using her computer. I snooped and found nothing to help with my quest, so I moved to the couch and waited with my knees pulled to my chin thinking of all the possible scenarios.

When my mother breezed in with Melvin tagging behind, she stopped as if running into an invisible wall when she saw me. Melvin did a jig to avoid running into her. "Are you okay?" Her brow creased, marring her flawless complexion.

"What happened to the other babies?" I blurted the words before I thought about how confusing they might sound, but my mother didn't appear confused. She exchanged a glance with Melvin who shook his head and walked out, closing the door behind him.

"Who told you?"

"Nobody."

Her eyes narrowed. "Then how did you know to ask me?"

"I saw the ultrasound picture on your computer."

"I see." For a few moments, all I heard was the sound of her high heels against the wood floor, cutting the silence like a knife hitting a chopping block. I wondered if she was going to address the fact that I'd used her computer without permission.

My mother stopped pacing. "When I was a few months pregnant, my doctor discovered I was carrying triplets. Carrying multiple babies is a strain on a mother's health, and your father and I knew there was no way we could handle three, or even just two babies. With our careers, it was going to be too much. Plus, we knew that with my political ambitions the public would frown upon a candidate who had opted to pay the third-child penalty. So we chose selective reduction."

I opened my mouth to ask what that was, but my eleven-year-old brain figured it out. A different question came out, choked and halting. "How did you decide which babies to kill?" My heart thudded.

My mother grimaced and then sat down beside me. "I wish you wouldn't think of it that way. It was a complex decision for your father and me."

"How. Did you. Decide?"

My mother sighed and rubbed my back as if that would somehow calm the agitation in my soul. "You were the biggest and strongest. You were thriving while the other two lagged behind developmentally. It was the right decision. The doctor said the other two fetuses wouldn't have been healthy." She studied me for a moment. "If we hadn't done that for you, you might've been unhealthy too."

I wondered if that was true, or if it was something my mother told herself to feel better. "Boys or girls?"

"Both fetuses were female."

I'd always wanted a sister, and I could've had two. I pictured myself with two other little girls playing dress up and sipping imaginary tea from the cups that were a cherished gift from my father.

"I never planned for you to find out this way. I was going to tell you someday when you were old enough to understand that sometimes we must make difficult choices."

"I'm okay. I'm old enough to understand."

But I hadn't.

⋊⋉

Ben had listened patiently, and when I finished, he studied me. "You realize if you'd been a little smaller your mother would've killed you instead, right?"

I refused to look at Ben.

"Vivica, I don't understand how you can even consider terminating. Especially now that you're telling me this."

"What about the fact that the rebels tried to kill my mother? You expect me to overlook that? Not to mention they could've murdered me. I was on the balcony with her."

"The Emancipation Warriors didn't kill President Hernandez or shoot your mother."

"Then who did?" I jumped up and clenched my fists. "You're so arrogant. You get me pregnant and then sit here and demand that I have a baby while you do nothing. All because of some stupid exclusivist belief. What makes you so sure you're right about God, anyway? What if there isn't a God at all?"

Ben stood, put a hand on my arm, and looked around. "Keep your voice down." He paused. "I don't want to fight. And I've already apologized for what I did to you. It haunts me every day. But killing an innocent child isn't going to make things better. You'll only feel worse."

"I think you'd feel worse." I didn't want to help ease his guilt. I was suffering. Shouldn't he?

Ben refused to meet my eyes but spoke evenly. "What if I proved that the Warriors had nothing to do with the assassination attempt? Would you be willing to let us help you hide?"

His calmness pacified me. It was a fair offer. "I'd be willing to think about it. But I'd have to have solid proof."

"Good. I'll tell Drake."

My guard went back up. "Drake? Why?"

Ben sighed. "We need his help. And he's good at what he does. You can trust him."

"I don't like him."

"He mentioned that." Ben smiled. "You're even. He's not exactly fond of you either from what I can tell."

My stomach flipped, and I wasn't sure why I would care that Drake didn't like me. But I wasn't going to let Ben know it. I forced my face into a smirk. "Good to know we're even." Then a question came to mind and I needed to know the answer. "Did Drake put you up to this?"

Ben nodded, and I wasn't sure why this knowledge disappointed me. "He knew you'd investigate, so you might as well have our resources. Do we have a deal?"

I held out my hand, and Ben grabbed it. "Deal."

# CHAPTER 14

The next morning I stood in front of the mirror and studied my abdomen. There was a small bump, but nothing that my clothes couldn't conceal. My height worked in my favor. I dropped my shirt and grabbed my school bag.

When I reached the bottom of the stairs, Officer Martina Ward waited with Melvin. My heart somersaulted, and I clutched the railing, forcing myself to remain steady. "Good morning," I said.

Officer Ward nodded.

Had my mother and Melvin found out about my pregnancy? Was Officer Ward here to take me to Pop Management to terminate?

"Vivica," Melvin said, "I'd like you to meet your new bodyguard, Officer Martina Ward. I stole her away from Population Management."

I started breathing again. Of course. Someone had to take Bobby's place. But Officer Ward?

Melvin smiled. "I'm sure she'll keep you safe. She comes highly recommended." Melvin's MD3 rang. "I have to take this. You two get acquainted."

I held out my hand, willing myself to remain cool. "Nice to see you again, Martina."

"I prefer to be addressed as Officer Ward."

"And I prefer to call you Martina. You work for me now. Not Pop Management."

"I work for your mother. I suggest that you not forget it." Martina's eyes narrowed. "Isn't it time for you to get to school?"

"Yes." I smirked when I thought of all the bodyguards I'd been through before Bobby. I'd have to make short work of Martina. "And by the way, you'll find out soon enough that you work for me too."

As soon as the retinal scanner confirmed my identity there was a loud beep. I froze and waited for Officer Jim to check the message on his computer while Martina lingered nearby.

He gave me a friendly smile. "No worries. We do need you to report to the nurse. Right away." He waved me on.

I nodded as I walked away, but my mind spun. It had to be for my mandatory pregnancy test.

Tindra appeared and grabbed my arm. "Wait 'til you hear what—" Her eyes widened. "Why is that woman from Pop Management following you?"

I sighed. "She's my new bodyguard."

"Oh my gosh."

I lowered my voice. "Let me know if you have any ideas on how I can get rid of her. She's not going to be cool like Bobby."

"Yeah. Especially after you stood up to her in front of everyone."

"Then she knows what to expect." I turned toward the nurse's office. "What did you want to tell me?"

"Oh, that." Her brow furrowed. "The police came to school yesterday to arrest $D^2$, but he wasn't here."

"No way." My stomach tightened.

"Yeah. The police had been investigating since his little outburst in class, and they finally found evidence. Rumor has it he split."

"Wow." How much longer before the same thing happened to Ben? I stopped next to the nurse's door. "I'll catch you later."

She sauntered away into the crowd of students, and I took a deep breath and pushed the door open.

# CHAPTER 15

"Good morning, Vivica," the nurse said turning away from an open supply cabinet. Mr. Greene was only in his mid-twenties, but a bushy mustache roosted above thin lips. "I need you to take a pregnancy test since your group went when you were absent."

I bit my lip. "I'm so sorry, but I went to the restroom right before I got to school."

"Figures, doesn't it?" He pointed toward the refrigerator. "Grab a water and chugalug. You can have a seat."

I settled in a chair out of the nurse's line of vision, sipped the water, and thought for a few minutes before removing my doc from my pocket. I needed to buy myself time to make a decision, so I disabled the tracking and hacked into the school's network. When I found the program they used for reporting the test results, I was ready, but there was no hurry. I didn't dare look suspicious.

I still couldn't believe I was going to these lengths to avoid termination, but I had to find the truth. I couldn't let Ben down. Maybe I already had. He kept insisting on using the word *kill*. Did it make him think less of me because I didn't think of termination that way? But hadn't I used the same word long ago when I'd learned about my sisters? Perhaps the gut reaction I'd had as a kid was the right one.

Draining the rest of the water, I made a production of throwing the bottle into the recycling bin. "I think I can go now."

Mr. Greene retrieved a narrow box from the cabinet he was organizing. Opening it, he shook out the plastic wand, scanned its bar code into his computer, and handed it to me. "Fire away." He went back to arranging boxes.

I choked back a laugh and shut myself in the bathroom, where I took care of business. The test would automatically report the results into the program. As soon as the test indicated positive, I entered negative in the program and crushed the test under my heel until the plastic cracked and the positive disappeared. Tossing the test in the trash, I strolled out of the restroom. "It's negative."

Mr. Greene hustled from the cabinet and glanced at his computer screen. "Super-duper. Have a good one."

><

Early the next morning, Melvin informed me that we would return to Union City because my mother was going to be released from the hospital. Before she returned home, she and I would attend President Hernandez's memorial service.

The service took place in a concert hall that held thousands. Representatives and personal friends of President Hernandez had journeyed from all over the country. Ambassadors from the European Union, the African Federation, the United Regions of South America, and the Republic of Asia were present as well as some members of the Council of World Peacekeepers. My mother and I were seated a few rows behind the Hernandez family, and a large security team, including Martina and Axel, surrounded us.

Though my mother was in a wheelchair, her black suit, makeup, and hair were impeccable. My mother acknowledged President Fortune and his entourage with a frosty smile. His face tensed before he nodded in return.

I looked behind me and saw Drake sitting with his mother and step-father. He winked, and I scowled. Seriously? Where were his manners?

The service lasted nearly two hours as President Hernandez's family, friends, and staff members eulogized him.

When it was over, we filed out of the concert hall and waited in the crowd for our car. Though the surrounding buildings and streets had been cleared, our bodyguards hovered.

I was so engrossed in people watching that I didn't see Drake until he bent next to my mother's wheelchair and held her hands. "Governor Wilkins, I'm so glad to see you here today. You look wonderful."

My mother beamed. "Why thank you, Mr. Freeman. I'm grateful to be alive."

"You'll still be our next president, I hope?"

What a liar.

"Yes, I plan to be."

"I'm sure I'll see you later tonight at President Fortune's dinner, but I just wanted to say hello."

President Fortune's dinner? This was the first I'd heard of the event. It seemed a little crass to have a dinner on the day of the assassinated president's funeral.

"I'm afraid I will not be attending. It was almost too much for me to be here today," my mother said. She was pale, and she'd argued with the doctors to be here because she wanted to show the country that she was strong and able to carry on.

"That's too bad," Drake said. "Have you considered sending your daughter in your place? I stand in for my stepfather all the time."

My mother raised her eyebrows. "I hadn't, but that's a marvelous idea." She turned to me. "How would you feel about that?"

Drake obviously had an agenda, and while I wasn't certain what he had in mind, I'd made a deal with Ben and needed to work with Drake—even if I despised him. I smiled. "It would be interesting." This was an opportunity to prove to my mother that I was grown up and capable of representing her.

"Melvin!" My mother waved, and Melvin rushed over.

"Yes, Genevieve."

"Please arrange for Vivica to attend Fortune's dinner party in my place. Drake Freeman will be her escort for the evening."

"Yes, ma'am." Melvin scurried away.

Drake knelt beside my mother again. "Thank you, Governor. I'll take good care of your daughter."

Since I'd come to Union City unprepared to attend a state dinner, Melvin spent the afternoon in a flurry trying to find an appropriate dress. After contacting Zelda for her recommendation of a designer in Union City, he presented me with several options in a size six. To his credit, Melvin did not draw attention to this fact but quietly observed while I modeled the dresses in my hotel suite. I settled for a one-shoulder pale pink chiffon creation with a silver embellishment at the waist. The dress reminded me of something a Greek goddess wore.

Promptly at six, I floated downstairs to the lobby to meet Drake. He was seated on a couch near a fireplace, and he stood when I entered.

So he did have manners.

Drake offered his arm. "You look lovely, my dear. That dress flatters you." The words were innocent, but the gleam in his eyes spoke otherwise.

I took his arm and gritted my teeth as we headed for the door. Martina followed. "Are you also a fashion expert then?"

Drake laughed and held open the door. "Let's just say I know enough to recognize what works and what doesn't."

Once we were alone in the back of the limousine, I relaxed. "Am I the only person who thinks it's odd that President Fortune is having a state dinner the very night of President Hernandez's funeral?"

"There are heads of state here from all over the world and all of the governors as well. He probably sees it as a chance to establish himself as president."

"I suppose my mother would do the same."

Drake nodded and then leaned over and whispered directly in my ear. "You and I have a mission tonight, so leave your doc in here."

I tried to focus on what he was saying, but it wasn't easy. "What is it?"

"Not here." He glanced at the window that separated us from Martina. "I'll tell you later. For now, pretend like you actually like me and focus on representing your mother."

I sighed and slid away from him. Maybe tonight would be the right time to get rid of Martina.

✖

The president's mansion stood in the middle of a fifty-acre compound outside of Union City. Though I'd seen pictures, this was my first visit to the place that might one day be my home.

Constructed after the nations had combined, the home was divided into three large sections built around a lake, each one decorated to reflect the heritage of one of the three countries that once existed in North America. The president typically chose to live in the section of his or her heritage, so President Hernandez had resided in the area that represented Mexico, though his family would soon return to their native region. Since President Fortune's family was from the former United States of America, he'd commandeered the corresponding rooms.

After security guards checked us in, Drake and I meandered to a large foyer where waiters served cocktails and guests mingled. Classical music played softly in the background and combined with the hum of chatter. In the middle of the room stood a white staircase embellished with gold. Behind the staircase was a sitting room with windows that covered the entire wall. It was dark, but outdoor lighting illuminated the lake and showcased the two other sections of the mansion.

"Miss Wilkins!" Governor Jensen and his wife approached, and he grasped my hand. "How is your mother? Is she here? I wanted to speak to her today at the funeral, but she left too soon." He shook his balding head. "Such a senseless tragedy."

"No, she's resting tonight. The doctors expect her to make a full recovery."

"That's fantastic. She's a lucky woman," Governor Jensen said and then turned to speak to a man who walked by with a glass of champagne in hand.

Mrs. Jensen smiled and stepped closer to me. "And also to have such a lovely daughter willing to represent her. I hope my children do the same someday." She nodded at Drake who had wandered away. "Are you two an item?"

"No, not at all. He's too old for me." There was also the fact that he was an arrogant rebel.

"He won't be for long." Mrs. Jensen's eyes gleamed. "My Edward is ten years older than me. Age is only a number that doesn't matter when you fall in love."

"I'm not going to fall in love with Drake."

Mrs. Jensen missed my protest as she flitted away to find her Edward. My mind wandered to Ben. Where was he? What was he doing? If he were here, I'd certainly be having more fun.

A waiter passed with a tray of hors d'oeuvres that looked more decorative than edible, but I snatched one and popped it in my mouth to have something to do.

Drake found me. "It's time," he whispered.

I swallowed and nodded, forcing myself to look normal.

"Relax, you look guilty."

I scowled. "I'm trying. It's a little hard when you won't tell me what's going on."

"Smile, Vivica." Drake grinned and took my elbow. "Let's walk. I know you hate me, but try to act like you like me."

I faked an adoring gaze. "That shouldn't be too hard. Mrs. Jensen wondered if we're an item."

"Don't start batting your eyes or people will know you're faking."

I rolled my eyes instead.

Drake led the way outside to a deck that overlooked the lake. He found a secluded spot and leaned against the railing, gazing out at the moonlit water. I looked back. Martina watched from a distance. "In a minute, you're going to slap me and run into the ladies' room."

"I get to slap you?" I couldn't help it. I sounded eager.

Drake laughed. "Yes, Vivica. Don't hold back either. I can take it. That lovely little silver embellishment on your waist contains a device capable of copying files from President Fortune's computer. It will also put a program on his computer that can give my organization remote access. Your dress was the only way we could get the device past security."

"You're joking, right? How did that get there? Surely Melvin isn't in on this?" I tried to think of anyone who would've had access to my dress.

"You can rest assured Melvin is fully on board with your mother."

Of course he was. How could I think otherwise?

Drake leaned against the railing. "I have other connections."

"Who?"

"Once you're in the restroom, make sure you're in a stall before you remove it. The security cameras in the restrooms are pointed away from the stalls. Come back out here to apologize. I'll be waiting."

"And you're still not going to tell me who put it there?"

"Did you listen to anything I just told you?"

"Yes."

Drake raised an eyebrow. "Repeat my instructions."

"Oh, no. You are not going to treat me like I'm in kindergarten." I put my hands on my hips.

"So you don't know?"

"Yes. I'm just not going to give you the satisfaction of repeating it."

"Fine." Drake smirked. "So how long are you going to hang on to Wimpy Ben?"

"Ben's not a wimp. And we're not together." My fingernails dug into my palms.

"Not because of desire. Poor boy tries to do the right thing and almost shakes your hold over him when you bat your eyes. Act like a damsel in distress, and he goes running back to you."

"That's not true. I do not. We're not even back together."

"Tell me, what drew you to him in the first place? Surely you knew he wasn't your type. Was he some sort of conquest for you?"

"I care about him."

"In your own selfish way. I've worked with him long enough to know that you're too much for him, my dear. And you always will be. Tell me you're not thinking of a future with him."

I looked away.

"Don't deny it. Why else would you be doing all of this?"

"You're just jealous." It was a childish thing to say, and, like many things I'd said to Drake, I regretted it instantly.

He stood straight and looked me directly in the eyes. "In case you've forgotten, your teenage drama is of no interest to me, but I do care about Ben's future as an agent. So I'm telling you to stay away from him. Let me handle this situation before you damage his career."

The crack of my hand on his cheek echoed across the water. "You're such a jerk!" I turned and fled for the ladies' room. Drake had baited me, but there was enough truth in his observations that I didn't have to act. Angry tears stung my eyes when I realized that's exactly what he'd wanted.

# CHAPTER 16

Once I was inside the stall in the ladies' room, I tugged at the silver embellishment piece. It snapped off and I examined it. Nestled on the back was a device so tiny that I found it hard to believe it could perform the functions that Drake claimed.

I reattached the embellishment to my dress before I flushed the toilet and made a quick show of washing my hands while clutching the device.

I stormed back outside to where Drake waited.

"Have you come back to apologize?"

"I'm sorry I didn't hit you harder."

I couldn't read his expression, but he wrapped an arm around my waist. "Give me a hug," he whispered.

"No way."

"Then how do you expect to make the exchange?"

"Fine."

I forced myself not to jerk away. Bending closer, I put my right hand on his shoulder and slipped my left hand into his jacket pocket and dropped the device.

He leaned over and whispered, "Good work."

"Leave me alone. I'm ticked."

"I am well aware of that, sweetheart. As I've said before, your drama is of no interest to me."

"But if you're going to make accusations, then I should at least be able to defend myself."

"I think you defended yourself quite well." He took a step back.

"What's next?" I asked.

"I am going to take care of business. You will go mingle."

"I want to help."

"No."

"Why not?"

"You've done your part. You'll get in the way."

"I can do more."

The muscle in Drake's jaw tensed.

"Really, I can," I said.

"Go mingle."

"But I—"

Drake's face was unchanged but his eyes flashed. "Vivica. Stop acting like a naughty child and do what I've asked you to do."

I threw out a few choice words and returned to the party.

><

I must have looked bored standing at the edge of the crowd, watching people drink more champagne than necessary during a cocktail hour, so a few governors' wives pulled me aside and pummeled me with questions about my mother. I made polite inquiries about their children, most of whom were older than me and probably had no idea I existed. While I mingled, Martina remained near the door watching my every move.

The change in the party's tone was so gradual I didn't notice it at first. In the middle of Mrs. Fox's interrogation, a commotion blazed near the front door, and I hoped it had nothing to do with Drake. Mrs. Fox's perfect brows puckered. The silence reached the corner where I stood. Was President Fortune about to appear?

Several women had mascara trails on their faces, and most of the men placed their arms around their wives. "Excuse me," Mrs. Fox whispered and moved toward her husband who drew her close.

"Ladies and gentlemen!" A man with perfect posture stood on the balcony that overlooked the room. I could only see his back, so I shoved to the opposite side of the room to see his face. "Tonight, I regret to inform you, there will be no dinner."

Martina was headed my way. I slipped into a cluster of people. Where was Drake?

"Thirty minutes ago, rebel forces bombed the Capitol building in Union City. It was completely destroyed."

Gasps filled the room and a few women wailed.

"President Fortune has already been escorted to safety. We ask that all of you leave as quickly as possible."

The crowd erupted.

"We have to get out of here!"

"What if they attack here?"

"Were there casualties?"

Individual voices faded when the crowd noise increased. Guests stampeded to the door. I scanned the room. Where was Drake? At least the chaos made it difficult for Martina to find me.

From the safety of his perch, the man waved his arms. "We have no reason to believe there will be an attack here tonight. Our military is monitoring the situation. Please remain calm."

A waiter with a tray full of empty champagne glasses jostled me, and when my arm waved as I regained my balance, I bumped his tray. The glasses shattered against the floor like the percussion in a chaotic symphony. I opened my mouth to apologize, but the waiter charged forward, oblivious to the mess in his wake. A vicelike hand clutched my arm. Drake. "Let's move," he said.

Drake maneuvered through the bedlam and guided me down a hall that led away from the foyer and living room.

"Did you hear the announcement?" I asked.

"Yes."

"Well? Do you know anything? Was it really the rebels?"

Drake paused. "I need you to hack into the security system."

I smirked. "You need me after all."

He ignored my comment and continued down the hall, dragging me with him. We came to a set of stairs that led to a lower level. "In case you've forgotten, your bodyguard is wondering where you are right about now. We don't have time for your ego. My tech people just called to tell me that Fortune installed cameras all over this compound that Hernandez never had. I didn't know about them earlier when I put the program on his computer."

We were in the basement, and floor-to-ceiling windows faced out onto the lake where Drake and I had talked earlier. He let go of my arm and opened a door, surveyed the area, and motioned for me to follow.

We stayed close to the house until we came to the next section of the building where President Hernandez had lived. The shadows hid us as Drake escorted me to a pool house that contained a bathroom, a kitchenette, a couch, and two chairs.

He pointed to the furniture. "Have a seat. We can't leave the property until the security camera problem is fixed."

I chose the couch. "Do you have a courier I can use?"

He pulled one from his pocket and punched a few buttons before handing it to me. "Can you use it?"

I examined it. "Yes. Now do you mind telling me if the rebels are responsible for the bombing?"

"To my knowledge, no. It's possible there's a rogue group I don't know about."

"It's also probable it's another setup by the government."

Drake nodded. "If the government creates a crisis, then they can rationalize to the public why war is necessary and why the Emancipation Warriors are enemies."

What would my mother do as president? Would she be willing to fake an attack on our own people to get rid of the rebels?

Drake glanced out the window. "Now isn't the time for pondering life's mysterious questions."

I glared at Drake and turned my attention to the courier. It took a few minutes, but I was able to hack the presidential mansion's security system. There were security cameras everywhere. "I'm loading the information. I'm also going to have to destroy the footage of us in this room and of you in Fortune's office."

"How much longer?" Drake glanced at the door.

"A few minutes." Not knowing about the cameras had made my job extra hard. "Come here and tell me where all you went."

Drake leaned over my shoulder and pointed at the various rooms as they appeared on the screen while I erased the histories and replaced it with generic footage that I created from innocuous recordings. "Try to hurry."

His breath heated my neck. "I need some space." Drake backed away, and I reset the time and date stamps on the computer, so no one would notice my changes.

"Okay, it's done." I held out the courier.

Drake tucked it in his jacket pocket. "Let's go." He grabbed my hand, but when he got to the door, he stopped. "Wait."

I could hear the footsteps.

"Get on the couch. Now." Drake's tone was so urgent that I obeyed without protest. But I was shocked when he sat beside me and put his arms around my waist. He looked at my lips and leaned closer.

The door creaked. "Excuse me. Are you two not aware of the evacuation order?" The man's tone was clipped and proper.

Drake straightened and I added a nervous giggle for good measure and put on my best innocent look. "What evacuation order?"

Mr. Perfect Posture squared his shoulders and looked at me with disdain. "I made the announcement twenty minutes ago. You must leave at once. The Capitol building was attacked."

I put my hands on my face. "Oh, my goodness. That's awful."

"Wow," Drake said. "We didn't hear it. We'll leave right now." I had to give Drake credit. He did look convincingly sheepish.

I smiled. "We're so sorry."

Mr. Perfect Posture shook his head. "I believe there is a woman looking for you. She's quite upset, and you fit the description she gave me."

I giggled. "Oops. That's my bodyguard. I don't know what she expects. It's not like I'm going to make out with my boyfriend while she's staring at me."

Mr. Perfect Posture sniffed and waited for us to exit.

When we were out of Mr. Perfect Posture's earshot, Drake looked at me and shook his head. "You have to be the world's worst actress."

"I am not. And is that the best scenario you could come up with?"

"What else did you want me to do? That was the only choice. Were you afraid I was going to kiss you?"

"No." I felt my face growing warm and prayed it wasn't as red as it felt.

"Liar." He elbowed me. "You might like it, you know. Which is probably what you're afraid of."

I bristled. "Can we please get out of here?"

"Absolutely."

>X<

When Drake and I found our limousine, Martina was nowhere to be seen. I opened the door and slid in. "We could leave without her. What do you say?"

"I think that would cause more problems than you need to deal with right now."

"Oh, come on, I love ditching my bodyguards."

"Well, you're not going to ditch this bodyguard ever again. Where have you been?" Martina climbed into the back of the limo and sat directly across from me. "Answer me!"

I shrugged. "Chill. We were just exploring."

"I watched you at the party when they made that announcement. You deliberately tried to get away from me." Martina's eyes narrowed. "Why?"

"Drake and I had planned to meet in secret. I had to find him to tell him about the bombing." I was pleased with this story because it made sense.

"Then explain to me why the butler found the two of you in the pool house making out."

I should have known Mr. Perfect Posture would rat me out. "If the world's going to end, you might as well enjoy the last few minutes."

"You always have an answer, don't you, Vivica?"

"I try."

Martina surveyed me for a moment. "I think we need an understanding."

"I agree."

"Your mother hired me to keep you safe. Don't think for one minute Melvin didn't inform me about your string of bodyguards in the past. And don't you dare think you're getting rid of me. I need this job."

I raised my chin. "I see. Then you need to understand that I expect a certain amount of privacy."

"Your safety is more important than privacy."

"Not if you value your job."

Martina pursed her lips. "You're up to something. I don't know what yet. But if you can agree to behave, then I won't waste my time trying to figure out what it is you're hiding. Understand?"

I didn't believe her. Her words sounded good, but her eyes told a different story. "I'm not hiding anything."

"Fine. We'll do this your way." She slid out of the limo. "Mr. Freeman, we're ready to go now."

But Drake was already gone.

# CHAPTER 17

I didn't care what Drake said. The next day I needed to see Ben, so I called him. He agreed to meet me outside of the tunnel that night.

Ben was waiting when I arrived, and I threw my arms around him. "Thanks for meeting me."

He held me tight for a moment, then released me. "Drake warned me not to, but I know when to ignore him. No one's following me." He sat and motioned for me to join him.

I settled into the dewy weeds and told him about changing the pregnancy test results. "I'm so confused about everything. I don't know what to do or feel or believe."

"I know. That's why I risked meeting you." His voice was earnest, his eyes kind. "Plus I have something to say, and I need you to promise you'll hear me out."

His eyes were what attracted me to him all those months ago. He took my hands and covered them with his own, and my pulse quickened.

"Okay, I promise," I whispered.

"I've been praying for you." Ben waited for my reaction.

I wasn't sure what to think. "Why?"

"Because you need Jesus Christ as your savior."

Why was he stuck on this exclusivist kick? "Whatever. I know you have your beliefs." Why couldn't Ben see that he was all I needed?

"I shouldn't have hidden them from you."

"Why? They're dangerous. And don't you think it's hateful to tell people who don't believe the same way you do that they're going to hell?" I pulled my hands away.

"It's worse to hide the truth."

I rolled my eyes.

"Okay," he said. "Then tell me how to get to heaven."

That was easy. "Be a good person."

"No one can ever be good enough to get to heaven."

"See, that's what I don't like. God makes rules that aren't fair."

Ben put a hand on my shoulder. "You promised to listen, remember? Let me finish."

Fine. Maybe if he got this off his chest, he wouldn't bother me with it again. I sighed but nodded for him to continue.

"Here's the problem. God is good. Holy. Even people who seem perfect can't measure up to God's standards." He closed his eyes momentarily. "I know it doesn't seem fair. But, our sins cause us to be God's enemies, and there has to be a punishment." He paused. "That punishment is death. But God created us and loves us, so he came up with a way for us to be at peace with him and go to heaven." Ben grasped my hand. "No matter what anybody says, it's the only way."

Something clicked, and I remembered the old man from the community center. "Jesus?"

Ben smiled. "Right. God sent his son Jesus Christ to take our punishment. If you'll admit you're a sinner and believe Christ died for you, you'll go to heaven."

"I'm sorry." I shook my head. "Your way isn't worth the risk."

"Salvation is free. But choosing to accept the truth has consequences."

"Yeah. Like being convicted of using hate speech."

"Or death." Ben reached for my hand. "This isn't easy. Promise me you'll think about it."

It seemed crazy. But he seemed so sure he was right. Maybe I should keep reading his Bible to find out for myself.

I squeezed Ben's hand. "Fine. I will."

"Cool." He smiled, and his brown eyes sparkled. "You're going to be praying, aren't you?"

⋊⋉

My mother slapped her MD3 on the dining room table. "The Council of Representatives has postponed my confirmation vote for president. It's so convenient for that rat who hijacked the presidency, isn't it?"

I broke off a piece of dinner roll. Commander's head rested in my lap, and he begged for a bite. "You're right. Fortune's a rodent with an agenda." I slipped the bread under the table and Commander gulped it.

My mother sighed. "Stop feeding the dog under the table, Vivica."

"Now, Genevieve," Melvin said, "can you really expect the vote to take place with the Capitol in ruins? They'll get to it."

"Don't 'Now, Genevieve' me. You know that Fortune is gunning for the presidency. The representatives could convene elsewhere. There are plenty of places." My mother threw her hands up. "What about that place where we had Hernandez's funeral? Where do you think they're going to meet to take care of other business?"

Melvin appeared to weigh my mother's words. "Do you want me to talk to some of the representatives and convince them to lead a charge to go ahead with the vote? Do you have any governors you would trust to use their influence?"

This calmed my mother. "Jensen and Fox have been helpful. Neither one has ambitions to be president, so I trust them as much as I trust anyone."

Which wasn't very much. My mother didn't get to be a governor by blindly trusting fellow politicians.

Melvin stood. "I'll call Governors Jensen and Fox right away."

My mother's face relaxed. "Thank you."

We ate in silence for a few more minutes.

"Vivica, there's something I'd like to discuss with you."

I nodded. Conversations that started this way were never good for me.

"Martina informs me that you've been disrespectful toward her. In fact, she's very concerned that you aren't aware how serious your situation is."

Of course Martina would paint it as concern. "I don't like having someone spy on me all the time."

"Your safety and well-being are more important than your happiness. Someone made an attempt on my life. You could be in danger too. I'll tell Martina to give you a little more space, but you must listen to her." My mother took my hand. "I'm only trying to protect you. I can't bear the thought of something happening to you. Someday you'll understand when you're a mother."

I squeezed her hand, but I couldn't meet her eyes because her words obliterated my refuge of denial.

She was right. I understood.

# CHAPTER 18

Tindra posed with a red polka dot dress. "Does this look like me?" I wrinkled my nose. "Not really. Those tiny dots make me dizzy." I pointed to a yellow halter dress. "What about that one? It's not obnoxious."

Tindra replaced the red dress on the rack and selected her size in yellow. "It's actually super cute. I'll try it. Are you going to put anything on?"

"I don't feel like it." Even though Tindra had talked me into going with her to the boutiques a few blocks from the governor's mansion, I hadn't tried on or purchased anything. My mood soured as the afternoon progressed because shopping was the last thing on my mind, and it didn't help that Martina stalked us.

"Come on." Tindra grabbed a black sundress. "You're trying this."

I yanked it away. "Fine."

Tindra elbowed me. "Quit acting like such a grouch."

"Sorry."

We shared a large dressing room, and the yellow sundress fit Tindra perfectly. She looked in the mirror and smoothed the dress. "Does this make me look chubby?"

"Seriously?" Tindra never looked chubby in anything. "Not at all." I tugged the side zipper on my sundress, but it traveled halfway up my torso and stuck. "This isn't going to work."

Tindra reached for the zipper. "Let me try."

"No." I removed the dress and grabbed my blouse. Tindra's eyes fastened on my midsection. I froze.

"You've got. To be kidding," she muttered.

"It's complicated." I turned away and put my blouse on.

"Not really."

"It is for me."

"Because of Ben?"

111

"It started that way, but now . . . I don't know . . ."

She whirled and gathered her hair off her back. "Unzip me."

I did and she tore off the sundress, letting it crumple on the floor. "I don't know what you're thinking or planning," she whispered as she dressed, "but if you think I'm going to help you, you're crazy." She flounced from the dressing room.

I put the rest of my clothes on, and when I came out, my stomach lurched. Martina had moved from her station by the front door to the chair outside of the dressing room. How much had she heard? And would she understand?

I went home and sprawled on my bed. It had been weeks since Drake had taken information from President Fortune's computer, and I hadn't heard a word from him proving his organization wasn't involved in the shooting. I buried my face in my pillow and wished for a second that when I turned over everything would magically be fixed.

Would prayer help? Ben seemed to think so, but I wasn't convinced. I finally decided prayer wouldn't hurt.

"God, I don't know if you care or not. Ben seems to think so, and I'm kind of desperate here. So could you please help me?"

# CHAPTER 19

"Please explain why I had to hear secondhand that my daughter is pregnant."

I huddled on my mother's office couch and clutched a pillow. Melvin sat on the opposite end. Commander whined outside the office door while my mother paced.

I knew the moment she'd summoned me to her office the day after my shopping trip that something was wrong. I picked a hangnail. Had Martina figured it out? Or did Tindra backstab me? So much for my prayer for help. "If it's secondhand, then you don't know it's true, do you?"

My mother stopped and faced me. "Is it?"

My hangnail started bleeding, and I put my finger in my mouth.

"Answer me!"

"Who told you?"

"So it's true?"

"I want to know who's spreading gossip about me."

She fingered her necklace. "It's a trustworthy source. And you never answered my question, Vivica."

"You never answered mine."

"I can't fathom why you wouldn't come to me. This is such an easy problem to take care of."

"I was going to tell you. But then there was the governor's ball and then the assassination attempt and—"

"You've known since the governor's ball? That was two months ago. I thought your mandatory test was negative." She muttered under her breath, and a vein in her neck protruded. "Surely you didn't tamper with the results."

I nodded.

Melvin groaned and dropped his head into his hands.

My mother stopped and let loose a string of profanities, while I burrowed deeper into the couch. When she finished, she took a deep breath and resumed pacing. "Why? Explain to me why, when you know what the law is, when you're a child yourself, when you have your entire life ahead of you, when you know this scandal could ruin my career, why would you do this? I suppose that rebel Ben Lagarde is the father."

I nodded.

"I'm still waiting for your explanation," she said. "Were you planning something with Ben?" Her eyes narrowed. "What did he talk you into?"

"It was my decision." I swallowed and whispered, "I don't want to kill the baby."

"Where did you even get the idea that terminating is killing?" Her faced twisted in disgust.

"If termination isn't killing, then what is it?"

She turned away. "I can't even look at you. Have I been such a horrible mother that you would set out to sabotage me?"

Why did she always have to make everything about her? I didn't get pregnant on purpose, and she'd never encouraged me not to have sex. All I'd ever done was try to be a daughter she could be proud of. "No, this isn't about you."

My mother laughed and looked at Melvin. "Can you actually believe she thinks this isn't about me? Can you believe it?"

Melvin's eyes widened.

"Then what is it?"

"I told you. Why do you never listen? I don't want to kill the baby."

"You mean like your cruel, heartless mother killed your sisters?"

I didn't have an answer. "I'm sorry."

"I don't care if you're sorry or not. We're taking care of this matter immediately. Melvin, find a doctor to perform the termination tonight. Someone trustworthy and willing to overlook how far along she is. Make sure the doctor understands it is necessary to make the medical records show that Vivica became pregnant *after* her latest test. Pay the doctor well."

Melvin stood and headed for the door. "Yes, ma'am."

Typical Melvin . . . always following orders.

"One more thing, Melvin."

Melvin paused with his hand on the doorknob. "Yes?"

"Send someone to arrest Ben Lagarde."

"No," I whispered.

"On what charges?" Melvin asked.

I tried to catch his eye, but he refused to look in my direction.

"Ruining the governor's life. I don't know. Plant evidence, make something up."

"Yes, ma'am." Melvin closed the door behind him.

I sat up straight. "Mother, please don't do this. We're not together anymore." I leaned forward, ready to drop to my knees and beg.

My mother held up her hand. "Enough. I don't want to hear it. He obviously influenced you. Go to your room and stay there until further notice."

⊁⊀

When I got to my room, I used the courier to call Ben, but he didn't answer. I considered praying for him, but dismissed the thought when I realized prayer had worsened my situation. I gritted my teeth and tried to make sense of my feelings.

I shouldn't have been relieved, but I was. The decision was out of my hands, and it made everything easier. I wouldn't be responsible for killing anybody. The baby wasn't meant to be born, or my mother would have never discovered my secret. If I was supposed to accept help from the Emancipation Warriors, it would have worked out. It had to be a sign.

I picked up my doc and called Tindra.

"You could've given me a heads-up. My mom called me into her office and blindsided me."

"What?"

"Don't play dumb. I know it was you. Who else would've told my mother I'm pregnant?"

"No way. I don't squeal. I think you're crazy, but I didn't tattle."

"Then who did?"

"I don't know. You've got that freak from Pop Management following you around. It was probably her. I didn't tell, I swear." There was a ring of truth in Tindra's voice.

"Fine. The point is, she knows."

"How'd she take it?"

"What do you think?" I sighed. "We're taking care of everything tonight."

"Good. I want my best friend back. This whole thing has been crazy. Don't you want to be free to have a life?"

Obviously. Who wouldn't? But it wasn't all about my life. It was about protecting a defenseless baby. The relief I'd felt a few minutes before vanished and resolve stood in its place.

"Tindra, I have to go. I'll talk to you later."

⋊⋉

The courier sat in my lap. If I didn't call soon, it would be too late. I thought I could trust Drake, but there was still no proof that the rebels didn't try to assassinate my mother. As much as I wanted to tell myself it was someone from inside my mother's political party, I couldn't be sure.

Someone rapped on my door, and I quickly shoved the courier behind a pillow on my couch. "Come in."

Melvin opened the door, and I saw Martina in the hallway.

"What's she doing out there?" I asked Melvin.

"Following your mother's orders to keep track of you until tonight."

"Seriously?" My entire body chilled. "I'm a prisoner in my own room?"

"I came to tell you everything has been arranged for tonight. You'll be leaving at ten o'clock for an undisclosed location. Make sure you're ready."

"Okay."

"And Vivica?"

"Yeah?"

He hesitated. "I thought you might want to know the police weren't able to find Ben or his family. We think they've left town."

I don't know how much longer I sat staring at the courier until I took a deep breath and dialed. Drake answered.

"I'm in, but I need your help," I whispered.

# CHAPTER 20

Drake listened as I explained what had happened and how I was a prisoner in my room.

"If you hadn't waited until you were backed in a corner, this wouldn't be a problem." Drake paused. "Is your window a possibility?"

"This isn't an easy decision. I even prayed, but God isn't helping. He's making things worse." I looked out my window. There was concrete below, and the window had sensors that would trigger the alarm system when I opened it. Plus, cameras monitored the outside of the house. "I might be able to finagle the window sensors so they're deactivated."

"Well, you're going to have to do something. I don't do miracles."

"One more thing. Is Ben safe?" I told Drake what my mother ordered and what Melvin had told me.

Drake groaned. "Yes, my dear. Lover boy and his family are safe. They left town yesterday. Ben is beginning his intensive field agent training."

My shoulders sagged, and I savored the relief that flooded my body.

"Vivica? Are you listening or thinking about lover boy?"

"Yes."

Drake sighed. "Whatever. Call me when you find a way out, and I'll tell you where to meet me. Be sure to pack light."

"What if I can't get out?"

"Then I guess I'll have to kidnap you en route to the clinic, which, I might add, is extremely risky and may not even be possible at this late notice. I'm not sure I'm willing to stick my neck out that much for you. And even if I wanted to, I'm too far away. So since you are quite clever and capable, I suggest you find a way out of your tower, princess."

"Princess?"

"Call me when you're out." Drake hung up. I wished he was standing in my room so I could slap him again.

But right now I had more important things to worry about. It was already 8:30. I went to my closet and stood for a moment. What does a girl pack when she's running away from home?

I dressed in a simple black T-shirt and a pair of jeans that I closed with a rubber band to extend the waistband. My running shoes would be the best choice. I shoved underwear and socks into my backpack along with another pair of shoes, a change of clothes, and a jacket. I scooped up toiletries and dumped them into a smaller bag that I stashed inside the backpack. The teddy bear my father had given me went into the bag with the unauthorized Bible and my digital photo album.

I stuffed the bag under my bed and sat down with the courier to work on my escape plan. The program I'd created to access the security cameras around the house wasn't working, and it would take time to fix it.

I glanced at my watch—9:18.

Further investigation proved the security system for the entire estate had been upgraded within the last day or two, and getting into this system was not easy. I finally figured the system out and worked on window sensors. The bathroom window was the best escape route because the roof extended under the window, and the drop would not be as far.

It was 9:45 when I deactivated the bathroom window sensor. I shoved the courier in my backpack and slung it over my shoulder.

I had just closed the bathroom door when my bedroom door opened. A fist thudded against the bathroom door. "Vivica, it's time to go. Now." It was Martina, and her harsh tone made me shiver.

I flushed the toilet. "Coming."

Could I make it out the window? I flipped the lock and pushed, but it wouldn't budge. Last summer's paint job had sealed it shut. I pushed harder. The paint cracked.

Martina rapped again. "Hurry up, or I'm coming in."

"I'm washing my hands." I turned the faucet on and then moved back to the window to try again. It opened, allowing fresh air to flow in.

Wait. The doorknob. I reached for the lock, but when I touched the knob, it rotated. I braced my feet and shoved the door as hard as I could, but Martina gave the door such a powerful kick that I toppled backward.

Martina's talon fingers bit at my arm, jerked me to my feet, and dragged me through the door. I swung my free arm, clipping the side of her face. Martina snarled and wrenched both arms behind my back. She gripped my wrists, and I flailed my elbows until she choked me in a headlock.

Martina yanked the backpack from my shoulder and tossed it on the floor. "So you were planning to run."

I tried to relax, but when I did, Martina tightened her grasp and dragged me into my bedroom where Axel waited. The dark spots in my vision grew prominent.

"What took you so long?" Martina asked. "Couldn't you hear the yelling?"

Axel removed a pair of handcuffs from his pocket and fastened them onto my wrists. "Can't handle the job? Maybe Population Management was a better fit."

"Shut up." Martina released my neck, and I breathed deeply, thankful for the rush of oxygen.

Axel glared at me. "Let's go."

Following Axel, Martina marched me down the servants' staircase that led to the kitchen. We went out the back door where one of my mother's executive cars waited. Axel sat in front to monitor the controls, and Martina shoved me in the back. A privacy screen separated us from Axel.

"My mother's not coming?"

Martina slammed the door. "No."

"Why not?" I had a few ideas, but I wanted to know if I was right.

"The less your mother has to do with this the better."

"What about Melvin?" Surely he could be there for me like he'd been in the past when my mother couldn't be.

"What does it look like?" Martina put on her seatbelt and scowled.

Of course. No matter how much Melvin cared about me, my mother and her reputation always came first.

"Where is the clinic?"

"You don't need to know."

"How long will it take to get there?"

"Why would I tell you that when I won't tell you where the clinic is?" Martina said it like I was a child lacking in intelligence.

My questions weren't profound, but thinking of questions to ask while weighing an escape plan wasn't easy. My best option was to escape on the way to the clinic, but without knowing how long I had, I wouldn't know when the best time to make a move would be. A faint hope remained that Drake would come to my rescue, but I had to act as though he wouldn't. Even if things were going smoothly, I wasn't sure I could count on him.

We were on the highway, traveling south out of town. I wasn't sure where all the clinics were since I'd never paid attention before. We were most likely going to the closest city, which meant I had about ten minutes to figure out an escape plan.

# CHAPTER 21

"Why did you take this job?"

Martina stiffened. "In case you can't tell, I don't do small talk."

I laughed. "Finding out why you wanted the job of being my bodyguard isn't small talk. So if you want to keep this job, I suggest you answer me."

"I don't answer to you."

"See now, that's where you're wrong. You may think you answer to my mother. Technically you do. But whether you like it or not, you're in charge of me. And I have to be happy. Bobby lasted because he and I had an understanding." Martina's face was unchanged. "Bobby knew his job was to protect me. You, on the other hand, seem to think your job is to run my life." I narrowed my eyes. "You may have a job to do, but I will still report on how nicely you do it. So, again, why did you take this job?"

The muscle in Martina's jaw flexed. "I need the money."

"You know my last bodyguard was killed, right?"

"Yes."

"So why is the money worth the risk?" The job paid well, but I had a hunch from the look in her eyes that something else motivated Martina.

"None of your business."

"Do you have any kids?"

"Again, none of your business."

I smirked. "In other words, yes." A hint of emotion flickered in her eyes, and I knew I was right.

"How many?"

"I never said I did."

"You didn't have to."

"One daughter."

"Single mom?"

"Yes."

I smiled. "I'm sure you want to provide your daughter with a better future, don't you?"

Martina looked away from me and stared out the window. I'd found her weakness.

"How much is my mother paying you?"

The lulling hum of tires against the road filled the vehicle, and it slowed as we exited the highway.

"Martina, how do you expect me to make a deal with you if you don't tell me what my mother is paying?"

She leaned forward. "Do you think I'm going to make a deal with a teenager who thinks she has access to money? Nothing you have is your own. You're only rich because your mommy is rich. And you quickly forget that I once worked for Population Management."

"No, I didn't forget." I shrugged. "You could pass my escape off as accidental and disappear with the money I can get for you." I'd have to hack into my mother's account since she'd cut off my allowance.

"No."

I hadn't expected Martina to say yes. The car turned, and we were in the city now. My thoughts were desperate as I groped at all possibilities. My mind rested on one that sickened me but was my last hope.

I steeled myself and spoke firmly. "Since you have a daughter, I hope you'll understand." I rested my hand on my abdomen. "I want to protect this child." I moved closer to Martina. "If you help them kill this baby, I will repay you someday when you least expect it. I will hunt your precious daughter down, and I will kill her. And I will have the resources to get away with it." The raw hate in my voice terrified me, but I knew I made an impact when fear ignited in her eyes. "Now there is a way to avoid that. Am I clear?"

Being so horrible felt like wearing clothes that were too small. Martina had to see I wasn't a good fit for such threats.

Revulsion sparked in Martina's eyes, overriding the fear. "Yes, you've made yourself clear," she said.

"Good. Then here's what you're going to do."

# CHAPTER 22

The car stopped. Martina turned from me. Axel's door opened and shut, and his boots thumped against asphalt. We were in an alley at the side of a building I assumed was the clinic. The door on my side opened, and I hesitated.

"Get out," Axel said, leaning forward. "What are you waiting for?"

I slowly slid out, aimed my foot at Axel's crotch, and kicked as hard as I could. Shock registered on his face as he staggered backward. Martina scrambled out. While Axel doubled over, I aimed my knee at his head, and the crack sickened me. He collapsed.

Martina removed my handcuffs, and I fished for the keys in Axel's pocket. When I stood, she stared at me, her expression full of hate.

"Get out of my sight."

I got into the car, disabled the navigation, overrode the car's automated transportation system so I could control the vehicle myself, and drove away into my new prison.

⋇

My first priority had to be getting rid of the car, and the second priority would be getting as far away from the Great Lakes Region as possible. If I wanted Drake's help, then getting to the Coastal Plain Region was the best plan since the courier was home in my backpack. I hoped it had a fail-safe in case my mother found it.

I stopped on the side of the road and scavenged for anything that might be useful. In the console between the two front seats were a flashlight, some napkins, and sunglasses. In the glove compartment there was tool kit. I left my treasures in the front seat and rummaged through the trunk where I found a tote bag that contained a large blanket, some bottles of water, and a bottle of champagne. I stuffed the supplies in the tote, placed it on the passenger seat, and continued down the road.

Ahead of me was a bridge that spanned a river, and I sped over bumpy terrain then veered right, toward the river. I stopped at the edge of the embankment, put the car in neutral, grabbed the tote, and hopped out. When I saw how close I stood to the embankment, my stomach plummeted. I scurried to the rear of the vehicle, stray twigs snapping under my shoes.

I planted my feet and braced my hands against the trunk. It budged. I took a deep breath and shoved. The wheels inched forward. The front bumper hung over the edge of the embankment, and the dirt on the edge of the bank crumbled. It needed a bit more momentum.

I braced myself again. My feet slid on the gravelly dirt, but the vehicle inched forward. Another push. The front end dropped. I shoved harder, lost my balance, and fell facedown in the dirt. I looked up in time to see the car slide over the embankment, clattering and crashing before splashing into the river below.

⋊⋉

I hiked along the wooded riverbank for at least a couple of hours before exhaustion set in, and I collapsed against a tree and guzzled water before wrapping myself in the blanket, shivering in the damp air.

My stomach roared. Why couldn't there have been food in the car? Should I open the bottle of champagne and drink it for calories? No. It might hurt the baby. Besides, being drunk wouldn't help.

The magnitude of my actions sank in. Would my mother ever forgive me? Then there was the issue of raising the baby. Could I do it? Did I want to? Maybe adoption was the best choice.

But as my head lolled against the tree and my eyelids grew heavy, the voice of fear reminded me I had to escape my predators before that decision was even relevant.

⋊⋉

*Snap.*

My eyes opened. The moon was a selfish sliver hoarding its light, and I drew my knees to my chest. Maybe it was just an animal. Either way, I didn't want to be discovered.

Holding my breath, I slowly turned my head from side to side. There were only trees and bushes. Plunging my hand into the tote, I clutched the champagne bottle's neck. I stood and crept toward the direction of the sound.

I jolted to a stop. A buck. We looked into each other's eyes, and the deer's face almost looked guilty, like a teenager caught in the middle of a prank. The buck had to be the twig snapper. He darted.

I returned to the tree where I'd left the tote and snatched it. I was awake enough to continue moving, though I'd have to cross the river to head south. Finding Drake in the Coastal Plain Region might be difficult without the courier, but staying in the Great Lakes Region was out of the question. It was impossible for me to cross the river here, so I trudged forward. At least I had an objective.

The trees grew more sporadic the farther I walked, and the bank grew less steep. Lights from a city dotted the horizon like hopeful beacons, but a faint hum, like the buzz of a wasp, clobbered my optimism.

A search drone.

I froze, trying to determine the direction of the noise and then decided it was coming from behind me. My heart thudded as I remembered what my mother had said about search drones. Police programmed them with the suspect's height and weight and released them into the areas where they believed suspects were hiding. I had to try to mask my heat signature until the drone went away. If it didn't, it would shoot me with a tranquilizer dart and tag me with a GPS locator. From there, the police would find me.

And that was the best-case scenario. The drone might be programmed to kill me.

Down the river was a marina with rows of boats tied to piers. I sprinted toward the marina in a zigzag pattern and cursed when I realized it was farther than I estimated. A buzzing crescendo pressed me to run faster, the tote bouncing against my side. Sweat dampened my forehead.

I reached the marina parking lot and dashed to the back of the building and onto a wooden deck that overlooked the river. Benches lined the railing, but their cover would be inadequate.

I followed the steps down to the pier-lined river. A row of houseboats floated to my left, some of which looked inhabited. I picked the pier that branched to the right and led to a row of pontoon boats.

I plunged into the shallow water, my feet sinking beneath the muck. Forcing myself into the muddy water up to my shoulders, I sloshed forward with a shudder. I picked a boat and ducked underneath, concealing myself between the pontoons. Water tickled my chin. The air was redolent with dead fish.

Shivering, I listened.

The drone's hum escalated, and a machine the size of a vulture hovered just above the rippling water and halted in the gap between the pontoons. My pulse pummeled my neck. A whimper slipped from my throat. With a red light blinking, the drone paused and leered at me.

Taunting me.

I slid beneath the murky water and clasped my hand over my nose and mouth. And waited. With lungs burning, I remained until desperation for oxygen vanquished my fear.

I emerged.

The drone was gone. I wanted to remain hidden, but violent trembling forced me to climb out onto the pier.

Footsteps sounded behind me. I whirled.

"That drone lookin' for you?"

# CHAPTER 23

A sinewy man stood next to a yacht. His only attire was a pair of cut-off denim shorts, and his gray hair was tousled.

"Yes," I whispered.

"Don't look like a jailbird to me."

I closed the gap between us. Would I see kindness in his eyes?

"I'm not." His eyes were full of suspicion but kindness radiated on his weathered face.

"Well, you mind tellin' me what's goin' on?"

"I'm sorry. I had to run away from some people who wanted to hurt me."

The man studied me as if trying to figure out why I looked familiar. I held out my hand. "Vivica Wilkins."

Recognition dawned in his eyes as he gripped my hand. "Governor's daughter?"

I nodded.

"Now why would you be wantin' to run away?"

"It's complicated."

"You a rebel?"

"Not really."

"Pregnant?"

I stared at the worn pier. "Yes."

"You're in quite a pickle, ain't you?"

"Yes, sir." I held my breath and fought against the urge to pray, remembering how poorly my last petition had worked. The man stared out at the boats, and the extended period of silence was punctuated by water lapping against the pier.

"I know just the person to help," he said. "If you want it. If not, scram and I'll never tell a soul I seen you. You decide."

Air seeped from my lungs with a whoosh. "Yes. Please. Help me." I sounded so pitiful I hated myself for the weakness.

"Name's Beau." He motioned for me to follow as he stepped aboard the small houseboat docked across from the row of pontoons. I forced myself to move forward, trying unsuccessfully to ignore what-if questions that sprouted in the fertile soil of my fear. What if he was crazy? What if he kidnapped me? What if his loyalty was to the government? My practical side pruned the growing questions. It would take a lot for my current situation to become worse than what I'd face if I returned home now.

I stood on the deck while Beau disappeared into the cabin. Two faded towels were spread over chaise lounges on the deck. Voices murmured, though I was unable to discern what they were saying.

Beau returned to the deck and had added a holey red T-shirt to his attire. A woman wearing a nightgown followed him. Her long gray hair was plaited, and her grandmotherly look comforted me.

"This here's my wife, Helen," Beau said.

Helen rushed forward and gathered me in an embrace, her cotton gown soft and comforting against my skin. "Don't worry, sweetie. We'll fix you right up."

"Thank you," I said. "Are you sure you want to mess with me?"

Helen chuckled. "Land, yes, sweetie. I promised my Lord a long time ago that I'd help any of his children in need no matter what. Now, let's go get you some dry clothes. You hungry?"

"Yes, ma'am."

As I followed Helen below deck, Beau was untying the boat from the dock. "Are we leaving?"

"That's right. We gotta get you to people who can help," she said.

We entered the galley that contained a small stove, sink, and refrigerator. Though the cabin was neat, the appliances and décor were years out of date. Helen went to a closet, removed a towel, clothing, and shoes, and pointed to another door. "Now get outta them wet duds. Feel free to wash that river water off in the shower."

I did, and after I dressed, I returned to the galley.

Helen filled a glass with water and pulled a jar of peanut butter from the pantry. "You ain't allergic, are you?"

"No." I took a long drink. "So, are you rebels?"

Helen laughed as she spread peanut butter on white bread. "I like to think of them people who align themselves with the government as the rebels." She cut the sandwich in half. "After all, they're the ones rebellin' against God Almighty and his ways." Helen put the sandwich on a chipped plate and handed it to me. I took a huge bite. "I decided a long time ago that I'd never answer to the government first. Beau's with me on that. We answer to God first."

"Aren't Christians supposed to obey the law?"

"Absolutely. But sometimes man's laws get so far from what God intended and told us about in his Word we got to make a choice. Obey laws that go against God. Or obey God Almighty. We choose God. And we're willin' to accept the consequences of breakin' laws we know ain't right accordin' to what's in the Bible."

"What about unanswered prayer? How do you answer to a God who doesn't bother to answer prayers?" I blurted the questions before my brain had a chance to filter them. I felt heat rise into my cheeks. "Sorry." I wanted an answer and sensed this wise stranger might be able to give me some direction. I looked into her eyes.

Helen took a seat across from me and folded her hands, resting them on the table. "What prayers has God not answered for you?" Her voice was gentle, and I appreciated the fact that she didn't appear to be judging me. I told Helen about my plea for help and how my entire situation became worse.

The boat moved in reverse out of the dock. Helen looked unfazed by what I shared, but the longer she took to answer, the more uncertain I became. Maybe she didn't have any answers either.

"God ain't always easy to figure out," Helen said. "Sometimes we think our prayers ain't bein' answered when he's really telling us no. Sometimes we gotta wait 'cause God is working at fixin' a situation, and we can't see the solution yet. I know how that goes. We've been prayin' for my daughter, Alma, and her husband to be able to have a baby for years. We're all still waitin' for God's answer." Helen smiled and shook her head. "He's sure takin' his time. Don't understand why. But I been a Christian long enough to know sometimes you gotta trust without knowin' why. As for you, someday you'll look back and see what God was up to."

Helen's words made sense, and I was willing to admit that her explanation was possible, even if I wasn't sure.

Helen patted my hand. "Don't make it any easier when you're going through it, but it's the truth."

I finished my sandwich and decided I didn't feel like dwelling on God and his ways any more at that moment. "Where are you taking me?"

"We got a contact in the Coastal Plain Region who's a part of a network that can hide pregnant girls like yourself." She put my empty plate in the sink. "We're gonna do our best to get you to him. There may be issues gettin' out of this region though. Security's real tight since the attacks."

I nodded. "I'm not surprised. What's your contact's name?"

Helen smiled. "I bet you've heard of him, especially since you run in political circles."

I knew the answer before she said it.

"His name's Drake Freeman. Handsome young man. Smart, too."

I hated to admit it, even to myself, but maybe God was answering my prayer after all. But I wasn't sure how I felt about the fact that Drake might be part of the answer.

⋊⋉

Helen called Drake and filled him in on finding me, and I wasn't surprised when she handed me her courier a few minutes later.

"I knew you'd find a way out," Drake said.

"You'd feel pretty stupid right now if you'd been wrong."

"At least I can rest assured that you're serious about joining our cause."

"This was all about me proving myself?"

Drake sighed. "No. I'm just making a statement. We both know everything happened so quickly that I didn't have time to come to your rescue. But I admit your resourcefulness makes me feel better."

"I'm so glad I could help you feel better. Tell me what happens now."

"You've created quite a stir with your disappearing act. I have a source who tells me your mother has launched a privately funded search team. I'll be interested to see what story they feed the media though. There's no way your mother will let news of your escape get out."

"You're right." For once Drake and I agreed on something.

"Beau and Helen are taking you to our meeting point."

"Which is?"

"The less you know the better."

"What if something goes wrong? Don't you think I should know?" His lack of trust rankled.

"You can trust them. I'll meet you and take you to the Coastal Plain Region. Border security is tight, but I have high enough clearance that I can get through easier than Beau and Helen could. Travel between regions has pretty much been cut off for the lower and middle classes."

I still wanted to know the rendezvous point. "Where are we meeting?"

"Just stay with Beau and Helen and you'll find out."

Drake hung up, and I scowled and handed the courier back to Helen who smiled.

"Is he always like that?" I asked.

"Don't know him that well, but he's got a good name for himself. One of the best the Emancipation Warriors have."

"How did the Emancipation Warriors get started?"

"I can tell you a smidge." Helen filled a glass of water for herself and refilled my glass before sitting at the table again. "Years ago Beau and I were newlyweds when the Union City Massacre happened. You know 'bout that?"

"It's how my great-grandpa and grandparents were killed."

"Sorry 'bout that. The rebels started the whole thing, but the government caused the civilians to die. Then blamed the rebels."

I'd never heard that before.

"Anyway, what we and a bunch of other folks learned from the rebels who staged that failed uprisin' was that if we was gonna overthrow the government, then we had to have more people and be better organized. So we found other people who felt the same and started organizin'. Everybody involved knew it would take years before we had the kind of numbers to think about makin' a difference, but we hung in there, taught our children, and kept recruitin'. Now there are people in every region in all kinds of places. Even the government. We're almost ready."

"When you 'make a difference' what exactly do you mean?"

"I mean a revolution."

The term startled me, but when I remembered Drake's talk at the Governor's Ball in March, Helen's declaration made perfect sense. I decided to press further.

"What do you mean, 'almost ready'? If your group is planning a revolution, haven't you already started with the attacks on the Capitol?"

Helen shook her head. "That ain't us. I've heard rumors that corrupt members of the government did it so they could turn public opinion against us and avoid a revolution. Or at least make it an easy fight. But they don't know how big a threat we are."

This statement also echoed what Drake had told me. "War really is inevitable, isn't it? I was hoping . . ." I didn't have the heart to finish. Why had I hoped the attacks would be isolated?

"The cost of freedom is high," Helen said.

Was freedom worth the cost? But then I thought about my escape. Wasn't I seeking the same thing?

"I gotta believe we're gonna restore freedom. Beau and I have devoted our lives to this cause." She motioned around the cabin. "This is the sum of our earthly possessions. Takes effort just for us to keep this boat. I want better for my grandchildren."

"Do you have any?"

"Our son has two girls."

"How old—"

"Helen!" Beau's voice was urgent.

Helen stood. "Stay here." She took the stairs two at a time, and I admired her agility.

Beau barked a few orders, but the hum of the engine drowned them out. Helen returned to the cabin, her face full of concern.

"We've gotta hide you. There's a government checkpoint down the river."

# CHAPTER 24

Helen strode down the stairs before dropping to her knees in front of the small pantry beside her stove. She opened the pantry door and ran her fingers along the floor. Pausing, she pushed and a panel slid aside, revealing a compartment that was so tiny that for a moment I simply stared. Surely she didn't expect me to crawl in there.

"Go. It's bigger than it looks."

"But—"

"Now. We're gettin' close to the checkpoint, and Beau can't slow down. It'll look fishy." Helen's gentle countenance was replaced by a no-nonsense expression. She waved at the black hole.

I grabbed my soggy tote and clothes and knelt in front of the pantry. I shoved the bag in first and crawled into the hole. Helen had told the truth. The hole was deeper than it looked from the galley. Though I couldn't stand, I'd be able to sit up straight with my legs stretched in front of me. What did they use this space for? Helen replaced the panel, deserting me in the darkened tomb.

I forced myself to breathe. It was only temporary. Being forced into a dark hole by a virtual stranger multiplied my fear. The soft whirr of the boat's motor diminished as the boat slowed. Straining, I listened for voices.

Instead, I heard heavy footsteps that didn't belong to the sinewy Beau or the agile Helen. The trudge present in the footfall indicated someone large had boarded.

Then a voice spoke that matched the footsteps.

"Just following orders. We have to search every boat that passes through." Axel. Blood pulsed in my ears in time with my racing heart.

"Why?" Helen asked.

"Escaped convict."

"Man or woman?" Beau asked.

"Young girl. Sixteen. Long blond hair. Tall. We have reason to believe she's a violent offender."

No doubt about it. They were searching for me. Even though I was alone in the dark, I rolled my eyes. Violent offender? But it made sense. People would be more likely to turn me in or supply information if they thought I was dangerous.

"We ain't seen nothin'," Beau said. "Be glad to keep an eye out for you though."

"If you see anything suspicious, call the authorities. Immediately."

"Will do, sir," Helen said.

There were more footsteps. Lighter. Almost like Helen's. "Anything here, Axel?" Those three words, spoken in a raspy voice, were enough for me to identify the speaker. My stomach roiled and the darkness edged closer.

Martina.

"They've not seen anything," Axel said.

"I see." Martina sounded skeptical. "Did you search?"

"No." Axel sounded sheepish. "I don't have any reason to suspect them."

"And that's why the governor put me in charge instead of you. I ran the boat registration. These two are suspected rebels. They've never been arrested, but they've been questioned lots of times. So we're going to search."

Doors opened and closed.

"Axel, go search on deck," Martina said.

The pantry door opened, and I cowered against the hull and held my breath. As the door slammed, I sagged, trapping an audible sigh.

"There's nothing here." Martina's determined footsteps seemed even louder in my cave. "Let's go. We can't waste any more time here."

"We'll keep an eye out for her," Helen said.

"I doubt it. But I think I ought to remind you that harboring a fugitive is a criminal act. With your suspected rebel affiliation, I wouldn't expect any mercy."

Beau cleared his throat. "We'll keep that in mind, missy."

"It's Officer Ward."

"Yes, ma'am, Officer Ward." There was a note of mocking in Beau's tone.

There was more stomping and a door slammed.

When the sound of their speedboat motor faded, the door creaked, and Helen's smiling face appeared. "You ain't claustrophobic, are you?"

I grinned. "Now you're asking?"

# CHAPTER 25

"She was sure pleasant," Helen said as we settled into the recliners in the salon.

I laughed. "Martina was my bodyguard. The other guy was my mother's." I explained to Helen about escaping from Martina, though I left out the part about threatening Martina's daughter. I didn't want Helen to know that about me.

"She's got somethin' to prove to your mother, no doubt."

"Right."

Helen started to say something, but Beau interrupted. "They're coming back!" He didn't appear but shouted from the bridge, which meant they were close.

Helen and I exchanged panicked glances, and I scrambled for the pantry. This time I didn't hesitate and dove into the burrow.

Why would Martina and Axel return? I tried to remember if we'd passed any other boats that might have reported seeing me, but I hadn't been paying attention.

The drone of the speedboat's motor grew louder. When it stopped, the sound was replaced with muffled voices and footsteps.

"You might as well make this easy. I know she's on board," Martina said.

"Who's that?" Helen asked.

I heard a throat clear. "The fugitive," Axel said.

"What makes you think she's here?" Beau sounded annoyed.

"This," Martina said.

What was she referring to?

"What's that?" I think Helen knew, from the tone of her voice, and I could tell she expected her fears to be confirmed.

"It's a bug. I planted it when we came aboard the first time." Martina sounded haughty.

My heart plunged to my stomach. Was there another way out of this coffin? I scooted forward until my feet hit a solid surface. Drawing my knees to my chest and bracing my hands against the walls, I thrust my feet forward. They thudded against the barrier. My back throbbed. I thrust again. More pain and the wall refused to budge. The baby kicked, and a twinge radiated through my right side. I had to try something different before I hurt the baby. I sat up and ran my hands along the wall hoping to find a crack, but the compartment was solid.

"What's that noise?" Axel asked.

"Dunno," Beau said. "It's an old boat. Makes funny noises sometimes like old houses do."

I scooted backward until I was at the opposite end of the compartment. Carefully rolling over onto my round abdomen, I drew myself up, faced the wall, and examined it with my hands. This time my fingers fell upon a narrow groove. I pushed forward and backward. No movement. My heart pounded so much that I forced myself to stop and take a deep breath. If the panic won, Martina and Axel won. That was not an option.

Martina gloated. "I heard everything that was said in this cabin. So not only do I know there's someone else on board, I know that you're hiding exactly who we're looking for. And you're right, Helen. I do have something to prove."

"Where is she?" Axel asked.

"If you got something to prove, then I suggest you find her yourself," Helen said. "It's a small space."

The answer was a gunshot followed by a thud that shook my tomb.

# CHAPTER 26

"Helen!" Beau screamed. I heard shuffling. Then weeping.

"What are you doing!" Martina shrieked. "Did you have to kill her?"

"I didn't like her tone," Axel said.

"Give me your weapon."

"No."

"I'm in charge of this operation, and I gave you a direct order. Surrender your weapon."

The shock of the moment passed. I hadn't moved since the gunshot. Springing to action and ignoring the lump that formed in my throat when I thought of Helen, I ran my hands along the top of the compartment, hoping to find the door that led to the pantry. I had to help Beau.

My hand rested on the trap door when a second gunshot pierced the air. Once more I froze. Beau.

Martina swore and confirmed my fears.

"I was putting him out of his misery," Axel said.

"He's not an injured animal." Martina's compassionate side shocked me. "We could have used him for information."

Perhaps compassion was the wrong word.

"I don't even know why you care. You're the one who figured out they're rebels," Axel said.

"Suspected rebels."

"Like it matters."

"What matters is I gave you an order. You've still not complied."

"Woman, you've pushed me around long enough. In case you've forgotten, we're in this mess 'cause you let her get away. Governor Wilkins appointed me to this team too. This isn't the military, and I don't take orders from you."

"You won't be taking orders from anyone if we don't find that girl."

I crawled away from the trap door that led into the pantry and turned my attention back to the wall where I'd found the groove. This time, I pushed to the side, and the panel slid open. Dragging my bag behind me, I wiggled through the opening into the next compartment and shut the panel. While I crawled, I ran my hand along the top of the partition, hoping to find a second trap door. Feeling nothing, I edged forward to the bow.

When I reached the end of the compartment, I ran my hands all over the walls and found the ceiling had a groove similar to the other panel, and I shoved it aside. Sunlight assaulted my eyes.

I poked my head out and observed my surroundings. The bow was small, but a narrow deck ran along the starboard side all the way to the stern where their speedboat was secured.

Would I have enough time to steal their boat?

I crawled onto the deck. The wood bit at my knees, but I gritted my teeth. If I could reach the starboard deck and stay under the windows, they might not notice me.

I turned the corner when the cabin door opened, flattening myself against the cabin wall. My heart sank when I realized I'd left the compartment door gaping.

"Martina, get out here."

"What?"

"Look at this."

"So that's where she was hiding."

Footsteps drew closer. Plunging my hand into the tote bag I'd carried with me, I clutched the neck of the champagne bottle and rose.

Axel rounded the corner, and I aimed the champagne bottle at the back of his head. It was a direct hit, and he collapsed at my feet in a pile of green glass, his head wet with champagne. I cringed. His tattooed arms were bigger than my thighs. Why had I never noticed that before? It took a couple of tries, but I rolled Axel over and took his Diablo 87. He groaned.

I stepped around the corner and saw Martina with her gun pointed at me. Whirling, I fled down the starboard deck. Martina fired a shot. A bullet whizzed by my arm.

When I reached the stern, I yanked open the cabin door, rushed in, and locked it behind me. Bile rose in my throat when I saw Beau's and Helen's bodies on the salon floor. Bullet holes pierced each of their foreheads. Axel's cruel executions made me realize I had more to fear from him than Martina, though I had no doubt she would take whatever measures were necessary to capture me, especially since I'd threatened her daughter.

Forcing myself to focus, I noticed Helen's courier was on the end table between the recliners where she'd left it. I shoved it into my pocket. It was my only link to Drake.

Thumps sounded on the cabin door. I peeked through the window. Martina was kicking the door. The flimsy lock wouldn't hold for long once Axel joined her, so I sprinted through the galley and into the berth where there was a door to the bow that I locked behind me. I plastered myself against the wall next to the window.

Martina gave up on the door, went to the starboard deck, and headed for the door I'd secured. I ran back through the cabin and out the stern door where I took the spiral staircase to the upper deck.

When I reached the upper deck, I stayed low and peered through the gap between the deck and the first rail. Martina was directly below me on the starboard deck, and she squinted as she looked into the cabin windows.

I pulled Axel's gun from my back pocket. Could I do it? Even though Bobby had shown me how, it had never entered my mind that I'd have to shoot someone. Guilt pummeled me when I remembered Martina was a single mom. What would happen to her daughter? But I had to remember she was the enemy.

I lay flat on the deck and aimed through the railing. At that moment Martina looked up. I pointed the laser guide at her chest and fired.

# CHAPTER 27

Martina fell against the railing then collapsed onto the deck. I scrambled to my feet and darted down the spiral staircase.

Martina's and Axel's boat was tied to the houseboat's stern. I hopped aboard and loosened the knot that secured the speedboat's stern. When I made my way to the speedboat's bow, Martina was no longer on the starboard deck. There was no blood. She must have been wearing a bullet-proof vest. With one hand I untied the knot while I held the gun with the other.

Martina would be well hidden and was probably planning to pick me off like a sniper unless I spotted her. But I couldn't see her. The steady beat of my heart increased with each second that passed. Where was she? I looked to my left. To my right. I had to find her. The knot was stubborn. Why couldn't I untie it?

"God, please help me."

The morning sunlight, my ally, warned me with a glint of light on Martina's gun. I ducked as the shot pierced the air.

There was a thump behind me. The bullet blasted a ragged hole in a seat cushion. Stuffing bled from the gash.

I flinched. Was I next?

I took a deep breath and yanked the knot again. This time it loosened, allowing the current to pull the speedboat away from the houseboat.

Martina fired again.

I aimed at the houseboat and shot at no particular target before I reached over and started the engine. I huddled under the steering wheel and put the boat in gear.

Another bullet pierced the seats in the back of the boat.

I returned the fire, lunged out of my hiding place, and pulled back on the throttle. The boat zoomed away, but not before Martina fired once again. This time the bullet whizzed over the top of my shoulder and pierced the windshield. I closed my eyes and turned away from the shattering glass.

When the glass settled, I concentrated on getting out of Martina's range. I traveled full speed for at least five minutes before I allowed myself to look back. Nothing but the river.

I slowed the boat, pulled Helen's courier from my pocket and hit redial.

"Drake Freeman."

For a moment I was so glad to hear a friendly voice that I couldn't speak. "It's Vivica."

"What's wrong?"

I told him quickly what happened to Beau and Helen. "What do I do now? Martina is after me. You know she's going to send backup. I can't stay on the river in one of their speedboats."

"You're right. You'll have to ditch it."

"Then what?"

"I've already traced your location. Get off the boat and get to shore."

"Are you sure?"

"Just get off the boat. We're already on our way. By helicopter." Drake ended the call.

I shoved the courier in my pocket and steered the boat closer to shore because there was no sense in making my swim longer than it needed to be. I had some serious concerns about swimming through the current, especially since I didn't want to ditch my clothes and shoes.

I turned off the motor and let the boat drift into shore. When it was close, I grabbed my tote, stood on the ski platform and jumped. I landed hard and nearly fell face-first into the sandy soil, but I put out my hand and caught myself on a tree root. I waited, wondering if I'd feel a twinge of movement from the baby. Feeling nothing, I moved up the bank.

I jogged through the woods hoping to find a clearing for Drake's helicopter to land. Birds chirped, and their blissful unawareness of the troubled world around them comforted me.

Pressing forward, I came to the edge of the woods and found a field. Shading my eyes with my hands, I surveyed the area. This was probably the best I could do. The uneven ground looked inviting, and I collapsed, wishing I'd thought to grab food and water from Beau and Helen's galley.

Thoughts of the kind couple arose in my mind, and the vision of their slain bodies soured my stomach. I hurled in the field. If I'd never run away, they would still be alive and able to spend time with their children and grandchildren.

I picked up a rock and chucked it. Even from the short time I'd been around them, I knew they'd willingly die for their cause. Hadn't Helen told me they were willing to accept the consequences of breaking the law? Still, it felt as though their blood was on my hands.

Then there was the issue with God. I could understand if he wanted to punish me, but Beau and Helen were good people. It was unfair that God would let such nice people meet such a violent end. Where had God been when Beau and Helen had needed him?

A hum in the distance distracted me, and I strained to listen. The staccato rhythm grew louder and more distinct. I scanned the horizon and saw the helicopter hovering over the woods. It moved over the field and lingered a few feet off the ground.

A man poked his head out and motioned for me to board. Gathering my meager possessions, I stepped over the rows of short, bushy crops, but when I reached the helicopter, I stopped. The man reaching his hand out was a stranger with light red hair and glasses.

"Apparently, my Kalvin Miller alias is effective," he shouted over the noise. "Meet your new husband, my dear."

My shoulders sagged. I took Drake's hand, and he helped me inside. "You could have warned me."

"That wouldn't have been as much fun." Drake nodded at the pilot. "You remember my brother Liam."

"Yes."

"Glad we caught you," Liam yelled.

"Me too." I sat and buckled my seatbelt. Drake handed me a headset with a microphone that matched the ones he and Liam wore.

Drake's face was etched with concern. "Are you okay?"

I adjusted the headset. "That depends on how you define the word.

I've escaped my own bodyguard not once but twice. I listened while two of the kindest people left on this planet got shot in the head for protecting me. And I got shot at myself. Other than that, yeah, I'm fine."

"I'm sorry you had to go through that." Drake sounded sincere, but his apology wasn't enough.

"I don't care if you're sorry or not. It's not like you've been much help!"

Drake frowned. "So the fact that I'm here now doesn't count?"

"If it weren't for me, I wouldn't even be here for you to help."

"Fair enough. I do want you to know that you're better than most field agents I know. I always had faith in your ability to escape."

"Whatever. You had no reason to believe I could get away from Martina. That's a cop-out, and you know it."

"I don't know what all you want from me. I'm pretty sure you don't even know yourself." Drake crossed his arms. "I can't always be your hero. Neither can Ben for that matter."

"Shut up."

"Gladly." Drake picked up his courier and scrolled through it. "Better things to do anyway."

I peered down at the farmland we were flying over, wishing for my life that had once been so simple. "What's next?" I asked a few minutes later.

Drake looked up from his courier and cleared his throat. "You get a new identity. And you get the privilege of posing as my wife."

"Yeah . . . about that second part." I glared at him, making sure I caught his eye. "No way."

"You don't get a choice. You need protection. I'm a trained agent, so you'll pose as my wife."

"Are you sure Ben can't be my husband? It would make more sense."

"I'm sure it does to you, but I can give you a thousand reasons why that scenario doesn't work. I'll not bore you. The answer is no. Ben doesn't have enough experience."

"How will he ever get experience if you don't let him do anything?"

"Ben has plenty to keep him busy. When he proves himself, he'll take on harder jobs."

"But this won't be that hard."

"You're a weakness for Ben. It would be very hard for him."

"Maybe you want to keep him away from me because you want me for yourself."

"Yes. That's it. My dream assignment is babysitting a spoiled, pregnant teenager who thinks she knows everything and argues for the sake of arguing. That's right. Ben was standing in the way of my living the dream." His handsome features twisted in a wry grin.

Drake's analysis of me hurt, but I deserved it. I'd driven him to it. I gritted my teeth to prevent retaliation. I folded and unfolded my hands, the whir of the helicopter filling the silence. I took a deep breath as I stared at my hands. "Do you think I'll ever see him again?"

"You really do have a thing for him, don't you?" Drake's face softened. "I'm sure you'll see him someday. Right now the security risk is too great."

"Drake, we're set to arrive at our destination in ten minutes," Liam said.

"Great."

"Just so you know," Liam said, "I think you two will make a very convincing married couple."

# CHAPTER 28

Liam landed the helicopter at an airstrip in the middle of nowhere. I wasn't even sure what region we were in. Drake led me into a hangar where several small planes waited. Two women worked at computers in a small office.

The first was Ben's sister Faith. Drake rushed over and pulled her into an intimate hug. I looked away. He was involved with Faith? Of all women?

The other woman with cat-eye glasses had given me the pregnancy test months before.

"Hello. We meet again," she said and headed for a table that had several black cases stacked on it. She clicked open one of the cases and started removing bottles. Then scissors and a cape. My stomach lurched.

She eyed me and held up a bottle. "How do you feel about being a brunette?"

I looked at Drake. "Is this necessary?"

"Yes." He turned to the woman. "Go easy on her, Ophelia. Nothing too drastic. Just different enough that she won't be recognized."

Faith shook her head and huffed under her breath. "Drastic would be better."

I scowled at Faith who gave me an overly sweet smile.

Ophelia surveyed me critically. "You know, Drake's right. But you have to look older. Definitely no bangs. Prosthetic teeth. When you arrive at your final destination a doctor will surgically take care of your eye color and retinas."

"Eye surgery?"

"No worries. It's completely safe and only takes fifteen minutes. Nanoparticles injected into your vitreous gel will change your retina enough to fool the scanners. And artificial pigment will make those pretty blue-green eyes brown."

I wrapped my arms around my waist.

Drake put his arm around Faith. "Vivica, I'm sure you know Faith. She's going to prepare your new ID."

"I didn't know you knew each other."

Faith smirked. "We've gotten to know each other better recently."

I was shocked, but I steeled my face so it wouldn't show. Why had I assumed Drake didn't have a girlfriend? I told myself to stop being stupid. It was none of my business.

Ophelia motioned for me to sit in the chair in front of her. When I sat, she draped a cape over my shoulders. "We'll start with your teeth so the machine can make the prosthesis while I do your hair. Open and hold still. I've got to get measurements."

I complied, and she held a metal stick with a ball on the end inside my mouth. It hummed and clicked before she removed it and plugged it into a small box sitting on the table.

Ophelia started applying color to my hair. "You're not going to make it too dark are you?" I sounded childish, but I'd always loved my hair color.

"Trust me. I know it needs to look natural. I'll even send some with you to use on the roots. You'll have to wear a bit more makeup if you're going to pass for twenty-three. I can help you with that too." She smiled and winked at me in the mirror.

Though I was flattered they thought I could pass for twenty-three, I wasn't sure why Ophelia thought I'd trust her blindly. I set my jaw, reminding myself that this was my only option.

"Trust me." She put her hand on my shoulder. "This isn't the first disguise I've created."

I took a deep breath as Ophelia turned to rinse the bottles in the next room. While my hair processed, I watched Drake and Faith huddle on the couch, sharing a computer. They appeared to be working, but their cozy pose annoyed me. Drake leaned over and whispered something to Faith, and she giggled, slapping him playfully.

Apparently, they had forgotten the rest of us were around.

Pushing thoughts of Drake from my mind, I forced myself to consider my future. Unanswered questions pursued me, demanding answers I couldn't produce. Would I be able to take care of a baby? Doubt nagged at me as my years of conditioning convinced me I was incapable. Why else would there be a law? In a way I understood the reasoning. I didn't have any qualifications to get a job. I was a minor. Added to those factors was the reality that I'd have to live in hiding the rest of my life.

Why had I entertained the fantasy of Ben marrying me and helping me raise the baby together? He'd never marry me. I wasn't one of his kind. Even if I changed, I'd always be the daughter of an enemy. I determined to move on for my baby if nothing else.

Fantasy aside, adoption was the most logical choice. But would I be able to give a child I'd fought so hard to protect to someone else? I'd have to. The baby would be safer and better off with them than me.

But what if no one wanted the baby? I hadn't even seen a doctor. What if there was something wrong with it? I decided to ask for a doctor as soon as possible. Surely there was someone in the organization who could provide medical care.

Ophelia put a hand on my shoulder, and I jumped. She grinned. "Let's rinse."

As she combed my hair the wet, brown strands made me cringe. I was more attached to my blond hair than I realized. "Don't cut it too short."

"I'll put some layers in it so it frames your face."

After Ophelia finished and blew my hair dry, she handed me a mirror. The change wasn't as bad as I'd anticipated. I took a deep breath and let it out. The light brown looked okay with my complexion, and I liked the softness of the cut. "It looks good. Thanks."

Ophelia rummaged through the cases. "We're not done." She produced two small packages and handed them to me. "Brown contacts for the ID pictures and to wear until your surgery." She demonstrated how I should pull on my eyelid and balance the contact on my finger. "Go ahead. Try it."

I wrinkled my nose and peeled back the seals on the first packages. The brown disks floated in solution. It was odd, aiming a finger at my eye, and I blinked and missed the first two times. On the third try, I managed to get the contact in my left eye. The right eye was easier. I grabbed a mirror. With every step, I shed a piece of my old life. Would I ever be Vivica Suzanne Wilkins again?

"We're not done." Ophelia slipped the mirror from my grasp. She put some makeup on for me, inserted the finished prosthetic in my mouth, and then stood back and surveyed her work. "Faith, we're ready for pictures."

Faith pulled herself away from her spot on the couch and set up a portable screen that served as a background with several color options.

I stood in front of the gray background, and Faith took my first picture. Then Ophelia styled my hair differently and had me change clothes before taking another picture, so I'd have a different picture for my national ID card and passport. I even had to put on a wedding dress and pose with Drake for a photo.

When Faith had the pictures, she created a new identification for me as well as an electronic trail for my existence. "Ready to see your new life? These creds will be on the new doc Liam will have for you. It'll look just like a government-issued one." She picked up her courier. "Birth certificate. Sarah Kate Abrams born on September 6. You're twenty-three years old." She swiped the screen, and a marriage license appeared. "On May 12 of last year, you married Kalvin Miller." She nodded at Drake, but her expression reminded me not to get used to the arrangement. "You're expecting your first kid, and one of our hackers has already registered and approved your pregnancy with Pop Man."

"Impressive work."

"Yeah," she muttered.

So much for trying to be nice.

In addition to the passport and national ID card, there was a diploma and transcript from a high school in the Coastal Plain Region. Faith shrugged as I studied the diploma. "It can't be from a fancy school like you're used to. Your school has to fit your new middle class position. I did make you an A student because you seem smart."

I ignored the barb. "Will I have a job?"

"Sort of," Drake said. "Officially, your alias works for a private company the government has contracted to distribute produce to cities throughout the country. Lots of travel involved."

"That doesn't sound safe."

"Right. But the government can track Sarah's doc, so she needs a legitimate reason to move around. We have a program that mimics the natural movement of a person in her position. That way the government will never suspect you're not actually moving," Drake said. "Unofficially, you'll be a hacker for our organization. There's lots of work you can do to help. I'll send a courier for that later."

"Good. I can live with that."

"You don't exactly have a choice at this point."

"No kidding." I tried to soften the words with a smile.

Faith scowled and handed me the wedding picture in a silver frame. "Be sure to display this in your new house. I'm sure you both will be blissfully happy."

"Whatever. It's only a few months," I said.

Three couriers rang simultaneously, and Drake, Faith, and Ophelia all exchanged glances before answering. No one spoke, and it was clear they were listening to some type of recorded message. Their expressions were grim when the calls ended.

Could I endure more bad news? "What? Something's wrong. Tell me."

"That was the general of the Coastal Plain Branch of Emancipation Warriors," Drake said.

"Wait. Like general of an army?"

Ophelia looked at Drake and he nodded. "Right," she said.

"You're kidding, right? You mean this movement or whatever is so organized that you have an *army*?" I felt stupid, like everyone was in on some colossal secret except me. I was tired of being left out. "So, what did the general want?"

"It's really more like a militia," Faith said. "The general wants all volunteers to report to their posts by eighteen hundred hours."

"Why?" I asked.

Drake smiled. "The war is starting."

# CHAPTER 29

"Now what?" I looked at Drake, Faith, and Ophelia, hoping one of them could give me guidance.

Faith and Ophelia packed up the materials they'd used to change my identity, and Drake was on his courier in the middle of an intense conversation. When he ended the call, I tried again.

"Do you mind telling me where we're going now?"

Drake shoved his courier in his pocket. He walked over to Faith and gave her a quick kiss on the lips. I looked away. How long were they going to leave me wondering about my new life?

Faith and Ophelia finished packing and left, and Drake turned off the lights in the office. "Let's go."

"Where?"

"To the helicopter. Liam's waiting."

"Then where?"

"Wherever Liam takes you."

"Just me? I thought you were going too." As much as I'd complained about posing as Drake's wife, I had looked forward to his familiar companionship.

"Not now. Not with the war."

We approached the helicopter. "You don't know where I'm going, do you?"

"That's right." Drake helped me inside. "The fewer who know the exact location, the better."

✕

I treaded through a rutted cow pasture while the helicopter faded out of sight. Clusters of barns and sheds dotted the farm. I found the white cottage that Liam had described. The cottage had a front porch lined with flower boxes full of petunias that stood about five hundred yards from the main farmhouse. A light peeked through the curtains on the windows next to the doors.

A man who had a goatee and looked about forty answered my knock. He grabbed my hand and shook it firmly. "Welcome. I'm Judd Barry." He removed his cowboy hat.

"Sarah Miller." For a second I was proud of myself for remembering my new name.

"This here's my cottage. Built it for my mother-in-law ten years ago. She passed away three months back, God rest her soul. Wonderful woman. Anyway, my wife and I are glad to have you. We've got two little ones. Twins. You'll meet them later."

"Great."

Judd studied me for a moment while stroking his goatee. "The start of the war has changed everything. You got a cover story worked out for where your husband's gonna be?"

"He drives a truck delivering produce for Agricultural Management. They promised me his ID would show up in the government database."

Judd nodded. "Good. Every so often we get someone here from Ag Management checking on our crops and livestock. Have to make sure we're giving our fair share to Big Brother. I just wanted to see if you're ready in case they get snoopy."

I pulled the framed wedding photo from my bag. "Will this help?"

"Perfect. Oh, one more thing. Just in case." He motioned for me to follow and led me to the short hall that led to the single bedroom. Opening the linen closet door, he ran his fingers along the woodwork. A trap door slid aside, revealing a compartment large enough for a person. "Inside there's a button that'll close it up."

"Good to know."

"Yep. Never hurts to be prepared. I'll let ya get settled now."

Judd donned his hat and grinned, and I returned the smile as he headed out.

✕

A month later I sat on the porch of the cottage rocking and bask-
ing in the humidity that rose along with the sun. After I'd settled, the
doctor had arrived to check the baby and to change my eyes. After
that excitement, the weeks had dragged while I read books, took daily
walks, and awaited news about the war. None came.

Judd's wife, Monica, strolled out of their farmhouse holding two
mugs, and she made her way to the cottage via the brick pathway that
connected us. I guessed Monica was around thirty-five, and her model
looks seemed out of place on a farm.

"Good morning, Sarah," Monica said as she handed me the cup of
decaffeinated coffee.

"Morning." I took a sip. I'd discovered that she was eager to share
coffee every morning before her children Emma and Jesse woke up. I
was thankful for the company.

Monica settled in the rocking chair next to mine. "Did you get any
sleep last night?"

"More than the night before." In addition to having to go to the
bathroom frequently and not being able to find a comfortable sleeping
position, nightmares plagued me. The images of Beau and Helen were
resurrected from the grave where I tried to bury them every night before
I went to sleep. Then there were the images of Martina and Axel chasing
me.

"I prayed that you'd sleep better," Monica said.

"What is it with you people and prayer?" I regretted saying the words
the minute they left my mouth because Monica would probably have an
answer since she was an exclusivist like Ben.

She looked at me over her mug, took a sip, and then cupped it in her
hands. "It works."

"Not for me."

"Are you sure?"

Before I could say yes, I remembered the frantic prayer I'd uttered
when Martina was stalking me. But maybe that was a coincidence. I
thought of the other prayer I'd prayed and how my situation had gotten
worse. Because of *that* prayer, Martina was chasing me and Beau and
Helen were dead. "I have about a 50 percent success rate."

Monica laughed, and her hazel eyes sparkled.

"I'm not sure what's so funny. I'm being honest."

"I know. I'm sorry. I'm not making fun of you, especially since I've felt that way myself. You just summed up those feelings of doubt so perfectly." Monica set her coffee mug on the table between our chairs. "Tell me this, Sarah. How would you describe God?"

I bit my lip. The truth was I'd never thought about it. "Well, I guess he's the great power that created the world. Or started the evolution process. He's there watching, and if you're good enough or do enough nice things, he'll pay you back and answer your prayers." I shrugged. "I guess that's why my success rate is so low. I haven't done enough good and too much bad. That's why bad things have happened."

"Do you believe God is good?"

"I don't know. God could stop the bad stuff in the world but doesn't."

Monica was slow to answer, and her silence was filled by chirping birds. "I don't have a pat answer as to why all the bad things happen in this world. I do know God doesn't cause it. But he does allow it."

A lump rose in my throat. "Why?"

"Because he made men and women with free will. God doesn't make us obey him or we'd be like puppets. He wants us to love and serve him because we choose to do so. And some people choose to ignore God, rebelling against him and causing others harm."

Some of what Monica said was starting to make sense. "I understand some people don't want anything to do with God. That doesn't explain the bad things that happen and why God doesn't stop them."

"I don't know the answer to that," Monica said. "But someday in heaven we won't have to worry about pain, suffering, or evil anymore."

"And that's why I should accept Jesus as my Savior, so I can go to heaven."

Monica smiled gently. "I see someone else has already talked to you. But, yes, that's true. Do you want to?"

"No." I stared into my mug. "I don't know."

"Don't put it off too long. We never know how much time we have left." Monica's tone was matter-of-fact and didn't contain a hint of pushiness.

I sipped my remaining coffee and wondered if it was true.

>X<

When Monica left, I went into the cottage to escape the oppressive humidity. I turned on the TV and flipped through the channels. A special report played on each station.

I turned up the volume. Footage of a building that looked like it had been destroyed by a fire filled the screen. Then the camera cut to another burning building while the reporter narrated.

"Government officials from all of the regions have concluded that the coordinated attacks on the community centers have to be the work of the rebel organization. Emancipation Warriors, they call themselves. Government officials believe these attacks are retaliation for the recent enforcement of the ban on unauthorized Bibles. Enforcement measures began in the Great Lakes Region and spread all over the nation as governors followed Genevieve Wilkins's example and opened collection centers within community centers throughout their regions."

More footage of a burning building filled the screen. I sank onto the couch.

A knock on my door startled me. I could see through the window it was Monica and her children. "Come in."

Monica rushed in and her four-year-old twins trailed behind. "I see you've heard." She pointed at the TV, and Emma and Jesse headed to the kitchen where their grandmother had kept a drawer of kitchen odds and ends they played with.

"Yes, but I'm a little confused about what's happening. I just turned the TV on."

Monica perched on the couch next to me. "They did it. They actually pulled it off."

"The rebels?"

Monica smiled. "This was the first battle. They started with the community centers. All over. In every region."

I gasped. "Wait. *All* of them?"

"That's right. There was a coordinated attack last night."

I shook my head and stared at the TV.

"The organization wants to do this with as few casualties as possible," Monica said.

"Yes." I grimaced. "But I wonder if the government feels the same way."

⟩⟨

A few days later, I lay on the couch in the cottage while Dr. Bonham studied the images on his handheld ultrasound device. "You and the baby look fine," he said. He was the doctor who had performed my eye surgery.

"You're sure?" I sat up.

"We can't be completely certain, but I don't see any abnormalities." He pushed up his glasses that kept sliding down his pug nose and held out the device for me to see the high-definition images. The baby was curled up so I couldn't tell if it was a boy or girl.

"And you're sure it's okay for me to have the baby here?"

Dr. Bonham nodded. "I'll be here. If there are any complications I can do an emergency c-section right here. I'd rather not, of course. But it's too risky for you to deliver in a hospital."

"My disguise isn't working?"

"For the average person, yes. But we can't risk medical personnel figuring out you're underage. Besides, hospitals are understaffed and overcrowded. I've done lots of home births. And many women have home births with only a midwife."

I'd heard of it. It sounded like a bad idea to me. "How many c-sections have you done in homes?"

"A few."

I was hoping it was more than just a few. "And they all ended well?" "Yes."

Was he telling me the truth? Once again, I had to rely on someone I barely knew. Monica had assured me Dr. Bonham could be trusted and had delivered her own babies.

Dr. Bonham removed a book with worn edges from his bag. "Read this. It'll help you know what to expect at a home birth. There's probably too much information, but I'd rather you have too much than too little. If there's something you don't understand, ask me at my next visit. Or you can always ask Monica."

I shuddered as I flipped through the pages. The book had color diagrams.

"I'll check on you in a couple of weeks. Call me if you need anything or have any problems."

"I will. Thanks." I closed the door and went to my living room. The book could wait. A brand new courier waited on the coffee table. Right before the doctor's visit, a girl about my age had finally delivered it to Judd and Monica's house.

I had a message from Drake. "Hey, it's your hubby. I know it's boring for you sitting around, so I thought I'd send you the courier to play with. Sorry it took so long. We've been busy. Let me know how things are going and how you like it. Talk to you soon."

I grinned, and couldn't wait to see what I'd be able to hack.

I turned on the TV and went to pour a glass of water. When I heard the words, "Governor Wilkins," I spun to raise the volume.

"Great Lakes Region governor and presidential nominee Genevieve Wilkins issued a statement that her daughter is currently spending time in the African Federation helping her aunt, Gwendolyn Simons, do humanitarian work."

A picture appeared on screen of my aunt and me hovering over a bed that held an emaciated child. Someone had done a great job doctoring the image because it looked authentic. I hoped the child wasn't real.

The reporter continued, "There has been no word yet from the Nationalist Party chairman on the status of Governor Wilkins's nomination, and no confirmation vote has been scheduled. There seems to be hesitation about switching over power at this time, especially in light of the recent attacks on community centers nationwide. A recent survey shows that President Fortune's approval rating is at 73 percent, which is one of the highest presidential approval ratings we've seen in recent years."

I pointed my courier at the reporter, silenced her, and began exploring the programs loaded onto it. I was thrilled to find the latest technology, and I set to work seeing what I could hack into. It took about an hour, but I finally figured out how to break into the new system that protected my mother's home, giving me access to all of the cameras. Looking at each of the rooms carefully, I decided that nothing important was happening. In fact, it appeared that no one but the housekeeper and cook were even home.

I glanced out of my window. Monica and the kids were playing on the swing set. I needed some fresh air.

# CHAPTER 30

The next day I lounged in a lawn chair and watched Emma and Jesse play in their sandbox. I loved their chatter and giggles, but after an hour in the sandbox, Monica herded the kids inside for lunch and a nap. I went in and monitored my mother's house by streaming the camera feed through the TV all afternoon. Nothing interesting was happening, so I called Drake to see if he could give me ideas about how to help.

He answered on the third ring, and I heard voices in the background.

"Hey. I love the new courier. You're the best husband ever."

Drake chuckled. "I try."

"So what about those things I'm supposed to be looking for? Besides spying on my mother."

"I'll get to that. How's your mother?"

"She's not home right now. Traveling for work I think."

"Okay. By the way, while I'm thinking about it, I don't want you using the courier to contact anyone but me, understand?"

"What if there's an emergency?"

"I'm trying to keep you safe. If you need to contact someone in the organization, I'll tell you."

"Oh, I see. So I have to obey you, then?"

"Why do you have such authority issues? I'm trying to protect you."

"I don't have issues."

"Then I'll spell it out. Don't contact Ben."

I wished I could reach through the courier and wring his neck. Why did he always have to read my mind? I hated being so predictable. Why should he care if I contacted Ben? He had his own girlfriend. "You can't order me not to talk to him."

"Remember, you're supposed to be married to me. If you blow your cover, I'm not coming to your rescue."

"I'm not going to blow my cover. And I don't need you to rescue me."

"How quickly we forget. What would you have done if Liam and I hadn't plucked you from that field and flown you to safety?"

"Why are you keeping score? I thought that kind of thing was your job."

"I'm not keeping score. I'm just reminding you, my dear, that you're not as independent as you think you are, and that being overconfident could get you and a lot of other people into trouble. You're good, but you aren't that good. Have you thought about what your mother and her agents would do to your new friends if they found you?"

I swallowed, trying to block the thought of Monica and her kids ending up in a pool of blood like Beau and his wife.

"Now, do you want some work or not?" At least Drake had the restraint not to gloat.

"Yes, please. I'm so bored here."

"We're investigating a man named Jared Canton."

"Why?"

"Canton used to be one of us. In fact, he was working undercover for the Emancipation Warriors. One of our best moles. His assignment was in Population Management. He prevented a few teen girls from being forced to terminate because he passed along information to us. But several of our agents started to get suspicious a few months ago that he might have turned. Strange behavior. Mysterious meetings with contacts we didn't know. Things like that."

"Are you sure he just isn't weird?"

Drake laughed. "Maybe. But Pop Management nabbed a few girls before we could get them out. Then he suddenly disappeared back in December. We've never been able to prove he was loyal to the government, but something was off. We thought he might be working for a third party.

"I went through the files that we snagged from Fortune's computer at the state dinner, and one of them is Canton's government personnel file. So now I suspect Canton may have been involved with Fortune's power grab, if Fortune was responsible for the hit on Hernandez and your mother. Either way, Fortune was interested. I don't have time to figure out why. And I need to know if there's another player we need to be watching out for."

"So you want me to do that?"

"Yes. I figured you'd want to find out who attempted to kill your mother."

"What would Canton's motivation be in spying for a third party?"

"Usually it's money. Sometimes status. A promise of power. It could have been all three. Anyway, I'm sending you Canton's Emancipation Warriors file along with what we have from Fortune's computer. See what you can come up with and let me know. And by the way, since you're doing work for us, take a look at the agent training manual on your courier."

We said our good-byes, and soon I was exploring the files that Drake sent. The agent training manual had tons of information that would be helpful if I were working in the field. But I was stuck here, so I closed the document and studied the photo of Canton. He was twenty-seven years old and had worked for the Emancipation Warriors for five years. Like Drake, he came from the upper class. Canton graduated from a prestigious university, received undercover field agent training at an Emancipation Warriors camp, and then landed a job in Population Management.

Further research revealed that Canton's family was well connected with the Emancipation Warriors. Canton's father and mother were agents. Canton had to go through a rigorous background check, and the interviews the Emancipation Warriors conducted showed his beliefs were consistent with the organization. It seemed to me that nepotism played a role in Canton's placement, and I knew from personal experience a child's view and his parents' views could differ greatly. Had Canton become an agent to please his parents and then turned?

The documents from President Fortune's computer showed the government had a very different picture of Jared Canton. According to his government personnel file, Canton knew all the right things to say. His answers to the government's questions aligned perfectly with The Nationalists Party's positions and philosophies. Not only that, Canton worked on a project with Officer Martina Ward.

I stood and stretched, rubbing the cramp in my rounded belly. Hours of sitting alone researching Martina had taken a toll on my body and mood. Though I made the connection between Canton and Martina, I kept hitting dead ends when I explored the project they worked on. There was something I was missing, and I needed to take a break and look at the problem later.

My stomach rumbled, so I headed for the kitchen and pulled some rainbow rotini and marinara sauce from the pantry.

I turned on the TV to keep me company while I waited for the pasta. There was a knock on my door, and when I opened it, Judd and Monica's daughter Emma stood on my step.

Her cheeks dimpled and her stubby pigtails bounced. "Hi, Sarah! I came to visit you."

"Come in, sweetie. Does your mommy know you're visiting?"

"Yes. She said it was okay."

I had my doubts. I didn't mind Emma's visit, but Monica was respectful of my space. "Let's make sure." I crossed the room and pressed the intercom button. "Monica?"

"Yes?"

"I wanted to let you know that Emma made it over here for her visit."

There was a pause and Monica took a minute to figure out what I meant. "Oh, okay. Emma, honey, you can stay for a few minutes. Then we're going to have supper, okay?"

"I want to have supper with Sarah."

"Honey, you can't just invite yourself to someone's house for supper."

"Monica, it's fine. I'm making pasta and marinara sauce." I winked at Emma. "And I could use the company."

"Okay then. Emma, be a good girl."

I held the box of rotini so Emma could see. "I like rainbow rotini because of the pretty colors. What do you think?"

"I like it too."

I smiled. "How about you help me set the table?"

Emma's face lit up. "I know how. Mommy taught me."

I handed Emma some place mats, napkins, and utensils, and she busied herself setting the table. While Emma worked, I imagined myself someday teaching the child I carried. No one had pressured me to choose adoption, but if that was the route I picked, the organization would support me and help me find a family who was willing to adopt. It seemed like it should be the obvious solution, but even the thought of giving my child to a stranger nagged me. I'd have no control. Would my child feel abandoned?

Absently, I stirred the marinara sauce. What would my life be like after the baby? I doubted my mother would welcome me home, even if I did give the baby up for adoption. What reason would she give for my permanent disappearance? Would the Warriors continue to hide me? Would I be able to finish school?

The uncertainties crowded my mind like an over-full elevator, and for a moment the heat from the stove felt suffocating. I took a step back.

"Sarah?" Emma ran over to the stove. "I finished the table."

I glanced at the table. "Good job." When I gave her a high five, she looked pleased. "I think our pasta is ready."

After I dished out the servings, we settled at the table. I picked up my fork but stopped when Emma stared at me with wide brown eyes. "What's wrong, sweetie?"

"Aren't you going to pray? We always pray first."

I felt warm. "Oh. Do you want to pray?"

Emma smiled and shook her head. "You pray."

There was no way I was telling this four-year-old that God didn't listen to me. I bowed my head and swallowed hard. "God, thank you for the food and for Emma's company. Thank you for sending her to me. Amen."

My prayer must have satisfied Emma because she grinned, picked up her fork, and started eating. I watched her and thought about the prayer I'd faked. Even though I was trying to impress a four-year-old, I realized maybe God did answer prayer. I was lonely and he had sent me Emma. And I hadn't even asked.

✗

After I walked Emma home, I trudged back to the cottage knowing that an evening of research called. I sat at my computer and examined the files I'd spent the afternoon searching. Was I missing the obvious?

The TV droned in the background, and I reached for my courier to shut it off. Before I could, the picture on the screen caught my attention. It didn't look right.

Normally, it was clear, but today it was fuzzy. What was most noticeable was the giant flag in the middle of the screen, but it wasn't the flag of the United Regions of North America. It was an old flag from the United States of America. I turned up the volume, and a deep authoritative voice spoke.

"And so we are using this broadcast time to tell the truth. As citizens of what was once a free country, you deserve to hear facts reported. That's why we are overtaking the airwaves."

The man's words began to make sense. The rebels were broadcasting a message to the masses. They somehow had pirated the national news stations. I grinned. Who orchestrated that? I'd love to be part of something so daring.

"Your corrupt government and its mouthpiece, the United Broadcast Company, have lied to you long enough. The Emancipation Warriors are not responsible for the death of President Hernandez. We are not responsible for the attempted assassination of Governor Genevieve Wilkins. We did not attack the Capitol. Rather, we hope to find the responsible parties and bring them to justice—whoever they are. Citizens, if you passively accept the lies you've been fed, there will never be change in our nation. We will never know the freedoms our forefathers experienced. The war has started, and it is time to choose sides. The Emancipation Warriors attacked and destroyed the community centers that played a role in violating our freedom of religion. As we intended, buildings were destroyed, but no lives were lost. Now we ask that you stand with us as we seek to take down the government that has turned against its people. We must—"

The screen went black. I used my courier to try to adjust it, but when nothing happened, I crossed the room to the TV. The power button was green. I punched it a few times, but the screen remained unchanged. I switched stations, but they all were dead.

The government had pulled the plug.

# CHAPTER 31

In the middle of the night, I awoke with a theory about Jared Canton and knew it was worth a call to Drake. The courier rang at least ten times before he answered.

"Seriously? Do you know what time it is?"

"I have a theory about Canton."

"In case you've forgotten, I asked you to find proof. Not form a theory."

I headed for the kitchen as I rubbed my lower back. "Look, sometimes having a theory is what has to happen before you can find proof."

"Oh, the infinite wisdom of a sixteen-year-old."

"I'll be seventeen next week."

"I have a lot going on, and I need to get some sleep, so out with it."

"When I was going through the Canton file, I realized he worked with my bodyguard, Martina Ward. Before she worked for my mother, she was a government employee too. Population Management." I filled a glass with water and sat at the kitchen table. "They worked on one case together, but I don't think that was significant."

"So what is?"

"I think Fortune was behind the assassination. Martina worked for him. And I think Jared Canton figured that out. That's probably why he disappeared. He may have even been killed."

"And you're basing this theory on what? Your dislike of Martina?"

"No. But, if I had to pick one of them to trust it would be Canton. There was nothing in his file that made me suspicious. He seemed like a solid agent."

"All our agents seem solid. I need you to keep looking for more proof."

"Drake, I've been over the files. That's the problem. I can't find proof. We have to find out if Canton is alive, and if he is, talk to him about what he knows. Can't someone work on this?"

"We're trying."

"Then try harder."

"Things are a little crazy right now. Did you see what happened tonight during our broadcast?"

"Yeah, I did. Quite impressive."

"Right now we're dealing with that and the threat of government retaliation. Our resources are stretched too thin to send someone on a wild goose chase. The agents I worked with are sure Canton turned. I have to trust them."

"But what if they're wrong? You gave me this task. I'm trying to help you get it done, but you won't trust me."

Drake paused for a few seconds and the silence grew uncomfortable. "I'll send you some more files on Canton. Right now that's the best I can do."

We were never going to agree on this. I decided to let him think he had won. "Okay. Fine. Good night."

I didn't care what Drake said. My gut was telling me Canton's relationship with Martina was the key. And if Drake wasn't going to help me find Canton, I'd have to find him myself.

✕

The next morning, I searched the new files Drake sent me. A couple of files on Jared Canton stood out because they included observations from the agents who suspected that Canton had turned. I read and reread the files, but their observations didn't convince me. Just because Canton didn't always play by the rules didn't mean he wasn't on their side. The best agents always played by their own rules.

And that's when the plan started forming in my mind.

The first step was to hack the government database to find information on Martina. Her service to the government was exemplary. She was thirty-five years old and had been recruited by Population Management after she attended college. She was from a middle class family in the Atlantic Region. Further research proved that before President Fortune was a representative, he was a faculty member at the college where Martina studied political science.

A quick look at Martina's transcripts revealed that she took three classes Professor Fortune taught. As interesting as that connection was, it didn't prove a conspiracy.

I turned my attention to the next part of my plan, which was to find the information on Jared Canton that Drake was holding back, so I hacked the Emancipation Warriors' database.

I searched for a while, but to his credit, Drake had passed on the most relevant information. Also, Canton himself hadn't recorded anything significant regarding Martina. While I was in the database, I found Ben's number. I dialed and hoped the third part of my plan would work.

"Vivica? How did you get this number?"

"I have ways of getting what I want."

"Yeah, you do. How are you feeling? How's the baby?"

I gave him an update, and he sounded interested in hearing details, so I gave him as many as I could. "So how's the agent training going?"

"Slow. I want to get out there. The war is going on, and I want to do more, you know?"

I grinned. This was perfect. "Actually, I do know. And I need help." I explained to Ben my assignment from Drake and how I was sure Martina was connected to Jared Canton's disappearance.

"So you think if you can find Canton, he'll magically have all the answers?"

"I don't know what I think, but I have to try."

"And you need my help."

"Yes." I tried to sound as sweet as possible.

"What about Drake? He's your supervisor. I can't just take over."

"Drake is busy. He doesn't have time to help me. Please, Ben?"

He was quiet for a moment, and I knew to remain silent. "All right. I've been wanting to check on you anyway."

My heart skipped a beat. "Really?"

"Yeah. I mean, I assume I get to see you, right?"

I smiled. "Right. Let me tell you what I have in mind."

Laying the groundwork for my plan with Ben was going to take longer than I thought, but if I was patient I'd be able to get the information I needed. I planted fake orders in the Emancipation Warriors' database and now had to wait for them to be passed on to Ben.

While I waited, I checked on my mother to see if she'd returned home. I opened the feed and smiled when I heard my mother's confident voice. A second later the video sprang to life. Gathered around the long table in the conference room with my mother were Melvin, Martina, and Axel. My stomach contorted.

"What's the latest?" my mother asked.

Martina's expression was grim. "The rebels have hidden your daughter well, and the lead was a dead end. It's taking more time than I anticipated. There may be some other possibilities, though." She hesitated. "With your permission I'd like to trace the person who gave you the anonymous tip about Vivica's pregnancy."

It hadn't been Martina? That meant my mother had lied because an anonymous tip couldn't be considered reliable.

"What good would that do? I'd assumed the tip came from her best friend."

"I did too at first, but my gut says otherwise."

"Very well." My mother massaged her temples. "What else do you have?"

"When I worked for Population Management, I discovered that one of my coworkers was a mole who worked for the rebels."

I leaned forward. She had to be talking about Canton.

"He was passing information to the rebels so they could protect the underage girls and adults breaking the term law. He got careless, and I intercepted a message." Martina smiled. "That's how I caught that girl from your daughter's school who was ready to go into hiding. They'd scrubbed the footage of her sneaking into the office, but we restored the original."

Of course Meredith hadn't been that careless. It all fit. Canton disappeared in December, and that's when they took her.

"Yes, I remember. What does this have to do with finding my daughter?"

"I know where my former colleague is and how to get information from him. He's a gold mine."

My heart sank. If it wasn't Tindra and it wasn't Martina who tipped off my mother, then it had to be someone within the rebels' network. No one else knew. Not only was Canton a threat, but the Emancipation Warriors really did have a mole.

"Governor, don't worry. Axel and I will find your daughter. Give us a little more time." Martina's hands clenched behind her back.

My mother and Melvin exchanged glances. "Fine," she said. "I'll give you two weeks. If you don't have anything solid after that time, you're fired."

"I understand," Martina said.

Hidden away on a farm, I'd managed to convince myself I was safe. But knowing Martina was making progress on finding me shattered that illusion. If she was determined to find me, then there was no place safe. I squeezed my eyes shut when I thought of Beau and Helen. I had no doubt Martina would do the same to Judd and Monica if she had the opportunity. There was no way I could let that happen.

⋈

"Drake, there's a mole in the Emancipation Warriors. What if Martina finds me?"

"The minute you're in danger, we'll pull you out, okay? But right now, even I don't know where you are. I only know the first names of the agents supervising you."

"Then how did you send me the new courier?"

"Do you know how many channels that went through? Besides it was addressed to Judd. Not you," Drake said.

"Okay. Fine. Do you trust Liam?"

"He's my brother. Of course I trust him. He's the one who recruited me."

"Stranger things have happened. Promise me you'll consider what I said."

"I will."

I disconnected the call and collapsed on the couch. Even though Drake wasn't my favorite person, I'd thought he was trustworthy. But now I wasn't so sure.

# CHAPTER 32

On a muggy July evening Monica handed me the last plate to dry. "That went quickly. Aren't you glad you let me help?"

"Thanks."

I'd made a birthday dinner for myself and invited Judd, Monica, and the twins over. Of course, since I was celebrating my real birthday, I couldn't tell them, but I wanted the company. After a fun evening and my mediocre cooking, Judd had taken the kids home to bed.

"Monica, do you have a minute? There's something I'd like to ask you."

"Sure." Monica leaned against the counter.

I twisted the dish towel in my hands. I hadn't expected it to be this difficult. "I've been thinking about the baby. I'm due in several weeks. And I don't think I'm ready to bring up a child. I mean, if I have to I will." I hesitated. "I've seen how good you are with your kids. So I was wondering if you ever thought about adopting one."

Surprise registered on Monica's face. "Let's have a seat." She nodded at the couch.

I wondered if this was a bad idea.

She smiled. "I'm so flattered you thought of us. I have to be honest though, Judd and I are happy with the two we have. Frankly, we don't have the money to pay the fine for an extra child. But, I'll talk it over with him, and I can promise you we'll pray about it." She took my hand. "We thought our family was complete, but God may have other ideas. If so, he'll provide the money for the penalty."

I nodded. "And you're okay with God's ideas being different from what you want? I'd have a problem with that. I couldn't trust him to make the right choices for me."

"Accepting Christ isn't having warm, fuzzy feelings about Jesus. It means doing his will. And while I trust that he's doing the best thing for me, it's not always easy. But it's why I can promise you Judd and I will give serious consideration to adopting your baby. We want to do God's will."

"Well, thank you for at least thinking about it."

"You're welcome. And I want you to trust that if Judd and I aren't the right set of parents for this child, God will provide someone else."

It was a nice sentiment, but I wasn't sure I believed her.

# CHAPTER 33

My courier rang in the middle of a dreamless night. Too incoherent to glance at the screen, I mumbled a greeting.

"Vivica, it's Ben. I got my orders. I'm on my way to Martina's house."

I blinked a few times, trying to process the words Ben hurled my direction. "Okay. So did you borrow the equipment?"

"Yep."

"How soon will you be there?"

"A couple of hours."

"Are you alone?"

"Flying solo for the first time."

His meaning was literal because he'd earned his pilot's license a few days ago. I combed my fingers through my ratty hair. "Okay. Be careful. I'm afraid Martina knows more about the Emancipation Warriors than we realized." I told Ben about the conversation I'd heard.

"Then I need to do this. So we can get to Canton."

"You're right. Be careful. Call me when you get to her house."

We disconnected, but I was too awake to return to bed. I longed to be on the front line with Ben, so I read the agent training manual on my courier. When I finished, I realized our plan was probably stupid, but if Martina conspired with Fortune and knew where Canton was, then we had to follow through.

Two hours later, Ben and I were ready. He'd put on the glasses with a camera that allowed me to view everything he was seeing.

"Martina and her daughter left ten minutes ago," Ben said. He was stationed in a car outside of her condo. "I'm going in now if you're ready."

"Yeah, I'm ready." There wasn't anything for me to do except observe. Ben disabled the lock, and I prayed his entrance wouldn't trip a silent alarm. He slipped in and closed the door behind him. The condo was small, but the furniture was arranged to make the most of the space. In one corner of the living room was a table with a computer.

Ben placed a bug underneath the end table next to the sectional sofa. Then he walked to the bedroom where he placed a second bug behind the mirror that was attached to her dresser. When Ben turned around, something caught my eye on the unmade bed.

"Ben!"

"What?"

"She didn't take her MD3. Hurry up. She'll turn around as soon as she realizes it's missing."

Ben raced to the living room and moved his courier closer to the computer to copy the data.

"Come on," I said.

Ben looked around. "We're fine for now."

I drummed my fingers on the table and buried my head in my arm.

When I looked up again, the computer screen in front of me was dark, and my first thought was that we'd lost communication. Had I bumped something when I put my head down? But there was a faint band of light at the bottom of the screen.

"There it is!" My eyes widened when I recognized Martina's raspy voice, and the band of light made sense. Ben was under the bed.

I held my breath and prayed. I strained to listen, but there was only agonizing silence. The baby swirled in my belly.

"He'll be okay," I whispered to myself as much as to the baby.

At last my view changed, and the rest of the bedroom appeared on the screen.

"Are you okay?"

Ben chuckled. "I'm dusty, but yeah, I'm good."

I took a deep breath. "Did you get the files from her computer?"

"Yeah, it had just finished when I heard the door."

"Thank God!"

"I'm out of here," Ben said. "I'll get the information to you soon."

# CHAPTER 34

A week later I decided Ben's definition of soon was different from mine. I needed the information from Martina's computer if I was going to find a connection, and he still hadn't delivered it.

I put on some sunglasses and headed outside. It was morning, but I could tell the day would be suffocating.

"Good morning!" I called to Monica and the kids.

"I have your blueberry bucket," Emma said.

I took it. "Thanks, sweetie."

In need of a distraction, I'd agreed to help pick blueberries, though the humidity made me question my offer.

Monica led us to the rows of plants situated near the woods on their property. "Now, kids, remember to leave the green ones."

"Okay, Mommy," Jesse said. They started picking the berries.

Monica smiled. "It's not hard. Just hold the bunch in your hand and roll your thumb over the berries. The ripe ones will come off." She held up her bucket. "By the way, you and I are picking the government blueberries. We'll have to give 85 percent of our crop to Ag Management."

"I'm sure it's for your own good, right?"

We laughed and got to work. After a few minutes, Monica broke the silence.

"I'm glad you came today because I've wanted to talk to you."

My heart turned over, and I wondered if she had an answer for me. "Okay."

Monica dropped a handful of berries into a bucket. "Judd and I have been praying about your baby."

"And?"

"I'm sorry, Sarah, but we just don't feel God leading us in that direction. As I told you before, I'm flattered that you thought to ask us, but neither one of us feels at peace about it."

I focused on the blueberries and ignored the tears that bit my eyes. If they didn't want the baby, that was fine. It takes a lot to adopt another person's kid and to pay the fine. But just admit it. Why blame God to make yourself feel better?

"Sarah, I want you to know we'll do anything we can to help you find a family for the baby. If you give me permission, I'll put word out among the Emancipation Warriors, and they'll match you with the right couple."

"I need some time to think."

Monica put a hand on my shoulder. "Please don't take this personally. We believe God has other plans."

"I'm not. I understand." I picked a few more handfuls of berries, tears threatening to spill. Time was running out. I was already at thirty-five weeks. "You know, I'm not feeling so very well. I think I'll go lay down." I dropped the blueberry bucket. It tipped to the side, causing a few berries to roll into the dirt. Clutching my baby bump, I fled to the cottage.

⊁⊀

That night I was getting ready for bed when Ben called.

"I'm about five minutes away. I'll hide my car and walk when I get close. And I'm sorry it took me so long. I thought I'd get away sooner."

I dressed and reapplied the makeup I had removed. As I styled my hair and pinned it back, I wondered if he'd even notice.

When he arrived, we hugged, my belly a barrier between us. He took a step back. His eyes flicked to my abdomen and then back to my face. I was so much bigger than when he'd seen me last.

"You look, uh . . . pretty." A goofy grin spread across his face.

I smiled. At least he'd noticed my effort to look good. "Thanks."

Ben dug through his backpack and handed me the cloning device he'd used on Martina's computer. "Let's see what we have."

I went to work, and Ben helped himself to a glass of water in the kitchen.

"This is a nice place to hide out," he said.

"Yeah, I'm lucky." While I copied the information to the courier, I filled him in about Judd and Monica refusing to adopt the baby. "I wish she would've just said they didn't want the baby instead of blaming God." I projected information through the TV and the keyboard onto the table.

Ben sat in a chair across from me. "Did they pray about it?"

"She said they did." I started typing.

"Well, take them at their word. It's a big decision to adopt a child. Don't you want the right family?"

"Yes, but I want it figured out."

"There's time."

"Easy for you to say. This whole thing has been simple for you."

Ben held up a hand. "I didn't come here to fight. I'm sorry they aren't going to adopt the baby. God will work something else out."

Of course, Ben would say that. Then he was off the hook.

"I wouldn't be so sure."

"Have you been reading the Bible?"

"Not recently. But there was an original one on my courier, so I could. It doesn't seem that relevant. I mean, how can something written so long ago apply to life today?"

"Because people are the same," Ben said. "Every generation does evil things."

Whatever. I studied the TV screen. "I think I have something."

Ben moved and sat next to me on the sofa. "What?"

I pointed. "Look at this essay. It looks like it was written in Martina's college days for Fortune's class."

Ben read for a few minutes. "Hmm. She's really critical of President Hernandez."

"But that's not all. At the time she believed Hernandez's successor would be my mother."

"I wonder what made her suspect that?"

"The party has been grooming my mother for years. And right now I'd be willing to bet they have their eye on her successor. Fortune threw a wrench in the whole plan. I don't think they anticipated he'd be as popular as he is."

We read in silence for a few more minutes until we came to the last line of Martina's essay.

*The key to convincing the masses that the Nationalist Party is unfit to handle the growing rebellion is to create a crisis and use the media to blame the rebels. Then the Nationalist Party leaders will appear inept and the country will accept new leadership. With the right people in place at the right time, we can take over the party and guide the United Regions of North America in a global direction.*

"I bet Professor Fortune liked the sound of this," Ben said.

"No doubt. But it doesn't prove that they're connected. We need more than that." I started reading another essay. I looked up at Ben. "You're not going to like this one."

*In addition to nationalism, one of the biggest obstacles to globalism is Christianity. There are those who believe that hate speech legislation is effective for controlling the exclusivist Christian voice. However, its suppression may only give birth to underground movements. There has to be an eradication of those who practice this faith.*

Ben pointed at the screen. "Fortune's comment is even creepier."

In red letters, Fortune had typed, *I agree. Start thinking of ways to make this happen.*

I rested my chin on my hand. "The problem is that none of this proves that Martina and Fortune actually plotted something. It only proves they agree. We need solid evidence."

"You're right. But it's more than you had before."

Something was bothering me. I paced the room for a few minutes. Ben started to talk, and I held my hand up. "I'm thinking." I stopped and faced Ben. "Why would Martina leave Pop Management?"

"Your mom pays more?"

"Probably. But Martina had a successful career. What if being my bodyguard was a ploy to get closer to my mother? What if Martina and Fortune plotted to kill Hernandez and my mother so Fortune could take over and implement these strategies Martina wrote about?"

"But your mother wasn't killed."

"Only because Bobby got in the way. So Martina got the job as my bodyguard . . ." I didn't want to finish the thought.

"But why wouldn't she finish the job? She's had plenty of opportunity."
I paced for a few minutes until a thought occurred to me. "I threatened her daughter."

"What?"

"In order to escape from Martina and Axel, I threatened to murder her daughter if she helped kill my child. You know . . . an eye for an eye kind of thing."

Ben nodded, but the disapproval on his face was unmistakable.

"Don't judge me."

"I'm not judging you."

"I was working with limited resources. I wasn't actually going to do it."

"But Martina doesn't know that. You must have been pretty convincing."

I raised my chin. "I was. And that's why she's not taken care of my mother. She wants to get to me first."

"All this may or may not be true, but it doesn't change the fact that we have to prove Martina is working with President Fortune."

"You're right. There must be something else. I'll keep looking."

"I'm sure you'll find it." Ben stood.

"You're leaving already?"

"I have to get back before I'm missed." He grinned. "This stop wasn't exactly authorized."

I hugged him. "Thanks for being willing to work with me."

"No problem." Ben moved toward the door but turned back. "One more thing. If you ever get back to reading the Bible, trying reading Matthew, chapter ten. I think you'll find that very relevant."

# CHAPTER 35

A week later, I plodded around the farm on a low-humidity morning, thankful for the reprieve. Chickens pecked at their feed, and in the pasture, cows grazed. Monica worked in her garden, and when she waved, I headed over.

"I don't suppose you want to help pick green beans, do you?"

"Would I be picking for you or the government?"

Monica laughed. "Don't look so horrified. I'm actually ready to quit. Would you mind grabbing one of those baskets?" She nodded at a basket full of green beans. "I just want to take them to the porch."

We put the baskets on the porch and went inside.

Monica opened the refrigerator. "Would you like some iced tea? I made some this morning."

"That would be great."

"Monica, I've thought about your offer to help me find a family to adopt the baby. I'm ready for help now."

She smiled. "I'll start today."

"Do you think there'll be anybody willing?"

Before Monica could answer, the doorbell rang. "Excuse me."

I sipped my tea, deep in thought about the baby, and it was only when I heard an edge to Monica's normally gentle voice that I started listening.

"Ma'am, you're welcome to check my garden and our crops, but this accusation is ridiculous. We've never withheld anything from Ag Management. If you'll check records and speak with Mark, he'll tell you we've always been cooperative. Where is Mark?"

"Mark has been reassigned. I need to search your property to take inventory." I froze. It was Martina. Who had betrayed me?

"Fine then. Where would you like to start?" Monica sounded calm.

"Who lives in that cottage behind your house?"

"My cousin Sarah and her husband."

"Is she here?"

"I'm not sure. When she's not traveling for work, she sometimes goes to town on Tuesdays. Ma'am, what does this have to do with our crops?"

I didn't wait to hear any more. I bolted to the back door and lumbered to the cottage. I had to make it to the closet. Throwing open the door, I ran my fingers along the frame, as Judd had done. Where was the trigger? My fingers caught it, and I pulled the closet door shut.

Sarah's doc. My courier. Martina couldn't see those.

I burst from the closet and retrieved both devices from the table. Just as I closed the closet door, the front door squeaked.

I slid into the compartment and pressed the lever to shut the panel. The panel swooshed. It had to seem louder than it actually was. I shook the thought off. I had to make sure the doc showed that I was in town and not cowering in a closet twenty feet away.

Footsteps sounded.

"Is this your cousin?" Martina asked.

"Wasn't she a beautiful bride?" Monica said, her voice pitched higher than normal.

They had to be looking at the wedding picture. Was my disguise good enough to fool Martina? I used the courier to override the doc's tracking and to send a fake signal from town.

It had to work.

The sounds of cabinet doors opened and closed while the compartment's air grew warmer. "Thank you for your cooperation," Martina said. "I feel certain you aren't hiding any agricultural products from us."

><

"Sarah?" Monica's voice was faint. "Sarah, you can come out. She's moved on to the farm down the road."

I emerged from the compartment and pressed a finger to my lips. Monica stood in the hall, and her brow creased with concern. Using my courier, I swept the cottage for a bug.

Nothing.

"That woman wasn't from Ag Management." I started to shake, and the baby kicked a few times. Could it sense my fear?

"I know. Judd's on his way home. We're calling Drake immediately. You'll have to move."

"I don't know how she found me." I babbled about how Martina had been chasing me. Monica called Drake and explained the situation. When she handed me the courier, I told Drake about what I'd done to the doc's tracking.

"Leave it behind. I'll keep people on it. They'll make sure Sarah still exists in the system until Judd and Monica have a chance to make it look like Sarah and Kalvin moved. Vivica, I want you to promise me you'll do exactly what they tell you."

"I promise."

Drake cleared his throat. "That was a little too easy. You don't have your fingers crossed do you?"

I bristled. "No. I'm freaked out right now."

"Good. That will keep you from doing something stupid."

"Why do you assume I'll do something stupid? I care about saving this baby, you know."

"Yes. I know. Now get moving. I'll be in touch."

"Drake?"

"Yeah?"

"Do you think the mole ratted me out?"

Silence.

"It's possible, isn't it?"

"Of course, it's possible. But the only person who knows your current location besides Judd and Monica is my brother. And he's not a mole."

"Are you sure?"

"I'm certain. Have you left the farm?"

"No."

"Have you told anyone else where you are or who you're living with?"

I closed my eyes. I trusted Ben completely. There was no way he'd betray me.

"You told Ben, didn't you?"

"Yes, I did."

"Then we're done here. Just do what Judd and Monica tell you."

# CHAPTER 36

Had Ben betrayed me? There had to be another explanation, but knowing Drake blamed me for the breach added doubt. The memory of Beau and Helen weighed on my mind. What if the same thing happened to Judd and Monica? What would happen to the children?

It was protocol to wait until night to move someone, but my situation was so critical—again—I needed to be moved immediately. I packed a small bag of clothes, and Monica added dried fruit, bottles of water, and almonds.

Judd entered. "I'm ready if you are. I've seen a couple of strange cars drive by."

"Are you being paranoid?" Monica asked.

"Maybe. Can't be sure though."

I handed him my bag, and while he loaded it into his truck, Monica and I embraced.

"I'm going to pray for you," she said.

"I hope your success rate is better than mine." I glanced around the quaint cottage that had been my haven. "Thank you. For everything."

Monica nodded.

Judd, wearing a cowboy hat, appeared in the doorway. "Let's go."

I climbed into the back of his extended cab pickup truck. Under the seats in the back he'd created a compartment. Judd held my arm as I struggled to fit with my belly. It was tight, but I could lie on my side. He handed me a pillow for my head and another to put between my knees for support.

When Judd replaced the seat cover, I closed my eyes to block out the claustrophobic feeling. The engine rumbled, and soon the hum of tires against the road lulled me to sleep.

"Sarah? You okay?"

For a moment I couldn't place the faraway voice, then I remembered Judd was addressing me.

"I'm fine. Sorry. I fell asleep."

"No problem. We're going to meet up with an agent who'll take you from here."

"Drake?"

"No. He's tied up and had to send someone else." Judd stopped the truck. "Wait here." The door slammed.

While I waited, paranoia crept in. What if someone had set Judd up? What if someone caught us? I didn't even have a gun.

The door opened, and the seat cover lifted. I squinted, expecting to be blinded by sunlight but was enveloped by darkness. I'd been asleep that long? A hand grabbed mine, and when I clutched it, I looked into the man's face. Though glasses framed his brown eyes, there was no mistaking the light of kindness that shone in them.

Ben.

# CHAPTER 37

Ben's expression and nod immediately sent the message that I was to act like I didn't recognize him. I squelched the joy that bubbled and observed my surroundings. Judd had parked at the back of an abandoned church, far from the road.

Judd removed my bag and transferred it to the small car parked next to the church. "Sarah, this is Nick Flanagan. He's the operative assigned to see you to your next safe house."

"Nice to meet you," I said.

"Same here." The edge of Ben's mouth quirked.

I held out my hand. "Judd, thank you for everything."

"You're welcome. You take care of yourself." Judd grasped my hand with both of his, then tipped his hat and rode away while I prayed silently for his safe return and for the protection of his family.

"All right," I said as we climbed into the car. "How'd you pull this off?"

Ben grinned. "Hey, I can be sneaky too."

"So where are we headed?"

"We're going to take a detour." Ben started the car and programmed the route. "I found Jared Canton. I went through hours of audio surveillance from Martina's apartment and finally found a useful conversation." He handed me his courier. "The file name is Ward."

I opened it.

"So you still haven't been able to break Canton?" Martina's raspy voice filled the car.

"I don't think he's holding out any more. I think he's told us everything he knew." It was a man's voice, but I didn't recognize it.

I paused the recording. "Do you know who she's talking to?"

Ben shook his head. "She never calls him by name."

I turned the recording back on.

"I think we need to move him," Martina said. "We haven't done that for awhile. I don't want his organization snooping around."

"I thought they were convinced he turned."

"So did I, but our mole tells me that someone has been accessing Canton's case files."

"Should we kill him?" the man asked.

I looked at Ben with wide eyes, and he nodded.

"No," Martina said. "I want to be sure he's served his purpose before we do that. Move him to the cabin in the Rocky Mountain Region. It's the most isolated spot I know."

"When?"

"Tomorrow."

The recording ended, and I stared for a moment at the stretch of road in front of us. "When did this conversation take place?"

"Three days ago."

"Do you have any idea where this cabin is?"

"Yes." Ben appeared proud of himself, and it made me smile because I could tell he loved being an agent. "Martina's parents own an old cabin way up north in the Rocky Mountain Region. They visit every summer. Travel records show they returned from a visit last week."

"Meaning they probably won't return for a while, and it would be the perfect spot to stash Canton."

"Right. It's worth looking into."

"How are we going to pull that off? Isn't someone expecting me somewhere? Another family to hide with?"

"Yes. I'm supposed to take you to a new safe house. But we both know this issue with Canton needs to be pursued, and the Emancipation Warriors aren't going to look into it. As far as they're concerned, Canton is a dead mole who betrayed them."

My courier rang.

"It's Drake. Where are you?"

I looked at Ben. "On our way to an airstrip," I said. Ben nodded.

"How close?"

I turned to Ben and repeated the question.

"Probably ten miles away," Ben said.

"I heard him," Drake said. "Let me talk to him."

I handed it over, unable to shake the horrible feeling creeping into the pit of my stomach while Ben listened and nodded. Then he returned the device.

"What's wrong?" I immediately asked into it.

Drake sighed. "Vivica, I'm so sorry to have to tell you this, but Monica is dead."

I wanted to push a rewind button and recapture the hope that dared to bloom the moment Ben took me away. That was supposed to save them.

"The kids?"

"We don't know. We think the people who killed Monica took them."

"What about Judd?"

"We're moving him. He was still on the road when Dr. Bonham found Monica."

Half-formed thoughts darted through my brain, and I couldn't seem to capture one of them long enough to form a coherent sentence. "My fault."

"Vivica, you can't fall apart right now. Blaming yourself will only make things worse."

"But it is. If I hadn't—"

"Ben isn't the mole. It was a mistake to tell him your location. But he didn't betray you."

"Is there more you're not telling me?"

"I'll tell you what you need to know. Focus on getting to safety."

"Don't you get it? There is no safe place. I'm not letting you put me with other people so they can get killed. I refuse."

"You think you can do this on your own?"

I choked back a sob. "I have to. Monica is dead because of me. Helen and Beau are dead because of me. Judd and Monica's children are missing because of me. Maybe I should just go back to my mother and terminate. It would be easier for everybody that way."

Ben reached over and placed a hand on my shoulder. The comforting touch caused a lump to rise in my throat.

"You've protected your baby this long," Drake said. "Do you really believe that returning to your mother is the answer? What makes you think she'd take you back?"

She had to. Otherwise she'd risk the public finding out that she'd lied about my being in the African Federation.

"I'm sick over what happened to Monica," Drake said, "but understand. Both Judd and Monica knew it was a risk to harbor you. Anybody who works for the Emancipation Warriors is in danger. We're at war."

"And I've chosen my side?"

"I thought you had."

"What about the kids? Is anybody looking for them?"

"Of course."

I couldn't nab one of the thoughts that bounced through my mind. "It's not fair." I hated that I sounded like a whiny child, but couldn't God have done something to help Monica since she was one of his followers?

"You're right. It's not."

Drake's candor surprised me, and I was grateful for his honesty. He cleared his throat. "Focus on getting to safety. I let Ben come after you, so don't blow it."

"Fine."

"Call me when you get to the next safe house."

I disconnected and clutched the courier, trying to process everything.

Ben broke the silence. "I can take you right to the safe house. We'll forget the whole thing with Canton."

"We can't. It's too important."

"Viv, don't you think you should get to safety?"

"I'm not going."

"Why?"

I scowled. "You have to ask? You're kidding me, right?"

"If you're worried about more agents getting killed, don't. This is a very different situation from what you came from."

"I want to go ahead with the Canton plan." I smiled and touched his arm. "Please?"

Ben shook his head. "Fine. We'll stick with the plan. But I'm going to have to talk the Emancipation Warriors into giving us a jet to get to the Rocky Mountain Region faster."

"How do they know what kind of plane to give you?"

"Drake puts the order in the system if my assignment requires a plane. The agent at the nearest airfield gets the order and makes sure a plane's available. They make the decision based on the range. I only need a single-engine to take you to the new safe house."

"So you're able to fly jets and not just single-engine planes?"

Ben hesitated. "Well, sort of."

That didn't sound good. "What do you mean?"

"I'm trained. But it's not likely they'd trust someone my age with a jet since they're so rare these days. Single-engine plane, no problem. The Emancipation Warriors have plenty, and they need pilots. That's why I trained."

Drake would never let us have a jet, and we needed to get to Canton as soon as possible. I accessed the Emancipation Warrior computer network from my courier. "I'm going to hack in and change the order."

⋊⋉

Early the next morning we left on a five-passenger jet and landed at a small Emancipation Warriors' airstrip in the Rocky Mountain Region. We borrowed a vehicle that was stored in the hangar for agents and drove along the coast into a deserted area once known as Alaska. A sign indicated we were near one of the few remaining hunting preserves in the country. The winding ride ended when Ben stopped the vehicle near a grove of spruce trees a mile from the cabin.

When we stepped out, Ben motioned for me to come around to his side. He removed a small duffel bag he'd brought from the plane. He unzipped it and handed me a Diablo 87.

"Are you sure you want me carrying a gun?"

"I trust you. It's just for backup. I don't expect you to have to use it." He showed me a few safety tips.

I tucked it in my back pocket, but was aware of its presence. Though

I'd used a gun to escape from Martina several months before, I'd never toted one like an expert.

The uphill hike was probably not far, but it felt like ten miles. I stumbled up the dirt path, shivering in the dark tunnel of trees. The baby kicked. I paused and took a drink from my water bottle. We had to be close.

Ahead of me, Ben stopped and held up a hand. He pointed at the hunter's cabin surrounded by trees. Made with flimsy looking boards, the cabin was more of a shack with windows. An outhouse with a crescent moon cutout on the door stood about fifty yards from the cabin. Not exactly a luxury vacation destination. He motioned for me to follow, and we left the path and circled the cabin. When we returned to the front, he stopped.

"I think the best way to approach is from the north side since it has the fewest windows," Ben whispered. "I'm going to look in the windows."

"Won't they see you?"

"If they start shooting, be sure to fire back."

How comforting. "Maybe I should look. You're the more experienced shooter."

"Stay here and keep watch." Ben jogged toward the cabin, and I pulled the gun from my pocket, grounded my feet, and held my breath. He flattened himself against the cabin wall and looked into the window. He must have seen nothing because he ducked around the corner.

A few seconds later, I heard the shatter of breaking glass. I sprang forward and headed toward the sound. When I rounded the corner of the cabin, there was glass on the ground, and a faded curtain fluttered through a broken window. I stood on my tiptoes and looked in.

Ben stood in the middle of the room with his hands up while Jared Canton aimed an antique hunting rifle at Ben's chest.

# CHAPTER 38

"Canton!" I yelled. He turned the weapon toward me, and I raised my hands. "We're here to help. We know you didn't turn on the Warriors."

Canton looked at Ben who shrugged. "I tried to tell you that," Ben said.

"Please, we need to talk," I said and lowered my weapon to the ground.

Canton stared at me for a moment with vacant eyes. "Get in here." He leaned the rifle against the wall.

I entered the cabin through the front door, mentally reviewing everything I needed to say. Ben sat on the threadbare couch across from the chair where Canton sat. I perched next to Ben and folded my hands in my lap.

Canton's beard was scraggly, his posture defeated. The tracking bracelet circling his ankle made my heart sink. That's how they were keeping him prisoner. If it came off, they'd know.

Canton followed my gaze. "If it comes off, it triggers these." He raised his shirt and pointed to two freshly stitched cuts on his abdomen. "Poison capsules. If one comes out, the other goes off. That way I can't take them out and cut the anklet."

"Are you sure?"

Canton scowled. "Yep."

"We came here to help," I said.

"There's no way the Warriors sent you."

"This is an independent investigation," Ben said.

"Interesting. You might want to be careful. The Warriors don't like rogue agents." Canton studied me. "You of age?"

"No."

"The vaccine fails again. No surprise though . . ."

"Why?"

"What are you doing here?"

"We believe you've always been loyal to the Emancipation Warriors," I said. "If we can prove it, then they'll send help. Right now they think you disappeared because you turned and started working for the government."

"Never mind that I spent five years of my life enduring the bureaucracy in Population Management so we could protect underage girls and women who wanted to have their babies. Do you understand what a risky assignment that was? And this is the thanks I get. Forgotten. Everyone assuming I'm the bad guy."

"I'm really sorry," I said.

He shrugged. "Not your fault. I suppose I should trust you though. You're way too big to run out here on a whim."

I cringed. Big? Couldn't he have used the word *pregnant* instead of big? I clamped my mouth shut. We needed this guy.

"What can you tell us about Martina Ward?" Ben said.

Canton leaned forward and rested his elbows on his knees. "I was close to making a break. Almost had enough information on Martina. But she figured out I knew. Now I'm here."

"What did you know?" I asked.

Canton buried his head in his hands. "Why do you even care?"

"Someone killed President Hernandez. Someone almost killed my mother. I think Fortune is behind it."

Canton's head shot up. "Wait a minute. You're *Genevieve Wilkins's* daughter. Well, this just gets better all the time." He sighed. "So you actually think having your mother as president would be better than Fortune?"

I studied my hands. "It's the lesser of two evils."

"A president should be more than the lesser of two evils."

I caught my breath.

"Shouldn't Hernandez's killer be brought to justice?" Ben asked. "His family deserves that much."

"There hasn't been justice in this country for years."

Ben and I exchanged glances. If we couldn't get Canton to talk, then we needed to leave. A grandfather clock stood in the corner of the living room. Only the clock's ticks filled the room.

Ben stood. "Let's go."

Canton sat up. "Wait. Can you do surgery?"

I grasped the arm of the couch. "You think if we remove the capsules at the same time, you can get out of here?"

"Yep."

"I don't know if I feel comfortable with that," Ben said. "What if we hurt you?"

"You can't hurt a dead man walking," Canton said, and his eyes narrowed as he looked at Ben. "Besides. You're an agent. Haven't you had some medical training?"

Ben thrust his hands into his pockets. "Yeah, but not—"

"Tell us what you know and we'll try," I said.

Ben looked at me and shook his head.

"About ten months ago when I was working in Pop Management as a mole for the Warriors, I suspected Martina worked for someone else too. Obviously, it wasn't the Warriors. I dug around and figured out her connection to Fortune." Canton paused and stared out the window. "I thought I was being careful, but that shrew figured out I was snooping. She and some beefcake kidnapped me. They kept moving me, and I ended up here."

"What was the beefcake's name?" I asked.

Canton shrugged. "Axel or something crazy like that."

While Axel worked for my mother, he spent his spare time as a kidnapper. Lovely. "Do you have copies of the actual evidence that connects them to Fortune? MD3 records? Minutes from meetings? Pictures?"

"Yeah. I hid the evidence on a microchip before I was kidnapped. Unless Martina and her thug figured out where I stashed it, you should be able to find it. Make sure the Warriors get it. That's the only thing that'll clear my name."

"Where is it?" Ben asked.

Canton stood. "Get the recording device on your courier ready. You're gonna need it to remember all the directions."

My hands shook as I clutched the sterilized scissors in my gloved hand and mentally reviewed the instructions Ben had given me. I knew that didn't inspire confidence in Canton who lay on the table that took up most of the space in the kitchen. We'd done the best we could to set up for surgery with the first-aid kit retrieved from the car and the emergency medical kit we'd found stashed in the cabin.

Ben held another pair of scissors. "We shouldn't be doing this. You could get hurt."

"I'll be fine," I said. "We made a deal."

"You made a deal."

I rested my hand on Ben's arm. "Relax. We can do this. There's too much at stake to quit now."

As Ben looked at me, a slow smile spread over his face. My heart leaped. What was he thinking?

Canton scowled. "Hey, lovebirds. Enough. Can we get this over with? I'm dead if you leave me and who knows what they'll do if they suspect you've been here. I might end up ratting you out." He put a stick in his mouth to clench because we didn't have anesthetic.

Ben and I began to cut the stitches. When I finished, I stopped and waited for Ben. The wound had begun to close, but I made a precise cut with a kitchen knife. It was no different than dissecting a cat in my anatomy class. Right? The wound opened and a second later began to bleed. I took a deep breath hoping it would stop the room from spinning. I spread the skin and dabbed the flowing blood. The silicone capsule looked innocuous nestled in the tissue.

Canton moaned.

"I'm ready," Ben said. "I'll count. On three. One. Two. Three."

I plucked the capsule from the wound. Ben held the other capsule in the air triumphantly.

Canton groaned. "Hurry."

We tossed the capsules on the floor, and Ben stitched the wounds while I used towels to soak the blood. Canton's face was pasty and expressionless. After we bandaged him, we cleaned the mess.

"We need to move," Canton said. I helped him off the table, but he held my arm loosely as if he were afraid of adding to my load.

Ben held up a pair of pliers. "We've got to get rid of your anklet first." He knelt next to Canton and severed the device.

Canton stood between Ben and me as we shuffled to the door. A faint click sounded when we reached the porch. I hesitated.

Ben and Canton exchanged panicked glances.

Cutting the anklet had triggered a bomb.

"Move! Now!" Ben shouted and pulled Canton away from me.

Supporting my belly with one hand, I rushed toward the tree line with Ben and Canton trailing me.

I turned back in time to see a blinding flash followed by a blast that propelled us to the ground.

# CHAPTER 39

For a few seconds, I lay on my back, trying to get my bearings while the baby kicked as if in protest to the jolt. The whole world was muffled and shadowy. Then I felt Ben's arms around me. He picked me up and carried me to the vehicle that he'd brought up the mountain while I'd prepared the tools for Canton's surgery. Ben buckled me in the front seat and returned for Canton, who was unconscious. Ben put him in the back seat.

I coughed. The smoke from the explosion grew thicker and seeped into the vehicle. "Are you okay?"

"Yeah. I've got to get you to the safe house, so I can find Canton's stuff."

I closed my eyes, willing the murkiness to clear. "I'm not going to the safe house. I won't put another family in danger."

"What makes you so sure you're going to a family?"

"I'm not?" I tried to ignore the pain shooting through my back.

"You're going to be living with a single male agent," Ben said as the vehicle propelled down the narrow path. "I'll be honest. He's weird. Harmless, but weird."

I groaned, then coughed. "Define weird."

"Most of the work he does for the organization is by computer. He's a hacker like you. Drake thinks the two of you might collaborate and benefit the organization."

"You still haven't defined weird. Being a hacker does not make a person weird."

"Well, I guess I didn't make that point clear enough. He doesn't work in the field and rarely leaves his cabin."

That didn't seem like enough to make a person weird. "There has to be more than that."

"He's in his late thirties. Never married. A bit antisocial. He has a good heart though. Loves God."

Great. I was going to be trapped with an antisocial, religious nut. But if he was antisocial, he probably wouldn't try to convert me. "You've met him?"

Ben shook his head. "No, but my dad's worked with him."

"I'd feel better if you'd met him."

"So that means you're willing to stay with Ted?"

I rested my head against the headrest, longing to close my eyes and go to sleep. I didn't want to admit it to Ben, but today's adventure had wiped me out. If I wasn't pregnant I'd still be tired, but the exhaustion seeped to the marrow of my bones. I took a deep breath. "I'll go stay with Ted on one condition."

"What's that?"

"You and I are going to find Canton's evidence first."

"No way. I'm supposed to take you to the safe house."

"I know that. You've said that a bazillion times. But you took me to Canton when you were supposed to take me to the safe house. And I'm telling you, I'm not going until I have Canton's evidence in my hand."

"What am I supposed to do? Ted's expecting you."

"Call him and tell him we'll be late. It's not that hard."

His cheeks grew red. "There's no need to be rude about it. I'm trying to help you. And protect our baby."

"Then let me go with you to find the evidence."

"You don't trust me?"

I closed my eyes for a second. "This isn't about you. Try to understand that. Fortune killed the president and tried to kill my mother. My mother, Ben. She may not be what you think of as a great mom, but she's all I have. Not to mention those psychos are after me too. We have to prove his guilt. If you don't help me, I'll do it myself."

He picked up his courier. "Fine. You win. And, by the way, I still don't think you trust me."

"I don't trust anyone but myself."

"I know." His jaw clenched. "That's your biggest problem."

✕

Ben disconnected the call. "I hate lying for you."

"Do you think Ted suspected?" I asked.

He shrugged. "Who knows? He seemed to believe we're running behind."

At the airstrip we left Canton in the care of two agents and spent the night on cots in a hangar divided with a curtain. The next morning while Ben did his preflight check, I settled into my seat and stifled a yawn. Sleeping on a cot while pregnant did not agree with me. A few seconds later my courier rang. It was Drake. What was I going to tell him? He always knew when I was lying.

"Ben, Drake's calling."

Ben glanced over his shoulder. "Handle him. He's calling you, not me."

I sighed and answered.

"So according to my friend Ted, the two of you are behind schedule."

I glanced at Ben. "You know these things don't always go as planned."

Drake laughed. "When you are involved, my dear, things rarely go as planned. Ted may have believed your excuse about running behind, but I don't. What are you up to?"

I weighed my options and decided to tell part of the truth since he was already on to my lie. He didn't need to know about the jet. "We believe we've found some evidence that will implicate President Fortune in Hernandez's shooting and clear the organization. Ben and I are pursuing that lead."

There was silence for a few seconds. "I see."

"I also have doubts about putting more agents in danger by living with them."

Drake's lack of response was unnerving and so unlike his normal argumentative self that I wasn't sure how to respond.

"Be careful."

"That's all you're going to say?"

"Vivica, you never listen. And really, I'm not surprised that you managed to convince Ben to do things your way. I'm tired of arguing with you. If you think it's best to go on a wild goose chase, then I'm not stopping you. I'm also not going to rescue you if you find yourself in trouble."

"Okay, then. I can live with that."

"I hope so." He disconnected.

"We've been cleared for takeoff," Ben said.

I buckled my seatbelt. "Drake didn't protest."

"He probably has other things to worry about."

"No doubt."

Through the window the scenery blurred as the plane taxied the runway. If Drake had argued with me, then I would've been certain I was doing the right thing. But his cool disinterest caused me to doubt my actions in ways that disagreement never could.

# CHAPTER 40

Fifteen minutes into the flight I was bored. Ben wasn't in the mood for conversation, so I climbed to the set of seats that faced away from the cockpit and turned on the small satellite TV. I watched the news for a few minutes, but the anchor's blather about President Fortune's administration sickened me. I punched the power button.

My back ached as I tried to relax into the seat. I stretched and closed my eyes only to find myself imagining Monica dead and her children crying for her. Tears seeped through my lids, and I heaved deep breaths until my stomach muscles rebelled. There were so many people dead and hurting because of me. Because of my choices.

I soaked through the handful of tissues in my pocket and leaned over to grab more from my bag. Ben's unauthorized Bible rested on the seat beside me. The suggestion he'd given me awhile ago came to mind. Why not read? It was better than crying.

I found Matthew, chapter ten, and began. When I came to verse thirty-four, I read it twice.

*Do not suppose that I have come to bring peace to the earth. I did not come to bring peace, but a sword.*

That was weird. Hadn't the lady at the community center said Jesus promoted peace and unity? I continued reading.

*For I have come to turn a man against his father, a daughter against her mother, a daughter-in-law against her mother-in-law—a man's enemies will be the members of his own household.*

Those verses made sense. As much as I loved my mother, she was now my enemy. No wonder Ben thought I'd find this chapter relevant, but the contradiction about Jesus bringing a sword confused me.

"Please, God," I whispered. "I need to understand."

*I am the way, the truth, and the life. No one comes to the father except through me.*

The words the old man at the community center spoke reverberated in my memory. They had to be from the Bible. But where? My courier had an original Bible. I removed it and did a keyword search for the verse. John 14:6. I read the rest of the chapter, and verse twenty-seven brought up the peace issue.

*Peace I leave with you; my peace I give you. I do not give to you as the world gives . . .*

I bit my lip. As the world gives. The peace Jesus was talking about was different. But how?

I recalled something Ben had said. That had to be it. Jesus came to die for our sins so we could have peace with God and go to heaven. If we believed, we were no longer his enemies.

But that belief excluded all other ways to God, and that wasn't popular. Now it made sense. Peace with God meant sacrificing peace with those who refused to accept the truth.

Even peace between mothers and daughters.

I knew what I had to do. "God," I whispered, "I believe Jesus is the way, the truth, and the life and that I can only come to you through him." I took a deep breath. "I can't even begin to list all the things I've done wrong. Please forgive me. I want the peace that Jesus gives. No matter what."

# CHAPTER 41

"Viv!"

My eyes flew open. Last night we'd stopped at an airfield in the Great Plains Region to eat and recharge the plane's battery. Ben had decided to sleep before continuing on early the next morning. I'd fallen asleep soon after we'd taken off. "Where are we?"

"Not far from Union City. We should listen to that recording Canton made," Ben said.

I yawned and disregarded the pain that throbbed in my lower back. "Good idea." I accessed the file on my courier and punched the play button. Canton's voice filled the cockpit.

"I hid the information in the most secure place I could think of—the National Archives. The building is guarded. Built with modern safety features. Plus, there are so many items, someone would have to know what he was looking for in order to find the file. Have either of you been in the building?"

"No."

"It's amazing. The majority of it is underground, and the histories of the former United States, Mexico, and Canada are preserved there. Each country has a floor devoted to its history and two floors where members of each country can store information they deem valuable to the history of our new country. You both have fake IDs?"

"Yes," we answered in unison.

"Here's where it gets tricky. Because you're both citizens of regions that were a part of the former United States, you'll have access to the floors where information can be archived."

"I don't mean to be rude," I said, "but wouldn't Martina think of storing something there?"

Canton chuckled. "Never been to the archives, have you? Even if she knew my alias, she'd have to know where I put the file. Anyway, on the seventh floor is the United States History archive. The floor is divided into sections based on centuries. In the nineteenth-century section find the Underground Railroad. Locate the Harriet Tubman section and look for a box labeled Moses. On the bottom of the box, lift up the edge and you'll find a microchip with electronic copies of the documents needed to link Martina to Fortune and Fortune to the assassination."

I stopped the recording. "Ben, this almost sounds too easy. There have to be things we're not thinking of."

"Yeah, I'm a little worried too. What about security cameras?"

"Obviously that's why Canton said we have to use our fake IDs."

"We'll be careful. I need to concentrate. It's time to land."

><

The Emancipation Warriors ran the small airfield thirty miles south of Union City where the National Archives were located. The rebels were operating the airfield in plain sight with help of citizens from the African Federation who owned the strip. There was no way the government would upset the world by raiding the airfield even if they suspected rebels were there.

Like the rural airstrips, there were vehicles for agents. We selected a car, and Ben programmed the route to the archives. It was late afternoon, but the National Archive building was open twenty-four hours.

I studied my new driver's license and passport that had arrived on my courier. I was twenty-two-year-old Ella McDermott born on June first. Since I didn't have a new doc that matched my latest alias, we'd have to try to access the archives using my courier. Even though the courier had a program that could allow its screen to mimic a doc screen, we were taking a huge risk. "Ben, do you think you should pose as my boyfriend?"

Ben nodded. "I think we have to. If they check records, they'll know we aren't married. Not that they will, but we never know."

"How long have we been together?" I asked.

"Since high school? If anyone asks, we can use information from our real relationship."

"Cool."

The car parked itself in front of the massive limestone building. "This is it. You sure you don't want me to go in alone?"

"No, we need each other," I said.

Ben started to open his door. "Wait. We should pray."

"You're right." I smiled as Ben spun and surprise flitted in his expression.

"Don't look so shocked. Your prayers have been answered." I told him about what happened during our flight.

A smile spread across Ben's face while he reached across the console to squeeze my hand. "I'm so glad."

Holding hands, we strolled into the National Archives building and smiled at the guard who sat at the desk near the entrance.

"ID please." His craggy face remained stoic when he took Ben's doc, which was issued to his alias. The guard looked back and forth at him a few times before returning it. I held my breath when the guard took my courier and gave me the same treatment. Then he entered the information into his computer and produced two fobs attached to lanyards. He scanned the fobs and handed them over.

"These will give you access to floors one, two, three, seven, and eight. You may also explore anything on the main floor, which houses documents and information for the UR of NA. Got it?"

"Yes, sir," I said.

"Enjoy your visit." His tone said otherwise.

Ben and I walked to the elevator, and when the doors opened, we scanned the fobs and pressed the button for the seventh floor, which was actually below ground, seven floors up from the bottom. We were alone in the elevator, but security cameras monitored us. We continued to hold hands.

The elevator door pinged open at the seventh floor, revealing a dimly lit room, and it took a moment for my eyes to adjust to the low light. A dingy path worn in the beige carpet led to rows and rows of shelves stacked with books and metal boxes. This carpet looked like it was a relic from before the Great Collapse.

"Wow," I said.

"Pretty amazing." Ben pointed to the directory on the wall. "Let's explore. You game?"

I understood. We couldn't appear purposeful. I studied the directory and found it just as Jared described. The floor was organized by century, with the most recent centuries closest to the elevator.

"I'm going to look at World War II history," Ben said.

"Okay." I lumbered to the Great Collapse section. Sharp pains pinched my back, but I took a few deep breaths and hoped they'd pass. I looked in a few boxes and flipped through several books and newspapers before I decided the section was so depressing I needed to move on.

I wandered up and down a few rows before I went to the aisles that housed nineteenth-century documents. It didn't take long to discover where the information on the Underground Railroad was stored. Harriet Tubman was easy to find. I thumbed through several books and moved a few boxes before I uncovered one resting on the bottom shelf labeled MOSES.

Ben was nowhere in sight. I listened. Nothing. The carpeted floors muffled footsteps, but I did hear the elevator ding. Pulling my courier from my pocket, I sent Ben a message.

Where r u?

I launched the cloning program on my courier before I slid it in my pocket and removed the Moses box from the shelf. While I sifted through the contents with my right hand, I located the microchip with my left hand and connected it to my courier to copy the information.

A few seconds later the information was stored. I'd just sent a secure transmission to Drake when I heard a muffled thud.

My heart leapt into my throat. I replaced the microchip, put the box on the shelf, and walked to the end of the aisle where I peeked around the corner. Nothing. Maybe a box fell.

The elevator dinged a second time. I quickened my pace and told myself Ben was probably engrossed in a history book.

When I reached the Pearl Harbor row, I located the source of the thud. The contents of two boxes were strewn throughout the aisle. I wished for the gun I'd left on the plane, and when my eyes fell on a thick, hardback book resting on the floor at my feet, I snatched it. I checked the courier for a message. Nothing.

At the end of the aisle I peeked around the corner. It was clear. The directory indicated the stairs were on the wall opposite the elevator. Even though I'd need to walk up several stories, I would not take the elevator. I passed the Great Depression aisle. Every so often I'd stop and listen, but the air-conditioner's hum erased other sounds.

The stairwell door was in sight. I passed the United States Revolutionary War aisle. Out of the corner of my right eye, I caught the movement of a shadow. A figure lunged. I raised the book and brought it down on the figure's head.

A woman growled and grabbed her head as she fell back against a shelf.

It was Martina.

# CHAPTER 42

"Axel! Over here!"

I waddled to the stairwell door, yanked it open, and trudged up the stairs as quickly as my legs would take me. The door below me opened and then slammed. My breath came in gasps. Why couldn't this have been a normal building where the exit was downstairs instead of up? I looked over my shoulder. Martina was closing the gap, while Axel plodded behind.

"Give it up. We've already got your boyfriend."

Adrenaline pushed me forward, part of me refusing to believe Ben would allow himself to be captured. I was at the tenth floor. I could make it. Just a few more flights.

Another sharp pain pulsated through my back. Clutching it, I burst through the door to the main floor and raced through the rows of shelves that held the history of the United Regions. I swiveled my head to the right and left and caught sight of an emergency exit. If I could just make it to the car.

"Please, God. Get me out of here."

I opened the emergency exit, and the evening's gentle breeze engulfed me, which made the screeching alarm more jarring.

When I was halfway through the door, Martina caught my arm and squeezed, but I yanked and kicked. My legs flailed several times before I made contact with her shin. For a second her grip loosened, and I jerked away and ran outside.

In the twilight, it took me a few seconds to realize I was in the back of the building. When I rounded a corner, I dragged myself toward our car in the parking lot.

But Ben had the car's key fob.

In the car window's reflection, Martina encroached on the space separating us while Axel trailed behind. I headed for the road next to the building and prayed for a vehicle to pass.

I turned south, but my pace slowed, and my legs felt as heavy and awkward as steel beams. I glanced back. Axel passed Martina and closed the gap between us. I stumbled and prayed for a miracle.

Someone. Something. Didn't God want to help me?

A wave of dizziness caused me to stagger, and beefy arms grabbed me from behind. I had no more strength to fight. Axel's grip increased my dizziness. "Not so tight."

Axel laughed. "Right."

Martina slowed to a walk as she approached. "Your mother will be happy to see you."

"Where's Ben?"

"We took care of him."

Fury pushed against my chest, giving me a second wind. "You killed him?"

Martina crossed her arms. "Not yet. He may have information. Axel, does she have a doc or other device?"

I felt Axel shrug. "You look. I'm a little tied up here."

Martina patted me down and dug the courier from my pocket.

"How did you find us?"

Martina smiled. "You have your moles. We have ours."

I tried to think, but the pain I'd felt in my back ever since the explosion grew worse and was compounded by a lack of oxygen. "You didn't have to kill Monica."

Martina pointed to Axel. "Actually, he did. I have to give her credit. She didn't say a word about you. She denied it to the end. It was her kids who squealed."

"Where are they?"

"They're safe."

I clenched my teeth. "Somehow I doubt that."

"The government will care for them and see that they are trained properly."

I did not doubt that.

Martina took a syringe from her bag.

"What is that?" I asked, trying to keep the panic from my voice. "Will it hurt the baby?"

Martina looked at me as if I'd lost my mind. "You do realize your pregnancy will be terminated soon. It doesn't matter." "What. Is. It?" I tried to fight against Axel, but he increased his grip. "It's a sedative." She reached over and thrust the syringe into my neck. I screeched, but a few seconds later, numbing warmth spread through my body and everything faded.

# CHAPTER 43

They had won. That's all I could remember. Everything else faded into a fuzzy, drug-induced haze. But whatever they'd used to knock me out had worn off, and the blessed unconsciousness fled, leaving behind a penetrating chill and shadow of evil. Trembling, I battled to recall what had happened. And who was responsible.

Slowly, I opened my eyes and stared at ceiling tiles. Sterile, like the white walls and stainless steel cabinets and sink. I tried to sit up, but after moving a half inch I fell back. The restraints were too tight. My arms were pinned to my side, denying me any chance to free myself. I shivered in the thin hospital gown, and an antiseptic smell tingled my nose. Was I in a hospital? A clinic? Prison?

The door creaked. My mother and Melvin entered. Her makeup, painstakingly applied, couldn't hide the bags that circled her eyes. Melvin's hair looked grayer than the last time I'd seen him. Maybe it was the light, but they both looked older than I remembered. Melvin dragged a chair across the tile floor. It squeaked, making me jerk. My mother sat and moved it closer. Melvin stood behind her with his hands on the chair back. She leaned forward, her blue eyes hard and determined as they stared into mine. There was no compassion, only smoldering anger. Why? What had I done? I looked away.

"Look at me, Vivica. Why would you try to destroy me?" Her controlled voice was quiet.

My eyes flicked to Melvin as if he could somehow supply the answer. For a second, compassion flickered, but then his nostrils flared, his resentment obvious. I took a deep breath and fought to remember. I had tried to destroy my mother? Me? Why?

"Answer me."

I clenched my fists and tried to concentrate. "I don't remember."

"You're lying." Her eyes narrowed.

I wilted into the bed and looked at Melvin, hoping for rescue. His expression softened. "Genevieve, she may be telling the truth."

"I don't believe it." She stood and towered over me. Why wouldn't she believe me?

"Why do you always fight me, Vivica?"

Tears welled in my eyes. She never noticed my attempts to please her. She only saw me fighting her.

"Are you trying to destroy me?"

Was I?

I closed my eyes to try to remember. A vicious cramp tore through my abdomen, and the pain conquered the murkiness in my mind like the rising sun burns away morning fog.

The baby. They hadn't killed my baby. Yet.

My mother glared, waiting for an answer. My mouth was so dry it was hard to form words. "I remember now," I whispered.

"Do you realize what we've gone through? If this gets out, the Party will never vote for me. Even if I have to wait for Fortune to step down."

Melvin grabbed the bed's remote control to elevate me.

"You have your story," I said. "I was in Africa."

"Did you resent me so much that you would actually take the enemy's side? What did I ever do to you? Was this about your siblings?"

"Yes. But not like you think."

"Then I would appreciate it if you would enlighten me."

"I'm not going to let you murder my child."

"So I'm a murderer?"

I looked away.

My mother grabbed my face and turned it toward her. "Listen to me. I've had enough of your self-righteous attitude. You have no right to judge me. You are my daughter. You are a minor. And tonight you will comply with the law."

"No." My protest was useless, but I needed to fight.

"You have no choice. Dr. Mortensen will terminate the pregnancy tonight."

I wrestled with the restraints and tears flowed. I was so close to my due date. Why had I insisted that we try to find Jared Canton? Why had I changed Ben's orders? I should have gone straight to the safe house. Would it have mattered? Someone betrayed us, and everything I'd fought for was going to be taken from me.

"You're going to let a doctor suck the brains out of your grandchild." I flailed, and the restraints hurt. But I didn't care. "You cruel, heartless woman! You don't deserve to be president!"

In my rage I didn't feel the pain from the slap that my mother inflicted on my face before she fled the room with Melvin in tow.

✕

The sterile walls crowded closer with every passing moment, and I calculated escape possibilities. The restraints held tight when I tugged and pulled. I could lift my arm no more than an inch, so reaching a surgical tool was impossible.

"God, please help me," I whispered every few minutes, but when no help came, I needed to accept the inevitable.

"Baby, I'm sorry." I took a deep, shuddering breath and forced out the words that I needed to say before the opportunity passed. "I tried so hard to protect you." Fresh tears spilled, and I shivered. "I love you."

I longed for a kick, as if it would mean that somehow the baby understood and forgave me, but none came, and I felt more alone than before.

I wondered where God was, and my doubts resurfaced. "God, why?" I wailed. I was partly responsible, but I'd been trying to do what I believed was right. No answer came, and my sobs grew uncontrollable.

And then I remembered something from my Bible reading.

God had watched his Son die at the hands of evil men. I still didn't have answers, but the God who fully understood the agony that tore my heart held me close.

# CHAPTER 44

The door swung open, and a tall, bald man stepped into the room. "I'm Dr. Mortensen." He wore a white lab coat, but the grim reaper's black robe would have been more appropriate.

"How much is my mother paying you to keep your mouth shut?"

Dr. Mortensen's eyes widened before his expression changed to a frown. "That's not something you need to be concerned about."

"Where is my mother?"

"She's in the waiting room with her assistant. Miss Wilkins, stalling will only delay the inevitable."

"I'm aware of that. I want to see her before you begin."

Dr. Mortensen sighed and looked at his watch. "I don't have time for games."

"It won't take long. Please. I have one more thing to say."

Dr. Mortensen pinched the bridge of his nose, but he left the room. I had a plan that was a long shot, but I had to try.

A few minutes later he returned, shaking his head. "She told me to tell you to stop playing games and to begin the procedure."

My heart sank. "Please try one more thing. Tell her I have proof that links President Fortune to the assassination attempt."

Dr. Mortensen raised his bushy eyebrows. "I take it you want to make a deal."

"That's right."

He left, and a few minutes later the click of my mother's high heels sounded in the hall. She wrenched open the door and slammed it behind her.

"I've had enough of your game playing. You will terminate. And you will return to live with me."

"Martina's going to kill you. She'll probably kill me too."

"That's ridiculous. This is a pathetic attempt to stall."

"There's proof." I hadn't had time to look through Canton's information, so I prayed he'd told the truth.

"You have no such thing."

"Listen to me. Martina has been working with President Fortune for years. Fortune wanted to get rid of you and Hernandez, so he could be the next president. But Bobby got in the way and saved you when Axel didn't. Don't you see? Martina stepped in to be close to us. I have evidence that can put President Fortune out and you back in. And you'll get it on one condition."

"I don't make you terminate."

"Right. Let me have the baby. Let me give it up for adoption. In return, I'll help you put Fortune away."

"How do I know you're telling me the truth?"

"Jared Canton holds the key."

My mother was a good actress, but she didn't mask the surprise that crossed her face when I mentioned Canton. "How so?"

"I did some investigating while I was away."

"There's actual evidence?"

"Yes."

"Where? Do you have it with you?"

"No. That witch you hired to track me down walked off with my doc. That's where I stored the information."

"How convenient."

"You have to believe me. Get the doc from Martina, and I'll get the information."

My mother began to pace. "I think you're lying."

I shrugged. "But if you're wrong, and I'm not, and you make me go ahead against my will, then you'll never know. Fortune will keep what's rightly yours."

My mother stopped pacing, and the conflict on her face was evident. "Fine. I'll retrieve your doc from Martina. But that's all."

"If I prove that I'm right, will you call it off?"

"No deals yet," she said and left the room, slamming the door behind her.

I tugged at the restraints that held my arms and noticed that the one that held my left arm was looser. Jiggling my arm, I tried to weaken it. "Please, God."

The door flew open again, and my mother entered holding out the courier. I took it, but the information that I'd copied was gone because of the security breach. It had activated a program installed by the Emancipation Warriors that wiped all data. Plus, I could no longer make transmissions. I felt like a giant hand was clutching my throat, closing off all the oxygen.

"Well?" My mother had her hands on her hips. "What do you have?"

"Nothing," I whispered. I shouldn't have been surprised. Of course, Martina would try to get the information.

"What do you mean, nothing?"

I felt lightheaded. "The information is gone. I'm sorry. I have another way—"

My mother held up a hand. "Just stop. I don't want to hear any more. You've lied enough. Martina told me that thing isn't even a doc."

"Why can't you understand that all I want is to save the baby?"

"Probably for the same reason you can't understand why all of this is for your own good." Her anger faded and disappointment took its place. She took the courier from my hand. "I'm sending in the doctor now." She shut the door behind her quietly.

I tugged at the arm restraints. Getting out of this clinic was my last chance. After a few more yanks my left arm flew into the air. I was free, but the leather strap still encircled my right arm.

I heard footsteps outside the door and moved my left arm close to the bar, so it appeared to be restrained. Dr. Mortensen nodded at me as he entered. He withdrew a vial of medicine from a cabinet and turned to face me. "While you were unconscious, we performed an ultrasound. As you may be aware, you're in the beginning stages of labor. So I'm not going to use the partial birth technique."

I nodded.

He held up the vial. "This is digoxin." He took a syringe from the drawer of cabinets across from me and filled it. "It will stop the fetus's heart." He turned on the ultrasound machine. "After the injection, you'll deliver the fetus through the normal labor process."

The syringe's needle touched my abdomen.

I jammed my left fist into Dr. Mortensen's temple. He thudded on the floor, and the syringe pinged against the tile. I prayed that no one had heard him hit the floor.

I freed the restraint on my right arm, slid off the table and rolled it in front of the door. Opening a few cabinets, I found my clothes stashed in a plastic sack and went to the window but hesitated and returned to the cabinets where I stuffed the plastic bag with medical supplies.

Turning off the lights, I peeked through the blinds and waited for my eyes to adjust. I was on the ground floor in the back of the building. There was a grove of trees. I raised the blind and tugged on the window's rusty latch.

"Come on," I said to the latch.

Dr. Mortensen moaned.

Footsteps squeaked in the hall. There was a rap on the door.

I wrenched the latch.

"Dr. Mortensen? Is everything okay?" I didn't recognize the woman's voice. "May I come in?"

I grabbed the doctor's stool, launched it through the window, and turned from the shattering glass.

The door cracked, emitting a sliver of light. The door thumped against the bed. "Help! Security!"

I lurched through the window, scraping my hand on the broken glass. Chilling raindrops embraced me, and I retreated to the trees behind the clinic, my feet sliding on soggy grass.

My hand throbbed and blood dripped. I moved as quickly as I could, but a cramp split my abdomen. My knees buckled.

"Stay in there." I leaned against a tree and gritted my teeth, willing the pain to stop. Even though I was technically full term, it was too soon for the baby to arrive. When I heard shouts behind me, I clutched my bulging abdomen and forced myself forward until I came to a road at the edge of the woods. Headlights loomed, so I ducked back behind a tree and waited.

When a truck passed, I crossed the road into a cornfield. Batting aside the wet stalks, I propelled forward, shivering in my saturated hospital gown and cringing each time the soggy stalks brushed my skin like the cold hands of death.

My contractions grew closer together.

With each step, I grew more certain that death beckoned, and for the first time, I realized that death was not the worst option when heaven waited. My pace slowed to a trudge. My toes were numb. Tears and raindrops mingled. Wet, suffocating darkness. One more step. Two more steps. Three.

The cornfield ended.

# CHAPTER 45

I stood at the edge of the field and observed the scene in front of me that was illuminated by a pole light. The farmhouse was dark, but there were several outbuildings that could provide shelter.

A contraction drove me to my knees, and I clutched wet grass in my fists and forced myself to focus on breathing.

When the contraction passed, I staggered forward and chose the red barn. A wave of giddy joy eroded some of my despair when the door opened.

The barn contained large pieces of farm equipment that loomed like metal monsters. A rusty truck sat in the corner. I shivered as I walked toward it. When I opened the passenger door, there was a faint smell of manure. A key chain dangled from the ignition. It ran on battery power but was an old model that required a driver.

I climbed in and moved a hunting rifle that lay in the seat onto the floor.

Another contraction stopped me before I could turn the key. I squeezed the steering wheel and breathed.

When the contraction eased, I turned the ignition. The truck started, and I thanked God for farmers who left keys in old work trucks. I turned off the engine and clicked on the dome light so I could dress, but a contraction, stronger than any before, stopped me.

I lay back on the truck's bench seat and breathed. It would pass like the others. It had to.

The contraction passed, but there was no relief from the pressure. I lifted my gown and felt between my legs. My stomach lurched when I felt the baby's head. Panic clawed at my chest, but I could not let it overtake me.

"God. Help. Me. Now!"

A contraction came again, and my body insisted that I push. I braced my feet against the truck's passenger door and pushed. And pushed. The contraction passed. My mind whirred as I tried to form a plan for when the baby arrived, but the pain muddled my thinking.

Another contraction. I gritted my teeth and bit back a scream. Push. Harder.

A baby boy appeared. My son.

# CHAPTER 46

I picked the baby up from the seat of the truck and cleaned him with my hospital gown as he wailed. Relief washed over me when I noticed his skin was a healthy pink. I held him close to my chest.

When I didn't find anything adequate for cutting the umbilical cord in the bag of supplies I'd snatched from the clinic, I staggered across the barn to the tool bench and opened drawers in search of something to clamp and cut the umbilical cord. I found a pair of scissors and some string and returned to the truck. My legs could barely support me.

I cleaned the scissors with wipes from the clinic and then clamped the umbilical cord using the string. My hands shook, but I managed to cut the cord and wrapped the baby in my sweatshirt. *Thank you, God, for Dr. Bonham.* When he'd left that book for me to read, I'd no idea how much I'd need its diagrams. The cramping started again, and I bit back a moan.

A few moments later I delivered the placenta. I emptied the bag of medical supplies and placed the placenta in the bag before cleaning and returning the scissors.

I dressed before I went to the barn door and peeked out. The rain had stopped, and the night was still, so I opened the large door used for moving farm equipment in and out. My stomach growled. When had I last eaten? I wanted nothing more than to just curl up and sleep but couldn't risk that.

The baby had fallen asleep, and I moved the truck out of the barn. When I got out to close the barn door, I cringed at the truck's rumbling motor. In the second floor of the farmhouse, lights blinked to life.

I scurried into the truck and put a protective hand on the baby before I jammed the accelerator to the floor. The truck skidded out of the gravel driveway and raced down the road.

That's when I saw the battery was almost dead.

# CHAPTER 47

I kept driving and fought panic because my mission was to protect my son. I had an idea, but it required the use of a computer or doc. If I could make it to the nearest town, I might be able to find a library that opened in the morning, but right now that was hours away.

There was a wall of corn on each side of me, and after about five miles, I saw a sign on my right: CRYSTAL LAKE CAMPGROUND. The wooden sign had an arrow that pointed to the right, so I turned. The narrow, tree-lined drive led to a deserted parking lot and a lodge. Maybe I could find a computer there.

I scooped up the sleeping baby and the rifle and shuffled into the lodge. Automatic lights came on, spotlighting me. I froze and listened for signs of life. There was a stone fireplace on the opposite wall, with a worn, oversized couch in front of it. To my right, there were restrooms, and to my left was a hallway lined with doors. When I didn't hear anyone, I moved down the hallway and stopped when I came to a door labeled *Camp Director*. It was locked.

I placed the baby and rifle on the floor and removed two pins from my hair. For a second I thought I was going to faint, and I clutched the doorframe. Not now. The baby needed me. I blinked at the stars floating through my vision.

*Thank you, God, for the Warriors' agent training manual.* The dizziness subsided as I bent the first pin and inserted it into the bottom of the lock. I put in the second pin and jiggled a few times before I used the bent part of the first pin to turn the lock gently. It clicked, and the door opened.

A grin spread over my face when I saw the computer. I arranged the baby in my lap, positioned the rifle within reach, and went to work. This could be my solution if I could find the right information. Maybe God had given me the answer I needed.

All the data that had been on my courier was backed up on the Emancipation Warriors' secure database. I knew what I was looking for as long as I could gain access to it. It took a few tries while I fought waves of lightheadedness, but I located my files.

I found the contact information I'd saved from Helen's courier months before. When I found the right number, I paused. Could I do it? Was this the right choice?

I opened the messaging program and typed the words that would be sent as a secure transmission to the courier of a woman I'd only heard about.

My name is Vivica Wilkins. I met your mother and father the day they died. I need to talk to you and your husband.

# CHAPTER 48

Gabe and Alma Zimmer lived on a farm twenty miles from the campground. When Alma had received my message and responded, she'd told me to stay put. They would be there as soon as possible. Even though I'd contacted them, I was surprised that they were willing to come out in the middle of the night to meet with someone they didn't know. How did they know it wasn't a trap by the people who'd killed Alma's parents?

I shut the camp director's office door and sat on the couch in front of the fireplace where I cuddled the baby. God had taken me to Beau and Helen's boat that day to let me know about their daughter and son-in-law who had been praying for a baby for so long. Though I didn't understand why God allowed Beau and Helen to die, I now realized that God was at work that day in spite of evil.

My eyes fell on a tablecloth covering a long table across the room, and I had an idea. I stripped the table and made a sling from the cloth. There was enough length that I could swaddle the baby and tie him to me. When this was finished, I relaxed. My eyelids drooped, and I'd almost nodded off when headlights flashed through the floor-to-ceiling windows next to the fireplace. I stood.

Adrenaline pumped through my veins, and my eyes darted around the room, searching for the best way to escape. I grasped the rifle and headed for the back door at the end of the office hallway. When I reached it, I cracked the door and peered into the darkness. I couldn't see anything but trees.

A car door slammed. I held my breath. "Martina, come check this out." I shivered when I heard Axel's voice.

"What is it?" Martina asked.

"Check out all the blood."

"What's in the bag?"

The bag rustled, and then Axel retched. I reminded myself to breathe.

"Give me that," Martina said. "Oh."

"What is that?"

"She had the baby. It's the placenta. Go check the lodge. There's no way she got very far."

I shivered and slipped through the door, quietly pulling it shut and begging God to keep the baby quiet. I needed to get to the road before the Zimmers arrived, or Martina and Axel might be able to trace the baby to them. Plastered against the building, I peeked around the corner at the truck. Martina shut the truck door and headed in the building. I sprinted for the trees as the baby let out an ear-splitting shriek.

I moved as fast as I could, but my legs were rubbery and spots danced through my vision. The road was in sight. I had to make it to the road. Someone shouted behind me. A gun blasted. The bullet hit the ground next to me, spraying dirt. I ducked behind a tree and dared to look. Another gunshot. Martina and Axel were about a hundred yards away. I fired the rifle. Nothing. Cursing at myself, I flicked off the safety.

When I fired a second time, I hit Martina's leg, and she collapsed. Axel kept coming. I fired two more times, and this time I gasped and dropped the rifle when the shot pierced his head. I'd aimed for his legs. He slumped to the ground. Martina struggled to her feet and fired another shot before she crumpled.

I fled. There were just a few more steps to the road, but it felt like a marathon.

One. Headlights. Two. The car drew closer. Three. Please, God, let it be the Zimmers.

I stepped out of the tree line. Four. The car slowed. A man rolled down the window, and a woman leaned over to see. "Vivica?" Blackness crowded my vision.

Five. Open the door. Bright dots. Sit. So many bright dots. Shut the door. "Go. Now. *Fast*." My voice was far away.

The car lurched forward, and I surrendered to the darkness.

# CHAPTER 49

I awoke in an antique canopy bed cocooned in a comforter. The room was painted a cheerful yellow, and slats of sunlight peeked through the blinds.

A note on the nightstand from Alma told me to feel free to shower and then dress in clothes she'd laid out. The note was propped against a bottle of juice and a protein bar. I ate, then showered for a long time, thinking through my decisions and asking God for the strength to do what needed to be done. My body felt foreign minus a baby, and I was grateful for the soft t-shirt and jogging pants.

Downstairs, Alma sat in a rocking chair, where she was feeding the baby from a bottle. She smiled. "Good morning."

I knelt beside Alma's chair and gazed at the baby. "Is he okay?"

"I think so. We're going to have a doctor from our organization stop by today to check on you and the baby."

"That's good."

"How are you feeling?"

"Tired. Still nervous they'll find us. I should leave here soon. I don't want the baby in danger because of me."

Alma raised the baby to her shoulder and patted his back. "We'll figure that out as soon as the doctor says you're fine."

"What are you going to name him?"

"Gabe and I talked it over this morning, but we want your opinion." The baby burped, and she cradled him. "What do you think about Isaac?"

I studied the baby's face, and my throat ached. He looked like Ben. Had I made the right decision? I nodded my head. "It's perfect."

Isaac's wail pierced the night, and I sat up in bed and tossed the comforter aside. My baby needed me. Rushing toward the nursery, I halted when I heard Alma crooning a lullaby. I tiptoed to the door and peered into the room she and Gabe had prepared with items they'd stored in their attic after another adoption had fallen through. Isaac drank from a bottle while Alma rocked. I gripped the doorframe and caught my breath. My painfully swollen breasts chastised me for neglecting my duty as a mother.

Even my body knew I'd made a mistake.

Escaping back to the guest room, I buried my face in the pillow and sobbed until my eyes were grainy. I'd tell them tomorrow I'd changed my mind.

*God, help me find a way to tell them. Don't let it hurt them.*

It was a ridiculous prayer. Of course they'd be hurt. But I had every right to take Isaac back. He was my son. Alma and Gabe would just have to get over it. I rolled over and yanked the covers up to my chin.

Minutes dragged as I remained motionless, staring at the ceiling fan that hummed above my bed.

I couldn't do it. Not when they'd waited so long for a child. And they'd been heartbroken before. Not when I could see in Alma's tender touch and Gabe's soft whispers, they already loved him.

Not when I wasn't ready to raise a child on my own. This realization made the tears begin again. *Oh, God, give me strength.*

Wiping my tears with the sheets, I finally got up and returned to the nursery. Alma had gone back to bed, and Isaac lay in his crib, his tiny chest rising and falling rhythmically. I gazed at him. His tiny ears and lips were shaped like my own. I stroked his soft blond hair and took a shuddering breath.

Isaac didn't belong with me. He was home.

I clutched the edge of the crib. "God," I whispered, "let him know he's loved. Let him know I loved him."

〼〼〼

When the doorbell rang two days later, I'd finished filling a duffel bag with clothes Alma had given me from the stash she kept for people in need.

I peeked through the side panel. I thought the man standing on the porch was Drake in a new disguise. But I wasn't sure.

When I opened the door, he grinned. "You look good. No one would ever guess you'd just had a baby."

"Shut up." I stepped aside, so he could come in.

"Sassy as always." He surveyed me. "Seriously, I'm glad you're okay. And the baby."

I scowled. "It almost wasn't okay."

Drake was calm. Annoyingly calm. "And whose fault would that have been?"

I glanced away. This wasn't how I wanted things to go when I saw Drake again. Seeing him so soon caught me off guard, and I wanted him to know I had changed. I looked back at him.

"It would've been mine. I insisted we track down Canton instead of reporting to the other agent. I altered Ben's orders so we could fly a jet."

Drake nodded as if he was having trouble comprehending that I was willing to admit I was wrong. "I knew about the jet. But everything wasn't your fault. If you'd gone with the other agent, Martina still would have found you. We had a mole."

"Who?"

"Faith." Drake looked at his feet.

My heart dropped. Ben's sister. "I knew she didn't like me, but . . . How did you figure that out?"

"I didn't. Ben told me his suspicions, so while you two were flying around causing trouble, I investigated."

"How did she find me?"

"Faith figured Ben would go to you, so she put a tracking device on his courier." For a second, I could only think about Ben, but then I looked at Drake's face and saw his confidence was shattered. I put my hand on his arm. "Are you okay?"

"Yes." His tone was clipped and let me know the subject of his relationship with Faith was closed.

"How long has she been working for them?"

"Not long. Martina found her and convinced her to turn on you. They had your alias info, but until they traced Ben, they couldn't find you."

Something clicked. "She's the one who told my mother I was pregnant."

"Yep."

It all made perfect sense except for the reason behind Faith's betrayal. "Why would she turn on the Emancipation Warriors?"

Drake's face twisted. "To save her own skin. She made the tip to your mother to protect Ben, but was careless about covering her tracks. Martina figured out Faith worked for us." His tone was filled with contempt.

I stared. "I can't believe she'd betray her own brother."

"There are lots of cowards who—" He shook his head. "Never mind."

"What happens to Ben now?"

"He's considered a domestic terrorist. He'll remain in prison."

Tears stung my eyes. "You mean he doesn't even get a trial?" I knew the answer, but it seemed so unfair.

"The government doesn't care about fair trials anymore. Not that they ever have."

His face softened. "I'm sorry, Vivica."

"What if the war . . . " It seemed silly to hold on to the hope that the war might somehow be the solution.

"You're actually right. The war could change everything. Don't give up yet."

"I haven't. What about Judd and the kids?"

"Judd's searching for them. I'm afraid they've probably been hidden away in a reeducation center for kids."

I ran my hands through my hair. I didn't think I could handle any more bad news right now.

"Don't give up on them either. Judd's a good agent." Drake put an arm around me. "Are you ready to go? I'm kind of on a tight schedule."

"Yeah. Let me grab my bag and say good-bye."

Alma was rocking Isaac in the nursery, and she stood when I entered. "Time to go?"

"Yeah."

She put her arm around me. "Keep in touch, okay?"

"I will." I leaned over and kissed Isaac's head. "You make sure to be a good boy for mommy and daddy, okay?" I refused to cry.

Alma beamed. "Thank you, Vivica."

A lump filled my throat when I forced myself to leave the room. Drake gave me a sympathetic smile as he led me to his truck. I appreciated the fact that he didn't try to speak meaningless, cheerful words. When I put my bag in the truck, I had a thought.

"Wait. There's one more thing I want to do." I rummaged through the bag, pulled out the sweatshirt I'd wrapped Isaac in after he was born, and returned to the nursery.

"I want Isaac to have this." My voice wobbled. "Someday you can tell him his birth mother wrapped him in it the day he was born."

Alma took the sweatshirt. "I'll be happy to do that." Tears filled her eyes. "Thank you for being a part of the answer to my prayers."

I nodded and fled the house.

It was a long ride to the airfield, and it was awhile before Drake broke the silence. "Now may not be the best time to bring this up, but I have a feeling you could use the distraction."

"You're right."

"I don't know if you've given any thought to your future, but we both know you have some skills that would be extremely valuable to the Emancipation Warriors. You have some connections that could be helpful too."

"What are you saying?"

"The Emancipation Warriors would like to train you to become an agent."

"And what do *you* think?"

Drake chuckled and shook his head. "I think you've shown you're resourceful and tough. I have to give you credit for that."

"Do you think I can handle it?"

"Why do you need my approval?"

I felt my face flush, and I raised my chin. "I don't."

"Good. Because I have my concerns, and you know what those are. I don't care to rehash them again."

"I've changed."

"Have you?"

"Yes."

Drake kept his eyes on the road. "I need you to make a decision right now because we're almost to the airfield. If you're in, I'll fly you to a training camp. If you're out, I'll give you an alias and take you to a family that's a part of our organization in another region. You can enroll in high school and go back to a semi-normal life."

"I want to be an agent." It was an easy decision. As long as I was hiding out, pretending to be a regular high school kid, I wouldn't be able to help Ben. I didn't want to try to fit in as a member of a family I'd never met. Besides, I had to fight for freedom.

"This can't be just about rescuing Ben."

I bristled. Why did he always anticipate what I was thinking? "I know."

"Good. I wanted to make that clear. Are you sure?"

"Yes, I'm sure."

Drake smiled. "I was fairly certain you would be." He turned, and we were on the road that led to the airport. "I have one other thing." Drake dug into his jacket pocket, pulled out a microchip, and handed it to me.

"What is this?" I examined it.

"That's the information you sent to me on Canton. I hate to admit it, but I'm glad you followed your instincts. We cleared him. He's working for us again."

"I can't believe you haven't released this."

Drake smiled. "It has to go through the right person."

"And I'm the right person?"

"Yes."

"And you're comfortable leaving the decision of what to do up to me? How do you know I have enough information to make the right choice?"

"I think you have all the information you need."

I clutched the microchip with the information implicating Martina and President Fortune. "I think we need to make a special delivery before I report to training camp."

"I thought so."

# CHAPTER 50

Drake stopped at the wrought-iron gate in front of the governor's mansion where I entered the access code. The truck glided through the gate and stopped.

"I'll wait here," Drake said.

I walked to the front door and rang the bell. Footsteps approached, and the door swung open. Melvin's eyes widened. "Who—?"

"It's me."

"Oh. Right." His eyes flicked to my abdomen. "What are you doing here?"

I swallowed over the lump in my throat. "I need to see my mother."

Melvin stepped aside and let me in, and I followed him to my mother's office where she worked at her desk and didn't look up when we entered. Commander spotted me from his nest on the couch and he flew off, jumping and dancing with me.

When the dog calmed down, my mother looked me up and down. "Where's the baby? I certainly hope you don't intend to come and live here." She stood and walked around to the front of her desk where she leaned against the edge and crossed her arms.

"No. That's not why I'm here."

My mother glanced at Melvin. "Then why are you here?"

I held out the microchip.

My mother lunged and snatched it from my hand. "Is this the evidence against Fortune?" Her eyes widened. "You really had something?"

"Yes." I patted Commander's head.

"Melvin, see what this is." Melvin scurried forward, grabbed the chip, and downloaded the information into the computer. My mother peered over his shoulder. For what felt like an eternity, they were both silent. Should I run while I had the chance? But there was more I needed to say.

At last my mother raised her head. "This is incredible. It's everything we need to prove Fortune set up the assassination and the attack on the Capitol." She clutched my arm. "How did you get this?"

I shrugged. "You don't need to know."

"Why would you do this?"

"If I don't, Martina is going to come out of hiding and kill you"—I paused to steady my voice—"and because I'd rather see you as president than Fortune."

My mother exchanged glances with Melvin.

"Everyone believes I'm in Africa. I won't tell anyone differently."

"So you want to come home?"

"No, I don't."

My mother frowned. "Where will you go?"

"It doesn't matter."

"Of course it matters. I'm your mother."

A laugh nearly escaped my lips, but it died when I saw her earnest expression. "Could we agree to disagree?"

Melvin nodded. "I think that would be wise."

My muscles tensed. Did he think I cared if he thought it was wise or not?

"You're joining the rebels, aren't you?" my mother asked.

I studied my feet.

My mother pursed her lips. "You know I could arrest you right now. And I should."

I glanced at Melvin. Our eyes met, and he looked away.

"You're on the wrong side of this," my mother said. "We're going to win." She held up the microchip and shook her head.

"I'd like you to do two more things for me."

My mother raised her hands and laughed. "What do you want? I'm already giving you freedom."

My chest tightened. "And I just gave you back your dream. I want you to promise me that you'll never try to find my child. I'm not keeping the baby, and you have nothing to fear from it living its life." My eyes rested on the portrait of my mother above her desk. New. Beautiful. Flawless. I caught my breath. She'd posed for a portrait while I was gone?

My mother glanced at Melvin. "Okay. You have my word. I will never try to find the child. Now, what else do you want? Money?"

After everything, she thought I'd want money? "Release Ben Lagarde from prison."

My mother stared at me before her lips tightened into a firm line. Then she turned and focused on her computer screen. Kneeling down, I wrapped my arms around Commander and buried my face in his head. Tears stung my eyes. The silence grew more smothering with each second that passed.

My mother looked up from her computer screen. "We're done here, so I suggest you leave before I change my mind and make you stay."

When I stood, Melvin nodded slightly, and I trudged from my mother's office.

><

"Do you think freedom is worth the cost?" I asked Drake as we rode away from the governor's mansion. "I mean, I'm choosing to go to war against my own mother. It seems wrong."

"My dear, you went to war against your mother months ago. You're just having trouble wrapping your mind around the fact that you're getting ready to fight an even bigger battle. You know, the two of you aren't that different. You're both independent and like to be in control. She's betting on the government. You've staked your life on the Emancipation Warriors."

And on following Christ. *For I've come to turn a daughter against her mother.*

"Tell me, honestly, did you really think you'd go home again?"

I stared at the rows of houses in the slums and remembered the day I'd tried to give the little girl money. Though it had only been a few months ago, it now seemed like eons. "No. I guess deep down I knew I'd never go back."

"Then it's time to move forward."

Accepting that reality was the first step into my future. There was a war, and I had to fight for the freedom of my son and the generations to come.

# ACKNOWLEDGMENTS

There are many people who helped this novel come to be, and I'm thankful for each contribution.

I'd like to thank the entire team at Kregel. Editors Janyre Tromp, Barbara Scott, and Dawn Anderson gave insights and suggestions that deepened and improved my manuscript.

To Credo Communications and my agent, Ann Byle: Thank you for taking a chance on me and supporting me.

To Dr. Dennis E. Hensley, who was the first professional to read my manuscript: Thank you for your guidance.

To Christian Writers Guild mentors Christy Scannell, Yvonne Lehman, and DiAnn Mills: Thank you for teaching me how to be a better writer.

Thank you to my family members and friends who prayed for me throughout this journey. And finally, thank you to my Lord and Savior, Jesus Christ.